THE
MURDER
CLUB

BOOKS BY ALICE CASTLE

A Beth Haldane Mystery

The Murder Mystery

The Murder Museum

The Murder Question

The Murder Plot

The Murder Walk

The Murder Hour

THE MURDER

CLUB

ALICE CASTLE

bookouture

Published by Bookouture in 2022

An imprint of Storyfire Ltd.
Carmelite House
50 Victoria Embankment
London EC4Y 0DZ

www.bookouture.com

ISBN: 978-1-80314-494-8
eBook ISBN: 978-1-80314-493-1

To Ella and Connie, with love

ONE

Beth Haldane's bottom was wedged on a sliver of vinyl ottoman the exact size and shape of a Dairylea cheese triangle. It was the day before the start of the autumn term, and she was in the school shoe department of Peter Jones. How did I end up here? she asked herself in despair. She'd had all summer to get this done but, inevitably, here they were at the last possible moment, in a very special circle of hell. There were bad-tempered squeals and shoves everywhere, and that was just amongst the grown-ups.

She shifted a little, trying to get a better purchase on the shiny surface. Inadvertently, she brushed up against her companions on either side in all too intimate a fashion. The woman on Beth's right gave her a vicious look. Her little girl was being fitted with a pair of red Mary-Janes which, in Beth's considered opinion, would not last a week in any playground.

Over in the boys' section was Beth's own beloved Jake. Now a sturdy eleven-year-old with bright, enquiring eyes and a rather curly, overlong head of hair (no time to get it cut now), he was laughing helplessly. He and another lad his age had struck up one of those instant friendships that Beth sorely envied. She supposed she ought to be over there, pushing him to decide on some shoes that would somehow perform the impossible feat of being practical and yet not hopelessly uncool, getting this ghastly chore over and done. But letting him choose his own was just one of the ways in which she was trying to give him a bit more autonomy.

It was a small reward for having pulled off the seemingly impossible feat of squeaking into Wyatt's School.

Anyway, she wasn't risking too much, was she? Boys' shoes were all much of a muchness. Ugly, black, clumpy things that would be clogging up her hall for the foreseeable future. He might as well pick something he liked. And if she moved, she'd never find anywhere else to sit.

Beth shut her eyes briefly. She really couldn't believe this – either this eleventh-hour footwear frenzy, or getting ready for Wyatt's. Shoehorning Jake into Wyatt's School had been her dream for almost as long as she could remember, pretty much since she'd first clapped eyes on his downy head in the maternity ward. Just thinking of his triumph gave her a little thrill which made the ottoman, the shoes, and even the mothers fade away. But the trouble with having lifelong ambitions was that when they were finally realised, you were left treading air like a cartoon cat shooting off a cliff.

Sorting out Jake's schooling had been her motivation for staying on in expensive Dulwich after her husband had died, had been the aim behind every penny she'd saved up since his birth (not that many, despite her best efforts), and had even been the reason why she'd applied for the post of archivist at the school itself. She'd hoped, sneakily enough, that working there behind the scenes would give her some kind of edge. It was fair to say that hadn't worked out. It had just got her a ringside seat at her first murder, while the rest of the staff seemed to take it in turns to assure her there was no preferential treatment on admissions. Luckily, she loved the job. And Jake had done her proud anyway.

But what was going to force her to get things done now? She could concentrate all her efforts on her role as archivist. She could even produce her detailed plan for the definitive biography of Sir Thomas Wyatt, the appalling swashbuckler who'd founded the school. Her employers had been awaiting it for far too long now. But she suspected she'd still have a gap at the centre of her life.

She supposed this was why people did all that mindfulness stuff. So that they stopped being so goal-orientated and concentrated instead on inner peace and happiness. Beth shut her eyes and tried to think calm, zen-infused thoughts. Immediately, her right-hand neighbour gave her a crafty shove and Beth almost lost her precarious inch of ottoman. Her eyes shot open and she stared at the woman, who fixed innocent eyes on her phone.

If mindfulness was hard going in Peter Jones, it was going to be impossible back in Dulwich. Beneath her heavy fringe, Beth's forehead was as finely concertinaed as a Venetian blind. But the pleats dropped out as Jake strolled over to her, swinging a big black shoe by the laces. Beth smiled up at him. 'Are you sure you'll want to bother doing those up every morning?' she asked, head on one side. Jake nodded impatiently, dropped the shoe and ran off to join his new friend, nimbly skipping over a brace of toddlers who were playing with some fluffy slippers, and dodging round a clutch of younger boys.

Beth frowned at the toddlers. Who on earth would bring innocent children here, on this, the last possible day to get kitted out for school? Maybe their mothers didn't yet know about the tyranny of term dates they'd shortly be subjected to, or maybe these kids had older siblings who were already in the system. The poor creatures, playing on the floor with discarded tissue paper and empty shoeboxes, looked happy enough, though the mothers seemed shell-shocked.

But then that applied to Beth too. They'd had about eight long weeks to get Jake shod. The days had been whiled away very pleasantly, but somehow they had ended up here at just the wrong moment.

Beth made a decision and stood up, hoping Jake was serious about the lace-ups and not just bored with the whole shoe thing. Now that she'd given up her corner of the seat, another nearby mother darted forward, but was too late. The two women Beth had been sandwiched between fluffed themselves up like broody hens and effortlessly reclaimed the space. Beth plodded over to the queue at the cash desk, taking a quick look at the price tag on the underside of the shoes and really wishing she hadn't. It would have been better if she'd just handed over her credit card without bothering herself with the fine print of the colossal sum she was actually spending. Suffice to say, it was more than her own shoe budget for many years.

'We'd like these, please,' said Beth, when she'd eventually reached the front of the line.

The assistant, who must surely have been on a heavy dose of tranquillisers to withstand a whole day in this department, took a quick glance. 'What size, madam?'

Beth looked at her in horror. The measuring! They'd missed out a whole step. They were truly going to be in this place forever. The assistant gave a knowing smile and passed Beth a tiny numbered ticket, like the ones they handed out at the village deli on busy days. 'My colleague will be over shortly. Just take a seat,' she added, as though it were the easiest thing in the world.

Beth suppressed a scream and glanced back over her shoulder at the carnage. The entire department was rammed. Grumpy mothers stood around, giving the evil eye to those who'd got a perch on the ottomans, while the children, completely overexcited by the anarchy, rushed back and forwards between the shelves. There were hardly any shoes left that would pass muster now. Beth clutched the black lace-up more firmly, determined not to let it out of her sight. Jake might be destined to struggle with them every day for months until he outgrew them, but they were a lot better than nothing at all. After the long summer, he was left with one pair of smelly old trainers to his name. And they were white, or had been once. There was no way they could get away with those at Wyatt's.

Beth would have seriously considered giving up the ghost, but the thought of Jake being the only child without proper shoes on his first morning stiffened her resolve. He wouldn't be bothered. But she would suffer the myriad mortifications of the bad mother.

She sighed and trudged back towards her ottoman without much hope in her heart. But when she approached, though the women stared at her, questioning her right to return, one look at Beth's face had both of them shoving up infinitesimally. She subsided gratefully. Just as she was getting settled, she heard her phone. Ugh. It was playing 'Bridge over Troubled Water'. In a mischievous moment, her 'boyfriend' – for want of a better word – DI Harry York of the Metropolitan Police, had programmed her ancient not-very-smart phone with witty theme tunes. This was the one for her mother.

Beth took a deep breath, hoping the phone would cut off. If there was a single thing that wasn't going to improve her day, squashed between strangers on the world's least comfortable seat, it was a conversation with her mother. The tune shrilled on, and Mrs Vicious-Stare turned to give her a look which could have stripped paint. There was nothing for it. Beth somehow wrestled her bag off her shoulder without throwing all three of them onto the floor, and lugged the phone out.

'Mum. Hello,' Beth said cautiously. Ever since she had asked for her mother's help in finding out some background information on old friends at the beginning of the year, Wendy had been even more circumspect than usual in her dealings with her daughter. The pair had never been close. Beth had been very much a daddy's girl, and had been heartbroken and stunned when her kind and gentle father had succumbed to a heart attack in his middle years. She'd even secretly blamed her mother's cholesterol-choked cuisine, especially when Wendy had abandoned her repertoire of fry-ups and steamed puddings right after the funeral and forced muesli and grapefruit on her bewildered children until they'd left home.

'Beth, is that you?' Wendy quavered.

Although still in her fifties, one of Wendy's most maddening affectations, if Beth had been forced to choose from the array her mother seemed to exhibit, was displaying all the quirks of old age. Anyone who didn't know Wendy better would have thought she was simply amazing for seventy-five, from her snowy hair to her carefully vague blue eyes. Beth suspected she was one of the few who realised her mother was only just middle-aged, strong as an ox, and would probably outlive them all. She suppressed a sigh and admitted that she was, indeed, on the end of her own mobile phone.

'But I'm a bit busy, Mum. Trying to get Jake's shoes for tomorrow, you know.'

'Tomorrow? What's happening then?' said Wendy.

Beth's irritation levels swung immediately up into the red zone. How could any grandmother worth the name remain oblivious to such a crucial day? Wendy really took not just the biscuit, but the whole tin too.

'Jake's first day. Wyatt's,' Beth hissed, concerned that every word was being overheard by the two mothers sitting like sentinels on either side of her. Not that she was ashamed of her boy; quite the reverse. But it didn't do to be seen boasting. It was such a tightrope walk, being a mum. You had to take pride in your child's achievements, of course. But you had to be super-careful not to shove those self-same achievements down other people's throats.

'Oh? Oh yes, of course. Don't worry, he'll be fine,' Wendy said, with all the airy unconcern of total indifference. 'But something dreadful's happened, Beth. You won't believe it...' She tailed off dramatically.

Beth took a deep breath. She knew from long experience that her mother was probably fulminating about some slipshod play at the Bridge Club.

Her attention wandered. She looked down at the little ticket in her other hand, and up at the electronic display near the till. Still five people in front of her waiting for fittings. Luckily Jake was very happily occupied, over in his corner, where a group of boys of about his age had now gathered and were all peering at someone's iPhone screen. Beth hoped it was just one of Jake's normal battle games and they weren't looking at anything dodgy. She didn't mind him blasting umpteen enemy forces out of the sky, but she wasn't at all keen on him discovering anything more salty via his peers. As if she didn't have enough worries, the dreaded talk about the birds and the bees was looming...

'...And then I found the body,' Wendy wailed in her ear.

Wait, what? Had her mother really said that?

'The body? Whose body? Don't tell me someone's...'

'Yes, Beth. As I've been saying. It's Alfie. He's – dead.'

TWO

The havoc of the shoe department faded into the background as Beth concentrated fully on her mother's voice for the first time. Why hadn't she noticed, until now, the strain and sorrow in those familiar tones? She'd been far too quick to dismiss her mother's concerns as trivial. But this really did sound like a tragedy.

'I'm so sorry to hear that, Mum. I can't believe Alfie is dead.' Alfie Pole had been Wendy's Bridge partner for ages. How awful, and very sad for Wendy. Beth felt sympathy welling up. 'You must be feeling really shaken. Would you like me to pop in tomorrow? After I've taken Jake in, of course. We can have a cup of tea. You can tell me all about it.'

It wasn't convenient at all. Only a few minutes ago, Beth had been contemplating the acres of free time she'd have now that Jake had got into Wyatt's. She'd even been wondering what on earth to do with herself. But she now realised that, actually, tomorrow would have been the perfect moment to get down to some serious work in her little archives institute. She could have sorted out the whole summer pile-up, and possibly even have caught a glimpse of that very rare beast, the bottom of her in-tray.

There was nothing for it, though. She'd just have to put all that on hold. She knew how bereft she'd felt herself when one of her friends had died recently. True, Alfred had been... well, how old? At least in his mid-eighties, thought Beth vaguely. So, it shouldn't really have been a shock. But age was no doubt a moveable feast. From where she stood, in her thirties, eighty-odd seemed like a fine innings. No doubt the closer you got to that point, the more it started to resemble spring chicken status, and even ninety began to seem like a life cut horribly short.

Sudden death, at no matter what age, was unquestionably hard to face. The loss of Alfie would leave a void in Wendy's constrained and well-ordered life. Beth made vaguely sympathetic noises but was rudely cut short by her mother.

'I don't think you understand, Beth. I'm not upset because Alfie has died. Well, I am of course, but that's not really it, not at all. It's the circumstances, you see.'

'Circumstances?' As usual, Beth felt as though she and her mother were on completely different wavelengths. What on earth was Wendy on about now? Already feeling harassed and by now more than a little tetchy, Beth was aching to get off the phone, her moment of empathy wearing thin.

She checked the electronic display above the cash register – still a couple of people to go – and peered around automatically to see where Jake had got to. He was fine, of course. But the background noise in the department seemed to have ramped up yet another notch, now putting it on a par, Beth was sure, with the main stage at Glastonbury. As well as the buzz of bored and grumpy children, mothers and assistants, some rambunctious little child was now loudly refusing to have anything to do with his mother's choice of sensible footwear, pointing instead to a pair of bright yellow trainers with all the bells and whistles, including light-up soles and orange Velcro tabs. They were seconds away from a full-blown, heel-drumming tantrum.

Beth smiled sympathetically at the red-faced mother's struggles. They'd all been there, and it wasn't pretty.

'Murder! It was murder, Beth. Do I really have to spell it out?' From her mother's exasperated squawk in her ear, Beth realised that Wendy, too, had come to the end of her tether.

As usual, the word got Beth's full attention. But it was ridiculous. Surely her mother couldn't really believe that anyone would want to murder Alfred? He was an inoffensive old man if ever there was one.

'You're not serious? Who would want to kill Alfie?'

'You have no idea, Beth. You really don't. The Bridge Club is an absolute hotbed these days.'

Beth struggled inwardly. On the one hand, there was the Alfie she'd met a few times – a placid, calm, white-haired chap, with courtly good manners and a twinkle still in his eye. He was one of the few who'd been able to hack it as Wendy's Bridge partner for more than a couple of sessions. Wendy liked to think she was the doyenne of the club, but Beth had heard the mutterings over the years – sporadic lapses of concentration and wild bidding had been mentioned. She was apt to blame her mistakes on whoever was playing opposite her at the time. Certainly, Wendy had had more changes of partner than either Elizabeth Taylor or Taylor Swift.

Alfie had seemed not only resigned to bearing the brunt of her erratic style and even less predictable outbursts, but had really seemed to relish playing with her, and they'd lasted longer together than any of Wendy's other pairings.

On the other hand, Wendy had definitely lost her maddening veneer of vagueness, and had come right out with what was bothering her. That in itself was quite startling. Beth was used to circumventing several layers of passive-aggressive obfuscation before being able to disinter Wendy's true meaning. But today, her mother couldn't be clearer.

'I want you to look into it, Beth. That's what you do these days, isn't it? After all, that's how you got my old neighbours into such frightful trouble.'

Beth seethed inwardly. Only her mother could blame her for someone else's brutal killing spree. But she tried to put her annoyance to one side and consider the proposition calmly.

The trouble was Alfie's age. All right, you were only as old as you felt, but from where Beth sat – on a smaller and smaller wedge of ottoman – you had to be feeling it a tiny bit at eighty-five-odd, didn't you? She was pretty sure that disinterested observers would be mumbling all the usual clichés about Alfie's death – 'a ripe old age' and so on.

'Look, Mum, I know you were fond of Alfie, and it's a terrible shame, but...' Beth's gaze roved restlessly around the shoe department as she thought of ways to fob her mother off without her noticing. Suddenly, she caught sight of their number flashing in bright pink neon on the board.

She staggered to her feet, burdened by her heavy bag, with the phone still clamped to her ear. The ticket was now crumpled into a tiny ball in her hot palm. 'Listen, I've really got to...'

'Beth! There's more to it than you know.'

'Oh, come on, Mum. I know it'll be murder for you, finding a new partner and all, but that doesn't mean—'

'You're not listening to me. It won't just be murder for me, it was murder for Alfie, too. He was poisoned, I tell you. Poisoned.'

THREE

It was utterly typical of Wendy, Beth thought the next morning, to manage to take the gloss off Jake's first day at Wyatt's – an epic moment that she, as a proud mum, had been working up to for what seemed like every moment of the past eleven years. Beth felt she ought to be photographing him in his uniform, treasuring the sight of him looking simultaneously absurdly young and heartbreakingly grown-up in the pristine black trousers and smart new blazer. She ought to be gazing at the school crest, emblazoned with the motto *'For God's Sake'* (which had presumably sounded a lot less whingey and petulant when Sir Thomas Wyatt had come up with it in the seventeen-what-sits) and drinking it all in. Her own boy, now a member of the most exclusive, most sought-after group in Dulwich!

But she didn't have a moment. She needed to hustle Jake to the gates and then rush to meet Wendy, before hurtling back to Wyatt's to do a smidgeon or two of work... and all this with Colin, her malodorous old Labrador in tow. All right, this last part was not actively her mother's fault. But the rest of it she totally blamed on Wendy.

Yet despite herself, she couldn't help being intrigued. She'd thought long and hard into the night about Alfie and about who might possibly have wanted to harm the old dear. To her, the whole thing just didn't compute.

'*Mum?* Are we leaving or what?' Jake shouted.

For once, the tables were being turned. Beth was getting chivvied into leaving by her boy. She suppressed a smirk, gathered up coat, bag and phone, gave Magpie a wave and clipped the lead onto Colin's collar. They were off. Wyatt's here they came – ready or not.

It felt odd, walking the familiar route but striding straight on past the gates of the Village Primary where Jake had spent so many happy years. Beth, looking through the gates somewhat wistfully, noticed that all the children inside now seemed so small, so young, compared with her boy. What a difference a few months made. Jake, plodding along fast, head down, absorbed in his own little world, scarcely seemed to notice, but Beth tried to take in every bit of this first journey to Wyatt's together, from the fresh scents of the flower shop they passed to the gusts of expensive perfume wafting from the glamorous Dulwich mummies towing little knots of children up and down the village street to their various destinations.

Waiting at the zebra crossing, glancing across at Jake, Beth's heart was full. If only her late husband James could have been here to see this day. True, he'd been a lot less obsessed with what he called 'all this Dulwich silliness' than she undoubtedly was. He probably would have been annoyingly down to earth about Jake's big day and would have teased her mercilessly for caring so much. He also wouldn't have been best pleased that she'd spent last night with an enormous policeman in her bed. Beth smirked reminiscently as she thought of Harry. No matter how exhausted he claimed to be after a long day tramping the cruel cul-de-sacs of south London, it was extraordinary the way he perked up once they were safely tucked in together.

Suddenly there came an impatient toot, and Jake's call of,

'*Muuuum.*' A Volvo had screeched to a halt for them and the woman at the wheel was barely keeping the vehicle at the biting point, dying to be off. Beth could see she had one tiny car seat in the back of an otherwise empty vehicle – Baby probably had an urgent appointment at the Montessori and her whole educational path would be blighted if she didn't get there on time.

Beth scurried over the crossing as quickly as she could, all but tugging her forelock, and the car zoomed off, burning rubber. Beth shook her head. Funny how mothers always thought their own child's age and stage was the most important. Whereas any disinterested observer could tell you the first day at secondary school, well, that really *was* the biggie, no contest...

As they wandered on up Calton Avenue, Beth realised that for once it wasn't Jake who was dawdling. He was out in front, the pacemaker, while she was bumbling along with Colin, her head full of dreams. She really needed to wake up. As they crossed the intersection with Court Lane, Beth caught sight of two familiar figures, and realised why Jake had been in such a hurry. It was her great friend Katie, with her son Charlie, Jake's partner in crime. The way the two boys greeted each other, with a swipe of their brand-new backpacks and a casual 'Hi', belied the huge grins which lit up both faces. Katie and Beth exchanged their own relieved smiles, each now certain that things would go well. Though both boys were confident and outgoing, it never hurt to have a friend on your side – particularly on a day when everything else was going to be new.

Katie and Beth kissed quickly on both cheeks and Katie bent to pat Colin, who licked her appreciatively. The formalities out of the way, the pair strolled on side by side, picking up the pace a little to keep up with Jake and Charlie. From the speed at which the boys were marching up the hill, backpacks swinging, one would almost think they were looking forward to this.

'No Teddy today?' Teddy was Katie's appalling cockapoo, the worst-behaved dog in Dulwich.

'I couldn't face it. He'll be fine at home for a bit,' said Katie, demonstrating her famous optimism. 'How're you feeling?' she asked Beth.

'Oh, you know. Butterflies. But they'll be in such good hands.'

'I think it's easier for you. You know the school so well, and you'll be there if there's any trouble.'

'Trouble? There won't be any trouble,' said Beth automatically, although no one knew better than she, by now, that evil could lurk anywhere in Dulwich, and Wyatt's certainly wasn't immune. 'Also, and talking of trouble, I won't be around this morning, at any rate. I've got to go and talk to my mother.' Unconsciously, she used the downward-swooping tone of voice she always fell into when discussing Wendy.

'Oh? What's up?' Katie asked lightly.

'You won't believe it, but she says there's been a murder at the Bridge Club. Only her partner, Alfie.'

'Not poor old Alfie Pole? I heard he'd just died. Awful. But he must have been nearly ninety...'

'Exactly. But now my mother is convinced that there's skulduggery afoot. Honestly,' Beth muttered.

Katie looked at her quizzically. 'I'm surprised, Beth. You're usually up for a mystery.'

'I know, but it's my mother. Ten to one it's going to be nothing, just a storm in one of her fancy-pants porcelain teacups. It'll be a total waste of my time. And I was going to start my book plan today...'

Katie smiled and nudged her arm. 'Oh, come on. I've heard that one before. Listen, how about I tag along with you? I know you sometimes find Wendy a bit much on your own. And aren't we in the mystery business together now?'

Beth looked up at her friend. Katie was her perpetual ray of sunshine. A gifted yoga teacher, and happy-go-lucky good egg, Katie had lifted Beth from the doldrums more times than she cared to remember. Whether she was as natural a detective was something that Beth was still taking under consideration. It was definitely true, though, that while three was usually a crowd, with Wendy it was definitely crowd control. Immediately, one of Beth's most pressing anxieties started to dissolve and she grinned her agreement.

'It would be brilliant if you could come. We'll just drop the boys then, shall we?'

The women exchanged glances, eyes wide. Both wanted to downplay the significance of the moment, for the sake of their sons, but Beth knew each was a mass of jitters.

In the end, it was all a bit of an anticlimax. Beth hadn't really noticed what had happened to previous new Year 7 intakes, as her archives institute was nowhere near their playground, but it turned out that the school very wisely limited the opportunity for parents to lurk and spook their offspring. Carers were politely stopped at the ornate wrought-iron gates, leaving the children to file in on their own. Pupils were then immediately whisked off to their new classrooms in seconds, while parents were left in knots outside the school premises, craning wistfully through the bars. Neither Katie nor Beth liked the idea of looking quite so desperate, so with unspoken accord they'd started to make their way back to the village when they – or rather, Katie – was hailed by a loud voice right behind them. 'Katieeee. *Lovely* to see you.'

Katie almost disappeared from view as Belinda McKenzie engulfed her in a huge hug, while Beth had to make do with a glancing blow from the woman's trademark giant handbag. She raised her eyebrows at Belinda's black and white faux-fur coat. It was bang on trend – if you were Cruella de Vil.

'I'm so glad Billy's in Charlie's class. They're so sensible, Wyatt's. They never separate best friends,' trilled Belinda.

Katie smiled brightly, while Beth did her best not to look too put out. Billy and Charlie had lived virtually next door to each other in Court Lane for years but, though on perfectly cordial terms, had never played together willingly, as far as Beth knew. *Jake* was Charlie's best friend. She hastily reassembled her features into a social smile as Belinda finally deigned to include her in the conversation.

'So, it paid off aiming high, then, didn't it, Beth? Jake got in after all. Well, you splashed out on all that tutoring. And, of course, you are working at the school...'

Behind Belinda's shoulder, Katie opened her eyes wide and silently shook her head from side to side. Beth took a deep breath and closed her lips on the many retorts that tumbled, one after the other, onto her suddenly sharpened tongue. How come Jake trying Wyatt's was aiming high, but for Billy it was the obvious course? How come it didn't count that Billy had been tutored from the moment Belinda had decided he looked a little too laid-back in the grainy black and white print-out at her twenty-week scan? Jake had endured just two terms' worth of extra teaching. And how dare Belinda imply that Jake had only got in through some sort of back-door nepotism? All right, Beth wasn't above having considered it, but that route had been politely shut in her face.

She tried to count to ten, got as far as three, and pinned on the best smile she could muster under the circumstances, though she was willing to bet it was as frayed round the edges as one of the ancient tapestries in Wyatt's Grand Hall. 'Lovely to see you, too, Belinda,' she managed, through lightly gritted teeth.

Belinda looked her up and down quickly, seeming disappointed not to have got a rise, and caught sight of Colin. 'Nice that you're helping Battersea Dogs' Home out with that mutt,' she said, and abruptly turned back to Katie, nearly taking Beth's eye out this time with one of the flying buckles on her bag. 'Coffee?' she said, in the peremptory tones that worked so brilliantly on her usual acolytes.

'Another time,' said Katie. 'Got to run. See you later, Belinda.' And with that, she grabbed Beth's arm and the two walked off swiftly down the avenue together.

'Phew!' said Beth, as soon as they'd gone a few paces. 'That *woman!*'

'I feel sorry for her,' said Katie, in quieter tones. 'Well, I did, until she was mean about poor Colin.'

Colin, hearing his name, looked round and gave his best Julia Roberts-meets-a-watermelon grin in appreciation.

'So, it's fine that she implied that Jake somehow cheated his way into Wyatt's?'

Katie squeezed Beth's arm. 'You know she's madly jealous of you and Jake. Always has been. You two never jump through all the hoops, but you still land on your feet anyway.'

'I never knew I was so gymnastically gifted,' said Beth drily. 'But why on earth would you feel sorry for Belinda, of all people? That's stretching compassion the entire length of Dulwich Village – and back again.'

'Well, look at her. She's all on her own. Trying to find a new gang. It's not easy, is it?'

Beth glanced back over her shoulder and, sure enough, there were little groups of mothers forming around the gates, but Belinda, in her magnificent monochrome finery, was standing aloof. She seemed ostentatiously glued to a brand-new phone, so shiny it must just have come out of its box, but as Beth watched, she peeped sideways at one likely gathering, took a step towards them, faltered and came to a halt again.

'What's happened to her old cronies?'

'I don't think anyone else's kids got into Wyatt's,' said Katie. 'Giles Trubshaw somehow squeaked into St Paul's instead, and really put Belinda's nose out of joint. The rest chose other schools. Probably so they didn't have to risk direct competition. And a lot have gone for the state option, of course.'

As usual, Beth felt a mild pang at the thought of a state school. Probably just as good, and no fees... Why, why had she been so set on throwing her money at Sir Thomas Wyatt's cackling ghost? Still, she'd made her decision now.

'Oh well, Belinda's still got Bobby at the Village Primary, so she'll carry on ruling with an iron rod in that playground. I don't have to waste too much sympathy on her,' said Beth bracingly.

'It's the beginning of the end, though, isn't it? The kids don't need her as much, so she can't really justify all the au pairs. So, no staff for her to boss around. And once they're all at secondary school, then there's so much less hanging out at the gates for the mums. That'll be a big lifestyle change for Belinda. I bet she'll go back to work soon.'

'I pity the City,' said Beth. But, almost despite herself, she did feel for the woman. Trying to get back on the career carousel at any point after having children was no easy matter, even for someone with Belinda's apparently bulletproof ego. Beth knew women who'd done it in so many different ways – carrying on working with nannies, giving up entirely, going part time – and she had never heard any one of them say it had been an unalloyed success. There was always compromise, juggling, logistical nightmares, and it always seemed to be the women trying single-handedly to juggle various different-sized and - shaped balls, even if they were married or had partners.

Sometimes, she truly thought she'd had it easy, with only herself and Jake to consider for so many years. In some ways, this mere thought was madness. Being widowed had been no fun at all, and the financial insecurity that even now was freaking her out about the school fees was a worry so well worn it was almost like an old friend. But not having to consult anyone else, or indeed try to please anyone else, had had its advantages over the years. Perhaps she saw that more clearly, now she had someone who, nominally at least, she could discuss decisions with.

An image of Harry flashed into her head for a second. So large, so uncompromising in his rough blue wool jacket, so used to being obeyed. That was the trouble with these commanding types... like Belinda, she supposed. There was definitely an initial attraction to the idea of an alpha male. All that swooning into strong arms was really rather lovely. But living with one was another matter. They just got to the point where they were astounded when people didn't do what they were told.

But she didn't want to compare her own beloved (most of the time) boyfriend to Belinda McKenzie. Drat the woman, she could spoil anything. And all right, Harry was bossy. But that was his job. He was used to being in charge. Someone had to be.

Beth gave herself a mental shake and tuned in again to Katie, who was trying to march her swiftly past the Aurora coffee shop, where Beth, left to her own devices, would always stop. All right, the coffee itself was terrible, but it was one of the few cafés in Dulwich where you could be sure that every word you said wouldn't be overheard and then breathlessly recounted all over the postcode before you'd even paid your bill.

'Hang on a second, Katie. I've said I'd meet my mother here.'

'Not Aurora's? You didn't tell me that,' said Katie with a moue of distaste.

'Well, I wanted you to come, didn't I?' said Beth cheekily, bending down and looping Colin's lead under one of the rickety metal chairs positioned hopefully outside, in case of a sudden September heatwave. Colin looked at her reproachfully with his big chocolatey eyes. She sighed and sloshed some water from the bottle in her bag into the battered old dog bowl on the pavement. She patted his head briskly then held the squeaky door open for her friend and ushered her inside. 'Anyway, they might have bought a new coffee machine to celebrate the start of the school year,' she added encouragingly.

FOUR

Katie walked in, paused and sniffed, then turned to Beth and shook her head once with infinite sorrow. Whatever the smell in the place was, it wasn't freshly ground beans being gently cosseted into giving up their delicious aroma, pretty much the elixir of life as far as Dulwich – and particularly Katie – was concerned. No, it seemed that the Aurora was ploughing on with its tried, tested and sorely lacking old appliances, and as a result it was going to be a wonderful place to have quiet conversations for another year at least. Beth was secretly jubilant, though she assembled her features into a mask of mild regret, for Katie's sake.

Out of the sea of empty tables, the women chose one in the corner, from where Beth could just about see Colin. She strolled to the counter to do battle with the feisty and unfriendly staff – it was only fair after dragging Katie here on false pretences – and returned with a couple of pastries to keep them going while they waited for Wendy.

'What time did you say to your mum?' Katie asked, eyeing the venerable-looking pains au chocolat a mite suspiciously before putting one gingerly on her plate.

'Nine o'clock, but you know her, she'll keep us waiting,' said Beth through a mouthful of pastry which, while still flaky, was not desperately fresh. She was hungry enough not to care. She'd been too nervous to eat this morning – and too busy exhorting poor Jake to cram down more of the cereal he had been chasing around his bowl with his spoon.

'So, tell me all about the summer – all the bits I don't already know, anyway. How's the new place coming along?'

Katie had one of the most beautiful houses in Dulwich, backing onto the park and with a kitchen that, even two full years after it had been finished, was still considered in the forefront of trendy design by those in the know. But she had just taken on a holiday home as well. She and her husband, Michael, a big fish in publishing, had been wringing their hands about whether or not to buy one for years. The idea was to give their precious Charlie a taste of country life, far from the artificiality of Dulwich society. The reality was that they were irresistibly drawn to areas that were full of other weekend refugees from the south-eastern pocket of the capital. Finally, they'd fallen hopelessly in love with a tiny cottage 'in the wilds of Cornwall', which turned out to be a picture-postcard village where stock-brokers outnumbered tin miners by about ten million to one.

Despite having been virtually perfect when they'd bought it, at what Katie admitted were steep London prices, they were now in full-on refurbishment mode. Beth, who'd been shown all the pictures on Rightmove, and who'd suffered enough pangs of envy to satisfy Katie that they were doing the right thing, had no idea how they could make the place better. Every inch of it looked delicious to her, exactly as it was. But if anyone could gild the lily, it would be Katie.

Sure enough, as they thumbed through the photos on Katie's phone, Beth could see the place was coming together beautifully. In a village already chock-full of Farrow & Balled gems, it was going to be the jewel in the crown. It had a deli-

cate latticework wooden porch and dinky little windows
studded either side, like sleepy, come-hither eyes. And it was
now painted the most delicate shade of lavender, with pure
white accents. What any remaining locals would think of it,
Beth dreaded to think. The original owners would have been
hearty fisherfolk, used to roughing it through freezing winters
and isolated summers. Katie's heated flooring, power showers
and Hungarian goose-down duvets were putting paid to all
that.

Though the advent of families like Katie's brought a
sporadic bonanza of trips to the area's water parks, they couldn't
compensate for the lack of a year-round population to keep
schools and shops open. Michael would be the first to fulminate
if the village post office-cum-general store shut down. But that
wouldn't stop him getting Katie to do a massive shop at Waitrose before getting to the cottage to 'tide them over' during their
stay. He'd probably pop in once or twice during the fortnight to
pick up firelighters or a pack of bacon, wince loudly at the
prices, then be astonished when the place wasn't there on his
next visit.

'God, it's so gorgeous, Katie. You are lucky.'

'Mmm, I love it to bits already. And it's so great for Charlie.'

'The fresh air? Lovely walks, the boats? Seaside nearby?'

'Yes. All that. So wonderful,' Katie said briefly. 'But the best
thing is that you can only get a wi-fi signal in the loo round the
back – and it's perishing in there, so the poor boy hardly both-
ers,' she said with a little giggle.

Beth couldn't help laughing along, though she wasn't sure
she'd go to such lengths to stop Jake playing Fortnite. And also,
ahem, she didn't quite have the best part of three-quarters of a
million pounds spare to accomplish it.

Just then, the door jangled, then moved in an inch and stuck
fast. Beth looked round. Wendy was on the other side of the
glass door, yanking ineffectually at the handle. Beth closed her

eyes briefly, then got to her feet and walked round, pulling the handle cleanly and proffering her cheek for the usual peck.

'Honestly, Beth, I can't think why you like this place,' Wendy said a bit too loudly. 'Even the door is defective, and that's before you so much as try the coffee.'

'Shh, Mum,' Beth said automatically, without the slightest hope that Wendy would take any notice. It was already too late. The waiter, behind his counter, threw down his tea towel and stomped off to the kitchen, from whence they heard the sound of fairy cakes being rearranged with maximum prejudice.

Once her mother was settled – which took an inordinate amount of time, and involved much flicking of gauzy scarves and reorganisation of long strings of beads – she looked around with the downward pull of her mouth that Beth dreaded.

'Not a soul in here. Of course. No one but my daughter can stand it, eh, Katie?' Wendy trilled a mirthless little laugh.

Katie smiled back automatically, and Beth's heart sank a little further. Getting Beth's friends onside against her was a typical Wendy tactic, first deployed in her teenage years. It had proved so successful that she still used it today. Beth drummed her fingers on the table, not caring that her irritation showed. Wendy darted her a glance, then seemed to remember who needed who, this time.

'Well, Beth. Who'd have thought I'd be asking your advice, of all things?'

'Who indeed?' Beth countered coolly, meeting her mother's blue eyes. A flash within their depths suggested that Wendy knew when enough was enough.

'I'm so grateful that you've got time for your old mother. Especially when I need you so much.' Wendy's hand came down on Beth's, silencing the drumming fingers and causing her eyebrows to lift in surprise. This was about as fulsome as her mother's praise had ever been.

'No one believes me when I say that Alfie's death was no

accident. Thank goodness my own daughter's on my side,' Wendy continued, now looking at Katie for simple reassurance rather than trying to divide her loyalties.

'Beth's amazing,' Katie said, nodding enthusiastically. 'If anyone can get to the bottom of this, she will.'

'Now hang on a second there...' Beth was already feeling uncomfortably warm. Two compliments in as many minutes? She brushed her fringe off her newly sticky forehead. Was it her, or was it suddenly tropical in here? And did she really want to be lumbered with another mystery, anyway? They always came at a price. She slid her hand out from beneath Wendy's tiny paw, and pulled nervously at the sleeve of her sweater, her fingers absentmindedly brushing past the scar on her forearm. They then automatically traced the silvery mark on her forehead, too. Messing with murders could exact a price.

It wasn't always just physical, either. Many was the night when she was roused from sleep by a horrible memory. Sometimes they were specific – the gleam in a madman's eye, the smell of a dank passageway she shouldn't have ventured down. Sometimes there was just a vague feeling of dread. But it was never easy to get back to sleep afterwards, even if the comforting bulk of a large Metropolitan Police detective was taking up more than half of the bed, and a crazed killer would have to crawl over him to get to her.

On the other hand, this was her mother. Could she really draw the line at helping her? All right, Beth's first foray into amateur sleuthing had been to try and clear her own name, when she'd been implicated in a murder. But after that, she had to admit she'd sometimes got involved out of not much more than idle curiosity. Would it kill her, as it were, to get involved in this just to put her mother's fears at rest?

Wendy's suspicions were bound to be groundless. Beth could just tell her now, forcibly, that she was wrong, that Alfie had died of old age, and to suggest anything else was ridiculous.

But maybe it was unfair to turn her back on her mother's obvious distress. As she watched now, her mother's cornflower blue eyes filled up with tears.

Part of Beth knew this very effective trick had been honed over the years as a supremely effective weapon against her father, who'd crumbled every time in the face of a weeping female. But her dad had been gone for many years. Was Wendy still able to turn on the waterworks at will – or was she genuinely full of sorrow?

Beth sighed. The jury might be out forever over that little matter. What was certain was that Wendy's daughter had been too well trained by this stage. She simply couldn't deliberately cause her mother pain. They might not often – or possibly ever – see eye to eye... but this was her mum. There was a bond there, tattered though it might often seem, that was unbreakable.

And there was a side issue. Beth could never really resist a juicy mystery. Maybe this time, there'd be no unpleasant shocks in the night. Yeah, right, thought half of Beth's brain. The other half was already turning over a new leaf in her notebook and sharpening a pencil in anticipation.

'I suppose you'd better tell me all about it, then,' said Beth slowly.

'Well, I've given you all I know already, dear,' quavered Wendy unhelpfully.

'No, Mum. If you really want me to do this, I'm afraid you've got to give me a lot more information than that. Us,' she said, glancing over to Katie, who was looking suspiciously eager to be included. 'Katie will be helping me, of course.'

Wendy glanced over to Katie in some surprise, but perhaps wisely held her peace. 'I don't suppose there's any danger of me getting a coffee, is there, before I start? My throat is so dry...' she said, essaying the tiniest little cough to underline her point.

Typical, thought Beth. Her mother did her best to alienate

the only waiter, then made it someone else's business to get him back on side. But they could all do with a cup of something. She wasn't sure if it was just a Dulwich rule, or one of the immutable laws of the universe, but a good story did always go down better with a tea or a coffee. She pushed her chair back, went over to the counter and peered sideways into the depths of the kitchen. As well as a worktop covered with fairy cake crumbs, there was a tangle of cups in the sink and an ominously hissing coffee machine that looked as though it had been new on the day Belinda McKenzie had first tried fillers. And that was a date lost, along with the woman's smile, way back in history. No sign at all of the waiter.

Beth tried a rather fruitier version of her mother's cough. Nothing. Then called out a tentative, 'Hello?'

Immediately, there was a cross rattle from the depths of the store cupboard. 'Coming, coming, *honestly*,' the waiter grumbled, as though Beth had been yelling at him for hours.

There was a slight face-off when he eventually emerged behind the counter again, smelling strongly of cigarettes and clearly having flouted all the standard health and safety regulations by smoking in the confined space of the storeroom, over the café's supplies.

How revolting, thought Beth, glaring at him. She really must move on from this place. As usual, nine-tenths of her adherence was from sheer stubbornness in the face of everyone else's lack of enthusiasm. She really ought to grow up. But she bit back a few choice comments and took refuge instead in a veritable blizzard of acid politeness.

'Three teas, please. Two Earl Grey and a builders', if you could. And some milk, if you wouldn't mind. Thank you *so* much.'

With the waiter now severely told off, in Beth's view at least, she sat down with her back to him and rolled her eyes lavishly. Katie hid a giggle behind her hand, but Wendy looked magisterially oblivious. She might appear as delicate as one of the Dresden shepherdesses she collected so relentlessly, but like many women of her age, or even the age she pretended to be, Wendy didn't mind being firm in pursuit of what she wanted, particularly to those she considered underlings. And the world, it seemed, was full of those.

'Now, Beth, if you'll just listen a moment and sit still, then I can get on with the story.' She rebuked her daughter, who fumed inwardly at the injustice.

'I was just doing your bidding...' Beth said mildly.

'Bidding? How did you know it was about that? Don't tell me someone's been filling you in already?' said Wendy, seeming alarmed.

Beth shrugged. 'I've no idea what you're talking about, Mum. Why don't you start at the beginning?'

Wendy gave Beth a reproachful glance and started to rearrange her jewellery, a default move when she was ill at ease. Once every bead was satisfactorily realigned, and once Beth had got her blood pressure down to normal limitations, Wendy was at last ready to speak again.

'The thing is, it was just a normal day at the club. You know?'

'The thing is, *we don't*,' said Beth, leaning across the table. A slight stiffening from Katie at her side gave her notice that she should calm her body language a bit. She drew back, and added more quietly, 'Perhaps you could talk us through it. A normal day, and then this day in particular. Then we'll be able to see if there were any differences.' Her tone was now exaggeratedly patient.

Beth was beginning to despair that they'd ever get any useful information out of her mother, but perhaps that was just as well. As far as she could see, the only crime that had been committed here was by the Grim Reaper, gathering an overblown specimen to his scrawny bosom. All right, the Bridge

Club wasn't exactly the most private way to go. But Alfie might have quite liked it. He'd been doing what he loved. And at least he hadn't been on his own.

Wendy was rattling her beads again, and turned to Katie. 'You understand how it is, don't you, dear?'

Katie, for once, looked politely baffled. 'Um, not sure I do, Wendy?' she said mildly. 'Just tell us in your own words exactly what happened that day.'

'That is, if you can remember,' Beth added heavily.

At the suggestion that her memory might be slipping, Wendy seemed to pull herself together. Sparing Beth a less-than-motherly glance, she started piecing things together. 'Well, I would have arrived at Belair House at about, what? Maybe eleven fifteen or eleven thirty a.m.... and then I would have left at about two p.m.—'

'I thought the Bridge Club started at ten? And carried on until about five? That's what you've always told me,' Beth interrupted sharply.

It had been a bone of contention for as long as she could remember. Bridge had always lain slap bang across her mother's days like an immovable boulder. It had meant that, whatever age Jake had been, Wendy had always been safely occupied twice a week on either side of toddler playgroups and playdates, then school, and even after-school clubs, and couldn't possibly be asked to lend a hand doing the odd pick-up or drop-off, unlike every other grandmother Beth knew.

Wendy avoided looking at Beth. 'There was a bit of a reorganisation of times a while ago...' she said confidingly to Katie. 'Well, some of the newer members wanted a bit of a shake-up. I can't remember quite why.'

Beth fulminated. She was willing to bet it was because they were responsible grandparents and wanted to help their children out. She took a swig of her bitter tea and grimaced.

'When was that reorganisation?' Katie asked, after glancing at Beth and realising she was too cross to speak.

'Oh, a few years ago... does this really matter?' Wendy was wonderfully vague. 'I think I'm remembering a bit more of what happened now...'

I bet you are, thought Beth. But then, what good did it do, getting cross with her mother yet again? Nothing would change Wendy's fundamental behaviour at this point. She took a deep breath and tried to keep an interested smile on her face as her mother continued.

'So, there we all were, collecting in the Bridge Room upstairs, as usual. You both know Belair House, of course?'

Beth and Katie nodded.

FIVE

No one who lived in Dulwich could be unaware of the beautiful white slab of a mansion house that stood at one end of the sweeping road through the village, like a Fortnum's Christmas cake smothered in royal icing. Once upon a time this Georgian masterpiece, which the hopeful always claimed showed the hand of the great architect Robert Adam himself, had been the glittering centrepiece of polite society in the area.

It had been built by a Whitechapel maize farmer-made-good, by the name of John Willes. Just as Beth's frenemy Belinda McKenzie today chucked her husband's money this way and that, trying to crowbar herself into prime position in Dulwich, so Willes had done his best to shed the shameful chaff of his tradesman status via this grand house. He'd have hosted balls and galas aplenty, with the great and good of the area dressed up to the nines in their best taffeta and lace. They'd have been happy enough to dance the night away by candlelight at Willes's house, though they'd no doubt laughed behind his back at their host's Rumpelstiltskin skills at spinning gold out of his humble corn. An invitation to a Belair House soirée would have been a very hot ticket indeed, in the days when a neighbour's hen stopping laying would have been a major talking point for weeks.

These days, Belair House was doing a fine job at keeping afloat in difficult times by hiring itself out to groups like the Bridge Club, as well as providing a perfect backdrop for weddings and lavish parties. Though these occasions were no longer held by candlelight, in all other respects they were as splendid as the thrashes of yesteryear.

'The Bridge Room used to be the ballroom,' Wendy confided. 'But the Bridge Club has been coming so long that, well, we've really settled into the place. Part of the fabric, you know, and they've rechristened the room in our honour.' She couldn't resist a quick preen. Belair House's glamour still cast a spell, more than two hundred and thirty years on. 'I always sit North/South with Alfie.'

Beth and Katie looked at Wendy blankly, and she snorted a little with impatience. 'Really, you two, don't you know anything about Bridge?'

Katie was content to shake her head very sadly, as though admitting to a grave personal failing, but Beth, as usual, rose unthinkingly to the bait. 'Why should we, Mum? We don't play.'

'Honestly, Beth, you do know the rules, you know you do. Your father and I spent so long trying to teach you and your brother. We tried to give you a good start in life...'

Beth snorted. Of all the social graces to concentrate on, was Bridge really the most useful? But she did remember those afternoons. Wendy would round her up, with her unwilling and fidgety brother, and force them to sit at the dining room table with their patient father, who obviously enjoyed the whole business about as much as they did. Wendy always managed to convince herself she was helpfully instructing her offspring in the art of Bridge-playing out of the goodness of her heart, but, even as a young child, Beth had suspected she was being used as cannon-fodder while Wendy honed her own skills in any way she could. Otherwise, the weekends passed for Wendy as Bridge-free wildernesses. Even twenty years ago, she'd been an extremely keen player. It was fair to say she was now some way towards becoming an addict.

Beth felt a twinge of sympathy for her mother. Even if this murder business with Alfie came to nothing – and she didn't, frankly, see how it could go elsewhere – she knew that the loss of such a kindly partner was a crushing blow for Wendy. She was very unlikely ever to find such a sympathetic conspirator in her Bridge crimes again.

'Those lessons you used to give us were *some time ago*, Mother,' she said as mildly as she could, congratulating herself on her forbearance.

Wendy gave her an irritated glance and swept on.

'Well, anyway, the players are named after the points of the compass. North and South are partners, and so are East and West. We sit at square tables, you see. So, you face your partner, while your opponents also sit opposite each other. We play duplicate Bridge at the club – that just means that the same hands are passed around all of the tables in turn. It's fascinating because you're not only playing your opponents at the table, but are pitted against all the other North and South teams in the room.'

Beth glanced at Katie and was glad to see that she looked just as baffled as Beth was feeling.

'You might need to explain all this a bit more,' said Beth, with what she believed was admirable restraint. Really, she deserved a medal for her conduct today. Maybe two.

Katie was starting to move anxiously from side to side. In Jake, Beth would have diagnosed an urgent need for the loo. She lifted a quizzical eyebrow.

'I'm getting slightly worried about Teddy. I thought it was better not bringing him to school for Charlie's first day, but I really shouldn't leave him for too long... You know what he's like, Beth.'

Beth nodded briskly. She knew only too well what he was capable of. Although he was now almost a year old, and had settled down a bit, he was still a particularly hare-brained canine, as far as Beth could tell. Despite her own unexpected ownership of Colin, she didn't pretend to know much about dogs.

Colin was more like a kindly uncle than a dog, anyway. Beth sometimes felt he was looking after her, rather than the other way round. She sat up straighter in her chair and craned forward to see outside. Sure enough, Colin was there and exchanged a resigned glance with her. Neither was having the morning of their dreams, but Colin seemed to realise this was something that needed to be done, and was content – or reasonably so – to sit it out until Beth had finished.

Teddy was an entirely different kettle of fish, if that wasn't hopelessly confusing her animal metaphors. Of course, in conversations with Katie, Beth always referred to him as 'lively' and 'so affectionate'. As with annoying children, such words rapidly became code for 'uncontrollable' and 'an utter pest' – the sort of things she would never, ever say directly to her best friend. Criticising someone's dog was as fraught with danger as breathing a bad word about their offspring, husband, or even, she realised, mother. Though here at least, Beth was quite likely to get in first and didn't usually mince her words.

'Oh, he's such an adorable dog,' said Wendy, apparently quite genuinely as she clapped her hands together enthusiastically. She won a beaming smile from Katie. Compliments for young Teddy were as thin on the ground as Aldi bags in Dulwich's high street.

'I should probably check on Colin too,' said Beth quickly, scenting a possibility of escape, even though she'd just satisfied herself that he was perfectly fine. Or at least being very patient.

'Colin?' Wendy looked puzzled.

Beth tutted loudly. 'Jake's dog, remember?' It smarted that her mother knew Charlie's dog's name so effortlessly, but not that of her own grandson's pet.

'Oh, yes. You still have that, er, creature with you, then?'

Again, Beth sighed. Her mother had been over only the other weekend, and ancient, sweet Colin had been very much in evidence. All right, they hadn't exactly acquired him in the normal way – Colin and Beth had accidentally adopted each other in challenging circumstances – but he'd been part of the family for almost as long as Katie's Teddy. But Beth did admit that Teddy was most definitely the more memorable of the two dogs. In her view, for all the wrong reasons.

'Oh, well,' said Wendy in an ominously small voice. 'I thought you two had cleared a bit of time for me. But if you have to rush off for your *dogs*, then so be it. I do *quite* understand.' She fiddled with the spoon in her saucer, dropping it to the floor.

Beth bent down and picked it up without comment, looked briefly and wistfully at all Wendy's trailing scarves, then polished it on her own coat sleeve before putting it back on the table. Normally, she'd just ask the waiter for another, but here in Aurora it didn't seem worth the inevitable battle.

'No, Mum, that's all right,' she said in resigned tones. 'I did say I'd stay for as long as you need. I know you want to give me all the details. In any case, Colin seems OK outside.'

'And I'll be fine for another few minutes. The house needs redecorating, anyway,' said Katie with somewhat forced brightness.

'Well, then,' said Wendy.

Beth prepared for more endless faffing with the scarves. She wouldn't have been at all surprised if Wendy had slowed down almost to a standstill now that she'd ensured her audience was going nowhere. So, she was a little wrong-footed when her mother burst into speech.

'The thing is, it's quite horrible remembering it all. I suppose that's why I've been dragging my heels a bit.'

'Of course,' said Katie. 'We completely understand, don't we, Beth?' Beth nodded briefly, marvelling as usual at her friend's kindness. In the face of Wendy's distress, Katie had apparently put all thoughts of the wreckage of her house out of her head.

'It was like this.' Unconsciously, both women leant nearer to Wendy as she finally embarked on her story. 'It had been a perfectly normal afternoon. Just the usual. Everything as you would expect.'

Talk about anticlimax, thought Beth, drawing away again a little crossly. Under the table, Katie pressed Beth's battered pixie boot with her own pristine Ugg. Her friend was right. There was no point in putting Wendy's back up again. They'd just be here forever. At least she'd started talking now, even if she didn't seem to have much to say after all.

'We'd played the first two hands, and everything had gone smoothly. Well, Alfie had been a bit hopeless on the bidding, but that was nothing new. I really had been feeling for some time that he was losing it a bit. Very sad, but at his age...'

Beth gave Katie a significant glance. Even Wendy seemed to be conceding that the pile-up of years on Alfie's plate was a factor. And there was still nothing, as far as she could see, that even so much as whispered at skulduggery. The man had not been in the first flush of youth, and there was no getting away from that fact. His death, while hugely poignant – especially for Wendy, mainly as she now needed a new partner – was hardly shocking.

'Isn't that what we've been saying, Mum? Alfie was, well, a little, erm, on the elderly side...'

'Yes, yes, dear, I get it, he'd had a good innings and it's

nothing special when someone like that drops off his perch, or whatever other horrible metaphor you want to use,' Wendy snapped. 'But darling, it was definitely more than that. The circumstances, you see.'

'I'm sorry, but I don't see why the circumstances were suspicious. You'd played a couple of rounds—'

'*Hands*,' corrected Wendy tersely.

'Whatever. Hands. Then poor Alfie dropped dead. Great shame. Terrible. No mystery,' said Beth, pushing back from the table.

'But don't you see? It didn't happen like that at all,' said Wendy crossly.

Beth sighed. 'Go on then. What is it that makes the whole thing so suspicious?'

'It's the *way* he died. And where. Alfie never wanted to go outside at breaktime. He felt – we both did – that it broke our concentration. We tended just to have a quick cup of tea, sitting with the others sometimes, sometimes not, but really keeping ourselves... well, I think young people say, "in the zone", if you two understand what I mean.'

Beth blinked. Was Wendy now suggesting that her daughter was somehow past it, too ancient to decode trendy phrases that she herself was perfectly au fait with? That was a bit rich. But Katie, next to her, didn't seem to have taken umbrage at all. Maybe Beth was taking everything too much to heart, as so often happened with her mother. How was it that family could always press the right, or wrong, buttons?

Beth didn't pretend to get much about her mother's way of life, and she certainly didn't see why Wendy had to treat a game of Bridge as seriously as if she were engaged in some sort of full-on battle with a bloodthirsty opposition. These were elderly folk playing a game, after all. But now Katie was nodding in sage agreement.

'I know how you feel. I'm the same at yoga, between classes.

Everyone wants to get gossiping, you know, start talking about what's going on with the kids or with work, but I have to be careful not to get involved, stay focused.'

'Yes, but you're the actual teacher, Katie, so you've got good reason to stay aloof, I completely get that. I'm not quite sure why you, though, Mum, would need to...?' Beth didn't want to seem rude, but really, sometimes her mother seemed to have the oddest ideas.

'Well, you may find it hard to believe, Beth, but yes, although I'm not an official teacher, some of the others in the club do look to me for guidance. Katie knows what I mean,' Wendy said with a warmth in her eyes as she beamed at Beth's friend, which rapidly cooled as she turned back to her daughter. 'It just so happened that the club director, Deidre MacBride, wasn't able to come to the session that day. She'd previously asked me to keep an eye on things for her if ever she wasn't able to make it. Just informally, you know. There's so much jealousy at the club, sometimes, you'd be surprised. But we knew where we stood, Alfie and I.'

'I'm sorry, Mum, I don't know where you stood? What do you mean?'

'Well, dear, if you need me to spell it out, we were unofficially in charge if Deidre wasn't around. We were one of the better pairs. Not to put too fine a point on it, Beth, and you know I don't like to boast.' Wendy lowered her eyes modestly for a moment, then ruined the effect by going on to blow her own trumpet in a lengthy solo. 'We were actually the top pair at the time. Alfie and I had an unassailable record. And I also have a much surer grasp of the rules than quite a few other players I could mention. Sometimes people are quite happy to deploy a bit of selective amnesia to win an extra trick or two. Honestly, I think you two would be a bit shocked at how sneaky things can get in that place.'

Beth and Katie exchanged glances. In some ways, yes, it was

a bit disturbing to hear that a peaceful game of cards could become so competitive. But on the other hand, this was Dulwich. People here had a tendency to play to win.

Some, like Belinda McKenzie, just made it their life's work to have the biggest, boldest bag in the playground. She relied on the fact it acted as a signifier that she also had the richest husband, cleverest children and largest house. Some preferred the simpler option of becoming CEOs of major companies. Others wanted to push their children further, higher and faster (and Beth rather dreaded the thought that she was in this camp). There was no logical reason to suppose these drives were put straight into mothballs as soon as their owners retired.

Wendy, of course, had never had a job to retire from, unless you counted harassing the other members of her family from the sidelines. And as far as that went, as Beth could attest, she had certainly not decided to draw her pension yet.

'So, you were sort-of in charge that afternoon. I'm not sure why that makes it more likely that Alfie was murdered?'

It was Wendy's turn to sigh. 'Sometimes I worry that you don't have my gift for empathy, Beth. Can't you read between the lines?' Luckily, she moved on swiftly while Beth was spluttering and trying to formulate a riposte which would stop short of causing nuclear war in the café. 'We weren't really supposed to leave the premises. We had to be on hand, in case someone had a complaint about the play. If there's a problem, if someone revoked, say...'

'Revoked?' Katie's eyebrows shot skywards.

Wendy turned to her patiently. 'That's when someone pretends, or even genuinely believes, they have run out of a suit. If they then trump someone else's card, and in a later round it turns out they could have followed suit all along, then they can be liable to a forfeit.'

'Honestly, people actually do that?' Beth's eyes were wide.

'There's a lot at stake. How many times do I have to tell

you?'

'But what? What's at stake? You don't play for money, do you?' Beth asked.

'There are more important things in life than money. Or haven't you discovered that yet, dear?'

Beth didn't think it was the moment to point out that, given her circumstances and her mother's inability or reluctance to help her financially, she'd had no choice but to get to grips with that hard truth a very long time ago. Most notably when her beloved husband James had died suddenly from an unsuspected brain tumour and left her as sole breadwinner and lone parent to a very small boy. There was silence for a beat.

'So, is it just the shame of losing? Or what?' Beth asked tersely.

'At my age, there's a lot of prestige tied up in doing well, you know,' said Wendy with some dignity.

Beth knew her mother was, in fact, a bit of a stripling compared with most of those in the Bridge Club. Indeed, Wendy's participation brought the average age down significantly. But Wendy had always clung to her ageing widow pose. Beth found this hard to fathom, although – together with her hectic (and apparently fabricated) Bridge timetable – it had allowed her mother to sidle out of any childcare burdens. When Jake had been tiny, she'd seen many a granny wheeling a toddler-filled buggy through the streets, and even now she wistfully watched doting grandparents in Dulwich Park on Saturdays when she did her solo kickabouts with Jake, something she was fervently hoping would soon come to an end.

On the Bridge front, Beth supposed that for many of the club members who'd retired from commuting to big jobs every day, or had successfully steered flotillas of children through the choppy waters of family life, continuing to exercise their sharp minds and get one over on their neighbours via Bridge was as important as such things had always been in Dulwich.

'So, people hate to lose face. And they're not averse to the odd bit of cheating...'

Immediately, Wendy sat up straighter. 'Oh, I wouldn't say that, dear. No, no. I mean, there are one or two members who like to remain, shall we say, purposefully hazy about the rules when it suits them. But overt cheating? Not at all.'

'So, what do you mean, exactly?' As happened so often in conversation with her mother, Beth felt herself to be losing the scant stock of patience she'd started out with. Wendy seemed to take one step forward, then deliberately pirouette backwards by a giant leap. At this rate, they'd be sitting in Aurora until next Tuesday, and probably be no further on then.

Katie was getting restless again. Beth could feel it, though her friend was so polite that she was hiding it well. Her sporadic stirring of the cooling, undrinkable tea told a subtle tale, and Beth didn't want to presume on her friendship too far. Katie helping her out in another mystery was one thing – and that in itself was potentially dangerous and almost certainly a terrible idea – but listening to her mother maundering on for hours and getting nowhere was too much.

'What I mean, Beth,' said Wendy, 'is that someone has to be on hand, just to make sure that everyone is playing with, shall we say, their best instincts uppermost. We would never say that someone is cheating. That would be a shocking aspersion to cast. Particularly when we have a number of retired lawyers in our midst; at least one of them an expert in slander. So I was terribly, terribly surprised when Alfie insisted on going outside at breaktime.'

Finally, Wendy had managed to get the crucial detail out. And not a moment before time, thought Beth.

'You weren't expecting Alfie to want to leave the building? So, he was acting out of character that day, doing something that was really unusual for him?'

'Entirely,' said Wendy, nodding her head approvingly at

Beth. For a moment, her daughter felt the glow of having got something right at last. 'Alfie would never usually leave me to deal with everyone,' Wendy continued. 'Because, you see, during the break everyone comes to the director with the problems that have been, well, not exactly piling up, but have, shall we say, begun possibly to accrue in the previous hands played, or even at past events.'

'Everyone likes to bitch about each other during the tea break.' Beth nodded.

Instantly, Wendy's little smile of approval was gone, and Beth felt the usual permafrost re-establish itself between them.

'Really, dear, must you put it like that?'

'Is that what happens, though?'

Wendy thought for some agonising moments, as Katie and Beth exchanged a quick glance. They were both going to have to excuse themselves soon. Even Colin couldn't really be trusted outside on his own all day, and Magpie definitely would be up to no good, either lolling on Beth's new cardigan, which she had foolishly left on the sofa or, her latest favourite pastime, snuggling and shedding generously on the few files of Harry's that weren't too top secret to bring home. Plus Beth should really pop in on her actual job and do some work, if she had a moment. As for Katie, Beth could see only too clearly the pile of rubble her gorgeous Court Lane house would be reduced to if Wendy didn't get down to it pronto.

'Well, I suppose you could call it that, if you must. And really, it is a crying shame. It's so much easier to sort things out as and when they occur, and that's normal practice in Bridge clubs. When I used to go all the way to Beckenham—' Wendy paused here to press a beringed hand to her fragile chest, at the thought of the momentous twenty-minute journey she'd endured occasionally years ago. 'Well, let's just say people weren't afraid to raise the issues at the table, right there and then. We're a little more restrained in Dulwich.' Her tiny smile was smug. 'But that kind of delicacy can lead to its own problems.'

'What sort of problems?' Despite herself, Beth was starting to get sucked into her mother's story.

'Oh, well, you see, unless the person complaining has a really brilliant memory for the cards, all the details can get a bit sketchy. I mean, who can remember who exactly was holding the ten of hearts, say, once the moment has passed?'

Beth shrugged at Katie. Her mother had a point. Beth herself would be hard-pressed to know what to do with the ten of hearts, even when it was actually right there in her hand. Would she remember she'd had it, even seconds after it had been played? She rather thought not. Then something occurred to her.

'But wait a minute, Mum. Didn't you say you played the same hands on each table in turn? If everyone who sits at, say, East—'

'Who *plays* East,' corrected her mother tetchily.

'Plays it, then. But you see what I mean. You can just look at the hands and work out who had what. If you have a record of who's sat where.' Beth felt as though she'd been rather clever as, despite her mother's claims, it had been many years since she'd willingly held a fan of cards and puzzled over their meanings.

'Yes, yes, Beth. But it's more difficult than that... once the moment's passed, well, it's hard to change things retrospectively...'

Beth looked at her mother shrewdly. It sounded to her as though Wendy was flannelling a bit. All right, she definitely seemed to enjoy the added status that went with this Deirdre MacWhotsit lady asking her, even unofficially, to deputise when she wasn't there. But maybe Wendy shied away from doing any actual adjudication. That would be no surprise. Wendy had never enjoyed getting involved in any of Beth's own tussles with her brother, Josh. They were rarer than they might have been in some families, as Beth and Josh's interests were so separate. He'd been an affectionate, though somewhat distant, big brother, but was so lackadaisical and carefree that he'd seemed years younger than responsible, hard-working (and perpetually anxious) Beth.

She remembered, now she was thinking about it, an absurd time one Christmas when she'd wanted to watch one channel on their tiny, ancient telly and Josh had been mad keen to see something else. They'd bickered over the remote, switching back and forwards like the fairies in Disney's *Sleeping Beauty*, zapping the princess's dress from pink to blue. Eventually, they'd settled on watching the third channel – there had only been three back then in the dark ages – which neither had wanted, but had both ended up laughing helplessly, knowing how silly they were being. Wendy, throughout this hours-long spat, had been conspicuous by her absence.

In any case, she was the type, Beth acknowledged sadly, that would always give a man's word more weight than a woman's, and that went double for her son over her daughter. It was enough to give a sour twist to her mouth, and she dragged herself away from the less than happy memories and tried to concentrate on what Wendy was saying now. And to keep an open mind. She looked at her mother challengingly.

'Yes, well, I suppose what I'm saying is that I wasn't best pleased with Alfie, sneaking away like that, leaving me to deal with everything... All right, Deirdre asked me, and me alone, to be her unofficial, occasional deputy,' Wendy went on, 'but Alf and I had always had an understanding. I needed his help. And during this particular break, well, it was a nightmare. Everyone seemed to have a problem, some from weeks ago when I hadn't a hope of knowing what the hands had been, and Alfie was nowhere to be seen. I mean, really, that man was the *limit*.'

SIX

There was a shocked pause in the little café. Even the waiter, who'd darted out of the kitchen for a second, dived back in looking horrified. Wendy fought to get her ragged breath under control, and Beth tried her best not to judge her mother for speaking ill of the dead. By the looks of her, Katie was doing the same, and they exchanged the briefest of eyebrow-raised glances. For Wendy, it had been a long, overtly angry speech. Beth couldn't recall the last time she'd seen her mother so wound up, displaying her emotions instead of cloaking them in as many layers of obfuscation as she wore scarves round her neck. She'd obviously taken Alfie's defection very much to heart.

'So you thought he'd just, what, sneaked off and left you in the hot seat?'

Wendy nodded, biting her lips.

'And you took that pretty badly, by the looks of things. I mean, you were pretty furious?'

'Well, at the time, when everyone was coming up to me with all these petty little arguments, I just felt overwhelmed. It wasn't until I'd been able to deal with the first few that I suddenly thought, where on earth is Alfie, and why isn't he giving me a hand? It wasn't like him, and I have to admit, I was not best pleased.' Wendy looked down at the scratched surface of the table where her cup was still half-full of unappetising, grey liquid.

'And what happened next? Did you manage to sort everyone out?' Beth asked.

Now Wendy started to look even more ill at ease and began a root and branch rearrangement of her beads, keeping her gaze averted from both women. 'Not really,' she mumbled.

'I'm sorry? Didn't quite catch that?' Katie leant forward.

Wendy looked up crossly. 'Well, if you must know, I sort of... well, left, too. I mean, I had to find Alfie, didn't I?' She appealed to the women across the table as though she were the accused in a particularly heinous Old Bailey trial, and they were the sceptical judges she had to talk out of handing down a death penalty.

'So you just, what? Flounced out of the room?'

'Well, really, Beth. I would never use the word "flounce". What does that even mean?' Wendy asked tersely, flicking her scarves up and down in a perfect demonstration, then rattling her beads until they sounded like hail on a tin roof. Katie suppressed a smile and Beth ploughed on.

'OK, then, you, erm, swept out... Where did you go?'

'Well, I went to look for Alfie, of course. He'd just left me like that. I wanted to give him a piece of my... well, I wanted to see where he'd got to,' Wendy finished a little shamefacedly.

Beth could just picture the scene. A ballroom full of angry, entitled Bridge players, all believing with every fibre of their beings that they'd been trumped or overcalled or out-bidded or whatever by their neighbours, and only Wendy to stem the tide. No wonder she'd done a runner. But Wendy being Wendy, she couldn't admit to it. And even now she'd like to blame as much of the situation as possible on her poor, long-suffering partner.

Even though he was actually dead and way beyond helping her sort out who'd been rather sneaky with the ace of spades the week before last.

'So... how long did it take you to find Alfie? And what did you do when you finally caught up with him?'

'That was the thing, you see,' said Wendy slowly. 'It was all so odd. I mean, he wasn't one for fresh air at the best of times, Alfie. All right, he had an allotment, and yes, his own garden was absolutely lovely, but he got people in to deal with all that.'

Really, thought Beth. You could pay people to garden your allotment? Only in SE21. Elsewhere, such hotly coveted plots had huge waiting lists and were only awarded to those who had a genuine interest in cultivating fruit and vegetables. But round here, you could delegate anything, even your hobbies. She didn't know why she was so surprised.

'I wasn't sure where to look for him, really. I mean, he could have popped to the loo.' Wendy lowered her voice as though discussing something highly disreputable. 'Older men, you know. Prostrate...'

Beth smiled at the malapropism, suddenly thinking of her dear friend Nina, who was a great one for a verbal mélange.

'But you didn't, you know, have a check?' Beth arched a brow.

'Well, how could I, really, dear?' Wendy said tersely. 'I waited outside for a while... but time was ticking on, and people started coming out of the ballroom and, I'm not going to say they were attacking me, exactly, but there had been a bit of a contretemps on table two and they really wanted me to sort things out...'

'And you'd promised Deirdre MacThing that you would. And you quite enjoyed that status, too?'

'Well, yes, dear. At my age—'

'Oh, come on, Mum. You're still young.' It was a well-worn

mantra, but it never failed to provoke a smile from Wendy. Today's was a little wintry, though.

'I just mean, you don't get a lot of pats on the back. Not if you live alone...' Wendy's voice was threatening to develop a familiar pattern of self-pitying quavers. Beth, though not entirely unsympathetic, had heard it all before. And, of course, she'd experienced the same thing herself, having been on her own for years after James's death. A fact that her mother always conveniently forgot.

'You're not the only widow in the village, are you, Mum?' she asked bracingly. 'But we get the picture,' she added, glancing briefly at Katie, who nodded. 'People were lining up to have a good old moan and get you to sort out their squabbles. And you'd much rather have done that with Alfie, your partner, at your side. For a bit of moral support. Fair enough. You must have been getting worried about him, by now, as well.'

'Yes, I was. All the more so as several of the gentlemen had, ahem, been and gone, and there was still no sign of Alfie. I don't know why, but I just wandered over to the big window, you know, the one that faces out over Belair Park.'

'Perhaps you were just trying to get away from everyone?' Katie suggested gently. Beth sent her a smile, as usual appreciating her friend's lovely, and extremely handy, combination of tact and shrewdness.

'Yes, that was probably it,' Wendy admitted. 'It was all getting a bit, well, difficult.'

Beth knew her mother really didn't *do* difficult. She'd managed to live on her own terms for years, unencumbered by the demands of a husband or children. Beth's father had been tidied away into his grave decades ago, and Beth had got used to soldiering on alone as best she could. The last thing Wendy would enjoy was being held at bay by a posse of querulous elderly Bridge players, all absolutely certain – as people in

Dulwich always were – that they were right and everyone else was wrong.

'And what happened when you were cornered by the window?'

'Cornered? That's an odd way of putting it.' Wendy sniffed defensively at Beth, but she didn't deny that she had been. Her face suddenly grew grave and she paused for a moment before going on, swallowing a mouthful of cold tea in what seemed to be a bid to steady herself. It didn't appear to work. She slapped the cup down and pushed it away forcefully, splashing a little onto the table. Both Beth and Katie reached for their phones protectively and rubbed off imaginary droplets. 'Well, however you want to describe the moment, that's when I – saw him.'

'Saw Alfie?'

'Yes, of course, Beth. Who else?' Wendy said tetchily.

Beth blinked, but supposed she should put her mother's snappiness down to emotion. It couldn't have been much fun to catch sight of her Bridge partner's dead body. But wait a minute.

'Did you know he was dead, then?'

'No,' said Wendy, looking desolate. 'No, I didn't. I just thought he'd escaped and left me to face the music with the rest of the club all having a go at me. If you must know, I was pretty fed up with him. And I went outside to give him a, well, a talk-ing-to.'

Oh dear, thought Beth. Guilt was so often a part of bereave-ment. God knew, she had felt awful enough when her James had died, feeling that if only she'd taken his handful of vague symptoms more seriously, she could have forced him to go to the doctor before things reached the doom stage. But Jake had been so young, and had needed so much of her time and attention...

Anyway, she couldn't afford to go down that rabbit hole of recriminations now. Here was a situation that she might well be able to help with. It wouldn't make good Jake's fatherless state, but in some small way Beth felt, with these mysteries she kept getting entangled in, that she was doing something for the wider community of Dulwich. Not that it seemed at all grateful so far.

'So you rushed outside to confront Alfie, get him to come back inside and give you a hand with all the arguments... and what did you find?'

'Really, Beth, must you drag me through it all again? I can hardly bear to picture the poor man...'

'It must be so hard for you,' said Katie immediately, putting a soft hand on Wendy's small gathered fist. 'We understand, we really do. Don't we, Beth?'

There was perhaps too much of a pause before Beth nodded her agreement. How could her mother expect her to help solve a crime, when she wouldn't describe it to her, or show her that one had even been committed? But Beth knew better than to say that. She did her best to ooze sympathy instead. She put her head on one side and compressed her mouth into a line, hoping to imitate an understanding smile. It seemed to work, because Wendy carried on slowly.

'I suppose I was in a bit of a, well, I won't say temper, I never get heated,' said Wendy, bunching her scarves.

No, thought Beth. That would be too easy. You like to poke a few cold daggers into your victims instead. But she was being harsh, she knew. Her mother wasn't evil, she was just... a mother. This sort of behaviour came as standard. Beth hoped she didn't do the same to Jake, but realised it was a time-honoured method of control used by women throughout the centuries. People without physical power had to deploy subterranean means to achieve their ends. She didn't like it, but until things changed, the human race was pretty well stuck with it.

'I raced round to the bench where I could see Alfie, just sitting there, with his back to the house. He seemed not to have a care in the world.' Wendy bit back a sob. 'I didn't realise it then, but that's because he wasn't *in* the world any more. Poor, poor Alfie.'

'So, let me get this right, you left the grounds of Belair House, and went into the park itself?'

Wendy glared at her resentfully through moist eyes, but Beth knew she had to plough on. 'I'm sorry, Mum, I don't want to spoil your moment, remembering Alfie and all, but we do need to get the details right.'

Wendy sighed. 'Oh, I suppose you do. You'll be no help, otherwise,' she said with a sniff.

Beth swallowed down a retort. Now that they were so close to getting the real facts, she didn't want to derail Wendy's train of thought.

'Yes, yes, I left by the gate. It was open; it always is in the daytime. I think they shut it at dusk, like Dulwich Park, you know?' Her mother was right, the gates were left open during the days then padlocked overnight. In the case of Belair Park, it was a little pointless, as the fence was not high. But still, standards had to be seen to be kept up.

'Wait a minute, your eyesight must be amazing, to see Alfie sitting on a bench in the park, from the window. It's quite a long way, isn't it?'

'It is, yes. The house hasn't kept all its original grounds but the lawns at the back are still extensive. But I wear my glasses when I'm playing Bridge, you know, dear. My sight may not be quite what it was, but I'm not blind. And besides, Alfie was wearing his hat.'

'His hat?' Beth wrinkled her forehead behind her fringe.

'Yes, he always wears a bright red bobble hat, winter or summer. It's one of his things, you know. Well, it was,' she added with a lugubrious sniff.

'And he was wearing it that day? It wasn't that cold, though.'

'You young people with your hot blood. It's not the same for us oldies,' said Wendy.

'Oh, Wendy, you're not old,' said Katie obediently, hitting exactly the right note. Wendy preened a little and gave Beth a triumphant smile, which she chose to ignore.

'So, you saw Alfie in his red hat. I suppose it could have been someone else wearing the same, or a similar hat, and you wouldn't have known the difference?'

'Yes. Except it *was* Alfie, of course. As I discovered when I went up to him on the bench,' said Wendy with a delicate shudder which caused her scarves to tremble like aspens in a breeze.

'And what, exactly, did you see?'

'Really, Beth, you needn't sound so prurient. This is upsetting, you know.'

'I'm well aware of that, Mum, honestly I am. But your eyewitness account is vital. I'm not going to get access to any crime scene photos, so if I – we – have any chance of getting to the bottom of this, we need to hear absolutely everything you can remember,' Beth said earnestly, looking at Katie for approval. Katie nodded her head vigorously.

'I see. Well, it's painful, of course, but I'll do my best,' said Wendy, composing herself with a brief shake of her beads. 'I went up to Alfie. I'd been walking quite fast, because we didn't have much of the breaktime left and he really needed to come back. Time was ticking on; we had several more rounds to get through that afternoon and there'd be hell to pay if we caused a hold-up. The trouble with the people at the Bridge Club is that they really like to stick to their schedules,' she said confidingly.

Beth sucked in her breath. Her mother was the worst culprit ever for this, adhering to her Bridge timetable more tenaciously than a reduced-price sticker to a birthday present. But Beth buttoned her lip and Wendy took up the narrative again.

'I was calling out, "Alfie, Alfie," as I got closer, and I thought it was very odd he didn't respond. If I'm honest, I thought he was being quite rude. First of all, he'd left me in the lurch. Then he was ignoring me. Well, of course he wasn't, but I didn't know that then. So I'm afraid I did shout a bit. And as I got near enough to the bench, I took hold of his shoulder and I – well, I shook it.' She shut her eyes, as if to banish the memory.

'What happened next?' Beth prompted, hoping to cut the theatrics to the minimum.

Wendy's eyes flicked open and gave Beth a hard stare. She turned to Katie instead and, to Beth's horror, the tears formed again, and this time broke the banks and started to trickle down well-powdered cheeks.

'He-he-he just sort of collapsed, onto his side. All in one piece. Not like someone who's asleep. More like a... a... plank of wood,' Wendy said, her voice rising to a wail.

Immediately, the waiter popped his head out of the kitchen. This might be the worst café in Dulwich but that didn't mean you could make a scene here. Outside, Colin finally raised his voice in protest. That was it, as far as Beth was concerned. If a dog as patient as Colin had had enough, then she didn't even want to think about what Teddy was doing to Katie's curtains.

'Listen, Mum, Katie and I have to shoot off now.'

'But aren't you going to *do* anything?' Wendy asked tremulously.

'Of course we are,' said Beth. 'First thing tomorrow. We'll check out the crime scene in Belair Park.'

SEVEN

Beth looked at her watch at nine the next morning. It wasn't like Katie to be late, especially when she'd got her way and insisted on meeting at her favourite café rather than the dreaded Aurora again. Jane's was packed already, and it was destined to stay that way until it finally shooed its clientele out onto the streets at seven that evening. Beth had only managed to grab a table by sheer luck – and the fact she'd accidentally-on-purpose kicked a toddler's well-chewed elephant toy under the counter. When he'd screamed the place down and his harassed mother had bundled him out, Beth had swooped.

As she waited, Beth wondered anxiously about Jake. He seemed to have survived his first day at Wyatt's yesterday without obvious scars, but he'd gone to bed early, *sans* the usual nagging, and had still looked a bit haggard this morning. She briefly wondered whether it was all going to be too much for him. Perhaps Belinda had been right; perhaps the tutoring meant he wasn't going to cope.

Thank goodness, she then spotted Katie's blonde halo of hair. Her friend paused on the threshold and Beth waved. She had already got the coffees in, ready for a good debriefing on

Wendy, but Katie plunged in straight away. 'Did you do OK with that Maths homework?'

'*What* Maths homework?' she asked in horror. Oh no. Don't say it was starting already. Jake had always had a bad habit of pretending tasks were 'optional', as she'd frequently discovered to her embarrassment and the teachers' frustration. She'd already told him that wasn't going to wash in big school. And he'd told her never to refer to it as 'big school' again.

'Don't worry. They're probably in different sets, or something,' Katie said. Instantly, Beth fretted that Jake had already been consigned to the bottom rung of the Maths ladder while Charlie was speeding away to the upper echelons. Katie was still talking, though. 'But listen, are you going later on?'

'Going where?' asked Beth, taking a spoonful of delectable milk froth from her coffee. Mmm, it was getting a bit cool but was still heavenly.

'The coffee morning. At Belinda's, of course,' said Katie with a little shrug.

'Not invited. Obviously,' said Beth.

'Really? No, she won't have left you out. She wouldn't... would she? Here, check your phone.'

'No point. You know what she's like. Ever since... well, forever, she's given me the cold shoulder. Or just tried to knock me out with that damned bag of hers, like she did yesterday. She's made a decision. She's not going to have me over again.'

Katie tutted. 'I can't believe that. Honestly, she's... silly sometimes.' Beth thought this was much too mild an assessment but remained silent. 'Would you rather I didn't go?' Katie looked up with guileless blue eyes, and Beth didn't have the heart to admit that, yes, actually, she'd much prefer it if Katie boycotted Belinda from this point on, out of solidarity.

'Course not. You go, and report back. I want to know everything. New au pair, new appliances, new girlfriend for Barty – the works.'

'She'll be getting rid of the au pair. And I'm sure she was talking the other day about tightening her belt.'

'That was just a boast. She was saying she'd lost weight, not that she wanted to economise. Hell hasn't got that chilly; not the last time I looked, anyway. You've probably got to shoot off, then,' Beth said, hoping she didn't sound too despondent.

Katie looked guilty. 'Well, I've got a bit of time... Listen, how do you think it went yesterday?'

'What, with my mother? The usual mess of twaddle, precious few actual facts... I think we'll need to know an awful lot more before we decide if we want to get involved...'

Katie looked shocked for just a moment. 'No, I meant with the boys. First day, and all.'

'Oh. *That.* I think it was fine. You know Jake, he was quite tight-lipped. Like he'd taken an oath or something. Deflected all my questions, even the really cunning ones. Wanted to ask what Colin and I had been doing all day instead. I can't believe he's using my own distraction technique against me.'

Katie nodded in solidarity. Though Beth reckoned Charlie wasn't quite as wily a customer as Jake, Katie too had spent years wheedling out the truth in the face of determined opposition. 'Charlie was the same. Maybe they just need time to process it all before telling us.'

Beth nearly snorted, but refrained in her best ladylike manner. She didn't want to cast aspersions on Katie's lovely optimism – and she didn't want to risk spraying her cappuccino foam around the café either. 'Jake was tired, though, no question. It's a lot, the first few days.'

She thought back to her own work debut at Wyatt's. Added to the enormous size of the place, and the dauntingly shiny air of competence that everyone radiated, for her there had also been the unfortunate matter of her boss's sudden death. She was willing to bet that, however things were really going for

Jake and Charlie, it wouldn't be quite as bad as that. 'I dare say they'll be fine.'

Katie's eyes were troubled for a moment, then she sipped her drink. 'Well, you know the place. I'm so glad you're on the spot.'

'I haven't exactly been ever-present so far. What with my mother yesterday, then going to Belair Park today...'

'Ah yes, that,' said Katie. 'Listen, do you mind if I take a rain check on that? The coffee morning... like you said, one of us should go.'

Beth looked at Katie. She'd never been sure that her friend was really dedicated to being the Hastings to her Poirot. And sidling out of an important fact-finding trip to a murder scene was not a promising sign. But, on the other hand, maybe someone did need to know what Belinda was up to.

'That's absolutely fine, of course,' she said. 'I'll let you know what I find out. And vice versa?'

'Scout's honour,' said Katie.

* * *

It wasn't until later, as she pored over a perfectly ordinary-looking bench in the deserted green space of Belair Park, that Beth remembered neither of them had ever been Scouts. Or Brownies, come to that, though Beth had tried to make up for that by eating her weight in them many times over.

It was a distinctly autumnal day. The shrubs tufting through the fence at the perimeter of the park were changing from green to rusty brown. Though it was almost eleven now, the bushes still looked drenched with the night's dew, or perhaps it had been drizzling slightly when she'd been in the lovely warm café. Fingers of cold stroked her neck and cheeks, reminding her that the year was all downhill from here, weather-wise at least. Presumably, two hundred-odd years ago, a rather grander planting scheme had held sway, but today this bit of Belair Park was mostly uninspiring lawn, an also-ran compared with Beth's favourite open space, Dulwich Park.

She focused on the bench again. What could it tell her? Surely something? But the harder she looked, the more uncommunicative it seemed. An iron frame, painted a municipal dark green. A very plain functional design. It didn't look comfortable. She sat down gingerly, not afraid of getting anything on her jeans – she really wasn't precious about them, and with good reason – but still filled with an irrational sense of revulsion. Someone had died here. There might be no outward sign, no remnants of police tape, no X marking the spot, but she did feel a lingering malignity in the atmosphere. Just as she was telling herself not to be so silly, that there was nothing supernatural clinging to the place and she was being ridiculous, there came a sudden shout of 'Oi!' Beth jumped a clear foot in the air.

When she came back to earth, she looked around frantically for the source of the noise. Who was yelling at her? The only person she could see was a little old lady with an even smaller dog on a lead, the mutt resplendent in a tartan coat. Surely such volume could not have emanated from such a diminutive form. As she watched, the old lady put her head on one side, the dog tilted his to the other, so that they looked like matching bookends. Cross bookends.

'Um, hello?' Beth ventured. The pair came forward. Slowly, very slowly. The dog, now she saw it more clearly, was very stout, the coat not buckled underneath its low-slung tum but held on with a piece of string. Its owner was no less generously proportioned; almost wider than she was high. Though Beth felt a momentary excitement at finally having met someone in Dulwich who was around her own height, the angry look in the lady's eye was definitely daunting.

'*What* do you think you're doing, sitting there?'

After the bellowed 'Oi,' Beth had been expecting to have to

decode a rich south London accent, but this sentence was all cut glass, of the type that once would have shone brightly on the dining tables of John Willes. Beth had an idea, and sat up straighter.

'I said get orf, not get comfy,' the voice came again, as the lady shuffled inexorably closer.

Beth considered her options. She could either continue to sit and be shouted at, she could stand and wait to be told off, or she could close the gap between them and maybe have a bit of a chat. She chose the third path.

'I'm sorry, what's the problem with me sitting there? This is a public park, isn't it?' she said as she loped forward.

As she'd hoped, the lady looked horrified. 'Don't you know what happened there, young lady? Such a short time ago. People have no respect these days. None at all. Shocking, shocking.'

Now that she'd got her way over the seating arrangements, the lady seemed to have lost interest in Beth and started to amend her trajectory and shuffle towards the park gates instead, her little dog plodding just as slowly at her heels.

'Hang on a second,' said Beth, catching up in a stride. 'Is there something about the place where I was sitting?'

The woman looked up at her – a delicious feeling that Beth couldn't help savouring – and then gave a loud, disgusted sniff. 'Well, if you don't know, then I'm certainly not going to tell you. We're not like those youngsters who waste their money tying flowers round lampposts and all that sort of silliness. Not at our age!' Then she started shuffling again.

Beth wasn't sure quite what she was being accused of, so she edged along to keep up. 'It's just, that bench, well, from what I understand...'

'Yes? And what do you understand, a gel like you?' This time, this little Miss Tiggywinkle of a lady had stopped short (very short) and was waving a shaking finger up into Beth's face.

'No respect. That's what it is.' At this, her minuscule dog started to growl, the sheer unfriendliness of the sound quite at odds with his jaunty tartan wrappings. 'That's right, Tinker. You tell her!'

'I'm very sorry, we've really got off on the wrong paw, er, foot. I just wanted to ask you... some questions, if I could? About that bench?'

'I thought I'd made it perfectly clear. I have nothing to say!' With that, the lady hugged her flapping coat around her, took a firmer hold of Tinker's lead and swept off. The trouble was that her steps were so mincing that her finest sweep advanced her by only a matter of centimetres.

Beth took half a pace forward and was abreast with her again. She took a deep breath, and plunged in.

'I'm just looking into the death of Alfie Pole. My mother, Wendy, well, she's in the Bridge Club that plays at Belair House, and she's asked me to investigate a little... Alfie was her partner.'

Immediately, it was as though a switch had been pulled. Both the old lady and the dog melted as fast as marshmallows by an open fire. 'Wendy? Well, why on earth didn't you say, dear? How absurd. Did you hear that, Tinker? Wendy asked her to. Wendy. Yes, Wendy. *Wendy, Wendy, Wendy,*' she cooed, rubbing Tinker's tummy as he writhed on his back on the damp grass.

Beth looked on, bemused. She certainly wouldn't have permitted Colin to get himself quite so thoroughly snuggly on the muddy ground, but maybe this lady was less phobic about the smell of wet dog. She hoped poor Colin was OK. She'd thought that she and Katie would be super-busy this morning, so she'd left him guarding the sofa, under strict instructions not to let Magpie near it. She had reckoned without Belinda's coffee morning disrupting proceedings. Bloody Belinda, forever lobbing a spanner in the works.

Now she felt obscurely guilty, as she was in a park, without her dog. It seemed wrong, somehow. She consoled herself that Colin might have accidentally eaten or stepped on Tinker if she'd brought him, as the little pooch was so weeny. Neither of them would have wanted that on their conscience. And if she didn't tell him about the park, Colin would never know. That was the great thing about dogs.

'Um, I'm trying to gather as much information as possible about that day, the day when Alfie, well, you know... on the bench. Just to put my mother's mind at rest, you see,' Beth said, edging round and trying to get more of the lady's attention. She was still lavishing tickles on Tinker's belly, but she gave him a final couple of pats and straightened up, smiling now at Beth.

'Good of you, yes, good of you. Infuriating woman, in many ways,' she said, quite airily.

'Excuse me?' Beth felt herself bridle. Was this woman talking about her mother? True, very few encounters with Wendy came and went without Beth thinking far more highly coloured thoughts about her – but then Wendy was her mother. She couldn't tolerate even mild criticism of Wendy from a total stranger. That was breaking all the rules.

'Heart's in the right place, though,' the tiny woman continued. 'So, she's got you looking into it, has she? Good for her. She did mention something of the sort, but I thought she'd never get round to it. You know what she's like.'

Beth, who very much did, seethed silently. Perhaps the woman sensed something, for she carried on.

'Well, let me think back. Not easy at my age, you know. But yes, there was definitely something odd about the way that poor old Alf snuffed it. You take it from me.'

Beth immediately decided to take nothing this woman said at face value. If she'd ventured an opinion about the day of the week, Beth would have checked and cross-referenced it thoroughly before trusting the information.

'What makes you think that?' she asked through narrowed eyes.

'Bit fishy, that's all. Fishy, wasn't it, Tinker?' she looked to her little mutt for confirmation, and the dog barked sharply. 'See?' she said, as if that was as good as a signed confession. And, with that, she was shuffling off again. Beth took a dainty side-step and stood in front of her.

'Listen, I really need more information than that. Did you see anything? Is that why you're so sure?'

'Ha! Not catching me that way, young lady. Wasn't born yesterday,' said the woman, adjusting the angle of her shuffle slightly and continuing on. Tinker's lead looped inexorably round Beth's leg and she shook it off crossly.

'Look, can we sit down and talk about this?' Beth asked, gesturing to the bench, then remembering and hastily adding, 'Not there, not there! Maybe inside Belair House?' Then she realised how long it would take them to reach it at the current rate of progress. 'How about *that* bench?' she asked instead, pointing to one a short distance away.

The old lady looked at her shrewdly. 'Want to pick my brains, do you? Hmm, I'm not surprised. After listening to all Wendy's gibbering, you probably want a sensible version of the story. Can't blame you. Well, do we have time, Tinker?' she looked down at the little dog, who put his head on one side for a moment, before yapping briefly once.

'Oh, all right then. He insists, you see,' said the lady, starting the long (for her) trudge to the bench.

Beth wondered if it would be very rude if she just sat down and waited, but decided instead that she might as well start on her questions while they were infinitesimally on the move.

'Taking you back to that day, did you see Alfie going out to sit on the bench?' she started.

'Nope. Must have missed that bit. Playing Bridge, you know. That was the point of the exercise, not keeping the members under scrutiny. Just became aware of it once the whole hoo-ha was well under way. Surprising how much that happens,' she reflected.

'Once you did see him, what did you think? Did you, er, know he was dead straight away?'

The lady paused. 'Nope. He was sitting bolt upright, but then, he always had a bit of a military bearing. Very nice shoulders, you know,' she added confidingly, with a reminiscent look in her bright brown eyes.

Beth registered surprise for a moment, then wondered. Was it possible that Alfie had been a bit of a catch? And if he was, what did that mean for her mother's interest in him? Beth shook off the uncomfortable feeling. The absolute last thing she wanted to be doing with her free time was probing into her mother's love life.

Wendy was entitled to have one, of course she was. It had been decades since Beth's father had died, and these days Beth was in no position to pretend that it was necessary to remain forever faithful to one's first love. But that didn't make it any easier to think about. Beth suppressed a shudder and turned back to the matter in hand.

'Listen, I'm so sorry, I don't know your name?'

The lady paused mid-shuffle and Beth immediately cursed her social instincts. She'd inadvertently slowed things down even further. But once she'd proffered a tiny hand and shaken Beth's surprisingly hard, the woman got back to shuffling quite quickly.

'Claire. Claire Greaves. Mrs Greaves to you. And you'll be young Betty.'

'Beth,' Beth corrected automatically.

'That's right, Betty,' said Mrs Greaves, finally reaching the bench and subsiding onto it gratefully. She turned a baleful eye to the other bench and shook her head sorrowfully. 'Poor old Alf. He had so much more left in him, if you know what I mean.'

For a second, Beth didn't quite realise what she was looking at. Mrs Greaves seemed to have something in her eye. Something enormous, given the contortions her face was taking on. Then it dawned on Beth that her companion was winking. Very, very slowly. Ugh. She had to move things on and try and find out something she *did* want to know about Alfie.

'Um. If you could just tell me why you think something wasn't quite right that day. You said...'

'It was the way he was sitting. Rigid, you know. But not in a good way,' she cackled.

Beth looked at her quickly. She was starting to get some odd ideas about the activities of the Bridge Club that she really didn't want to explore.

'Yes, quite a gathering there was, by the time I got here.' This didn't surprise Beth at all. She was only astonished that the whole matter, and poor old Alfie, hadn't been tidied away by the time Mrs Greaves straggled onto the scene.

'Of course, I had my electric chair that day.'

'Electric?' Beth ventured.

'Well, I call it that. Like that nice Stephen Hawking's chair – but faster. Amazing thing. And I can put Tinker here in the basket,' she said, smiling, while the wiry little dog showed the whites of his eyes for a moment in what looked like terror.

Beth blinked briefly at the vision. 'So, you were here soon – well, reasonably soon – after... it... happened?'

'After he died. Yes. Why is your generation so mealy-mouthed about death, I wonder? It's coming to us all, you know. Even if you're *gluten-free*,' she said with surprising venom.

'I don't have a problem with gluten,' Beth said defensively.

Mrs Greaves snorted. 'You'll have a problem with death, though, I'll be bound,' she said tersely.

Beth wondered for a moment. Well, yes. But was that unreasonable? She thought not. Death wasn't good, in whatever

form it took you. She wanted to use her time, while she had it.
All the more reason to crack on now.

'So, if I can ask... what did Alfie actually look like? Were
there any signs of, erm, foul play?'

Mrs Greaves thought for a moment. Beth waited breath-
lessly, and the whole of the park seemed to breathe quietly with
her. There was the mildest sound of dripping from the wet
foliage, a husky panting sound from Tinker, very distant traffic
noises from the village. Quite peaceful. If she hadn't been
waiting for crucial information, Beth might have taken the
moment to relax. As it was, she was at screaming point by the
time Mrs Greaves opened her mouth again.

'I'm sorry, what were we saying?'

Beth ground her teeth silently. 'I was just asking you how
Alfie looked, you know...?'

'Oh yes. Ghoulish lot, your generation. In my day—'

'Um, any thoughts on Alfie? You did say earlier you thought
things were a bit "fishy"?' Beth couldn't quite believe that she'd
got her hands on a witness, only to be baulked by the woman's
complete inability to divulge any information.

'Rigid. That's all I can say, really. A bit too, you know,
upright. Usually people slump a bit. Seen a few, over the years,
and generally people are horizontal, not vertical. Hmm. That's
all I can say really. Flo would know, of course.'

'Flo? Flo who?' Beth racked her brains for a Flo that Wendy
might have mentioned. 'Is she in the Bridge Club, too?'

'Flo? No, don't be ridiculous, dear. Of course not. She
worked at the undertakers. Years ago, now.'

'Um, you think I should ask her, though?' Beth considered
the thought. Perhaps it wasn't as batty as it sounded. If this
person worked at a funeral parlour, she'd certainly know a thing
or two about corpses. If there really was anything peculiar about
Alfie's posture, then she'd be the ideal person to chat to. 'Where
would I find her?'

'Who?'

'Um, this Flo you suggested?'

Mrs Greaves cackled again, and this time had to delve in her pockets for a battered old cough sweet before she could go on. 'Don't be silly, dear. Flo won't tell you anything.'

'She won't? Why?'

'Six feet under, dear, that's why,' said the old lady, laughing again at her own extraordinary wit. At her feet, little Tinker echoed his owner by opening his mouth in a big hairy grin.

Beth got up from the bench, propelled by a sudden burst of irritation. This was getting her exactly nowhere. Then she sat down again abruptly. Unless she was very much mistaken, there was another member of the Bridge Club coming their way. It was Miriam, a sort-of friend of her mother's, who'd been tangentially involved in Beth's investigation of an artist's death last January. In fact, it was really Miriam's dog Liquorice that she recognised. He was a bigger version of Tinker; she remembered Miriam and her friend describing him as a Heinz – fifty-seven varieties. His stubby tail was like a metronome on allegro, his bristly coat was studded with bits of leaf, and he had a chunky twig clenched in his teeth. It had clearly been a busy morning.

Miriam raised a hand in the air in vague greeting but looked set to march onwards. The collar of her jacket was pulled up against the chill and she had a scarf wrapped round her neck. She seemed deep in thought. Beth couldn't let this chance pass her by, though.

'Miriam, hi. Won't you join us?'

Miriam looked up, seeming confused, then took a closer look. 'Hi, Claire, I thought it was you. And... erm? I do know you, don't I?' she said, squinting at Beth.

'It's Betty, Wendy's daughter,' announced Mrs Greaves loudly, drowning out Beth's attempts to put her straight. 'She wants to ask you lots of questions about Alf. You know, poor old Alf Pole.'

'Alf?' Miriam all but leapt out of her skin. 'What on earth for?'

'Oh, Wendy's got a bee in her bonnet. Thinks there was something up with him.'

Miriam seemed to weigh the matter, while her dog took advantage of her indecision to pad forward and say hello to Tinker. The two enjoyed a good sniff of each other's bits and bobs before Miriam appeared to decide. Then she wedged herself onto the bench between the two women. It was all a little more intimate than Beth liked to be with virtual strangers, and altogether too reminiscent of the shoe department at Peter Jones, but she was excited enough about the prospect of getting more information not to edge too far away. She didn't want to seem unfriendly.

'So, you were there on the, erm, fateful day, were you, Miriam?' she asked.

Miriam sighed and shook her head, her precision-cut grey bob fanning out around her. Her lipstick was a vivid slash in a pale face whose tone was not a million miles from her ashy hair. Altogether, Beth thought she looked like a well-heeled woman who was determined to come over as 'alternative'. Her clothes – a donkey jacket that Harry York would have loved (and would have looked devastatingly handsome in), her shiny Doc Marten boots, her thick magenta tights and curiously pleated red cotton skirt – would have looked at home on a twenty-something student at Central St Martin's art school. But they were all suspiciously clean and fragrant, which, Beth rather thought, was not authentic. Or hadn't been in her own student days, at any rate. If David Hockney had decided to dress as a woman of a certain age and sit on a London park bench... but Miriam was speaking.

'Well, yes, I was there, unfortunately. I rather wish I hadn't been. Poor old Alf. One moment he seemed fine, the next... well, you've heard. When I say that, it was probably about twenty minutes, to be fair. Long enough for him to have a heart attack or whatever it was.'

'Wait, were you actually playing with him right before it all, ah, happened?'

'Well, yes, as it turns out. Wendy and Alf were North/South. Wendy always plays South. Even though she's one of our more, ah, able-bodied members, she likes to stay put. All her scarves, you know. So, Jules and I were East and West, although Jules's hip is giving her such pain these days,' said Miriam with a sympathetic wince.

'Oh, I see, the East/West team move around, do they?' Beth asked. Both women looked at her as if she had two heads. 'What? I'm just learning all this stuff.'

'Yes, East and West move, North and South sit at the same table all through the session. Apart from during the break, naturally. And North does the scoring. I think that's one of the reasons Wendy likes to be South,' Miriam said confidingly.

Beth looked blank, until Claire Greaves took pity on her.

'Well, she's never really got the hang of the scoring,' she said, as though it were perfectly obvious. 'And, between you, me and the park gates, I think worrying about losing her scarves is just a pose,' said Mrs Greaves with a smirk.

'Honestly, it's not,' said Beth, who had a cupboard full of scarves that Wendy had accidentally left at her house over the years. One day, she'd drive them to Wendy's and dump them back where they belonged, along with her misplaced beads. But little though she liked some of Wendy's quirks, she wasn't quite happy with others laughing at them. 'Can we just get back to Alfie?' she asked a little stiffly. 'He wasn't showing any signs of being ill, or of anything being off, before he went for the break?'

Miriam thought hard. 'Well, it's some time ago now,' she said apologetically. 'And we don't talk that much between hands. You know, some of us are quite serious about the Bridge.'

Beth knew her mother fell into this category, though today's revelation that she couldn't manage the scoring system was surprising.

'Not even a bit of chit-chat, about the weather, say?' Beth couldn't really imagine any English gathering that could function successfully without adequate discussion of what the day offered, in terms of precipitation, aeration and illumination.

Miriam sighed. 'I don't think so... wait a minute, something's coming back to me...'

Beth hung on, breathless. The three women's shoulders rubbed against each other. It was a bit like being in a strange seance, as she tried not to move and derail Miriam's train of thought.

'Oh, it's gone. Damn, I really thought I had something there. Does that ever happen to you?' Miriam asked, turning her head to one side and then the other, her iron-grey locks brushing Beth's shoulder.

Beth bit back her irritation. No, it didn't, because she was still in possession of her full quota of marbles. Though more days like today might well see her losing them. 'Claire? Erm, Mrs Greaves? Anything?'

'Any what, young lady?' said the older lady in stern tones. 'Oh, I see. Reminiscences about dear old Alf. From his last day on earth. Well, I wonder, now. No, that couldn't be relevant. And you wouldn't be interested.'

Beth nearly jumped down her throat – difficult when she was separated from the woman by Miriam and two dogs. 'What? What? Anything would help at this stage.'

'Oh, just that he seemed worried about his allotment. You know, I always tune out a bit when men talk about gardening. Don't you, dear?' she asked Miriam, who nodded. 'Can't get excited about mulching. Never could, even in my youth,' she added with her trademark cackle.

Here, Beth couldn't blame her. 'But what was he saying

about it? It's funny, my mother mentioned it, too. But she said Alfie didn't actually do much of the work himself.'

Mrs Greaves looked at her darkly. 'Really? She said that, did she? She can be quite perceptive at times, your mother. Despite all that frou-frou.'

Again, Beth fought against annoyance. It was true that Wendy had moments of strange far-sightedness. And it was also undeniable that her mannerisms could try the patience of any available saint.

'Well, can't sit here all day discussing gardening. I've got jobs of my own to be getting on with,' said Mrs Greaves, levering herself off the bench with some difficulty and wrapping Tinker's lead around her fist.

Miriam didn't need any further prompting but shot up as well and was soon hurrying off in the opposite direction, with Liquorice at her heels. Beth sat for a moment or two longer, mostly to give both women time to get clear.

She, possibly uniquely of the little trio, did have important claims on her time. Jake, Colin, Harry, housework, Wyatt's... but the more she thought about the weight of chores and responsibilities that awaited her, the comfier the cold bench seemed.

EIGHT

Despite Beth's gloomy moment on the bench, everyone seemed to manage perfectly well that day without her micromanagement. When she'd picked Jake up in the afternoon, he'd been quiet but seemed happy enough. And Colin had apparently coped on his own for a few hours without either gnawing the furniture, or being gnawed in turn by Magpie.

Supper was produced, eaten and cleared without incident, though she had to cover Harry's helping with a plate and stow it in the fridge, yet again. No doubt something had come up. She supposed she ought to try and train him to let her know, but it was a lot more peaceful to let such niceties slide and just be happy to see him when he did deign to appear. She knew her mother would have had a lot to say about this arrangement. Much of it would have been along the lines of 'Why buy the cow, if you're getting the milk for free?' There was some truth in such views, but then, Beth was also getting something free, without the bother of a permanent man about the place and all the compromise that could involve. Perhaps they both benefitted.

Although everything had plodded along as usual, a germ of

an idea was developing at the back of Beth's mind. By the time Jake had finally consented to take himself upstairs, the germ had become a full-blown virus that had worked its way around to Beth's frontal lobe, and she picked up her phone to call Katie, her mind abuzz.

'Beth! I was just about to ring. What did you make of that Geography homework? I've never really understood what the savannah was all about...'

'What? Erm...' Even to her best friend, Beth didn't want to admit she'd had no idea the boys had an assignment. Geography, indeed. Surely she wasn't losing all grip on her son's education on only day two of the new regime? She'd just have to hope that Jake might have got round to it all by himself at some point during the evening, without her noticing. Yeah, right, a little voice said. 'No, no, I'm not ringing about that, Katie. I've had a bit of a brainwave.'

'About the gladiators' project, for Latin?'

Oh my God, thought Beth. Please, not a project. She'd seriously hoped these were a primary school chore that she'd left far behind, along with other menaces like soft-play centres and nits. Gladiators, of all things? The teachers were having a laugh. 'No, no, not that,' she said quickly, fending off the very notion as successfully as any *retiarius* with his net. 'About Bridge. And Alfie.'

'Oh.' Was it Beth's imagination, or did Katie sound a bit, well, reluctant?

'You do still want to help out, don't you, Cagney? Or are you Lacey? You're the carefree blonde, obviously. I'm the brunette with the bad flick hairdo and the fat arse.'

Katie giggled softly, then said with a sigh, 'I don't know, Beth. It's just that, after these first two days, I've seen how much support Charlie is going to need from me...'

Beth was baffled. She'd seen the very opposite from Jake. He was getting on with things as if he was still going to the

Village Primary every morning. Yes, he was tired out, and yes, maybe he was a bit pale... and he'd been a bit slow to get his stuff together this morning, seeming to linger a bit in the hall, playing with Colin... Hang on, was she just seeing what she wanted to see? Was he actually finding it tough going? Then she shook her head.

'Do you really think so? I'm not sure it's so good for them...' she ventured.

'What's not good for them? What do you mean?' Katie was defensive.

'Well, they're big boys now,' said Beth. 'OK, Jake's not big, but he'll grow... one of these days. Don't you think it's important for them to, well, start fighting their own battles? Like the blinking gladiators. Sort themselves out, for a change, without us interfering?'

There was a beat of silence. 'I'm not sure, Beth. Particularly at such a crucial phase. I need to be there for Charlie.' Katie's voice was quiet but insistent.

'But you can't be there for him. You can't be in the class-room, or in the playground, or even waiting in the playground after school, any more. And even if we could, wouldn't we actually be getting in their way? Stunting their development? Stopping them from learning how to manage for themselves?'

'But they're still so young, Beth. And it's going to be GCSEs any minute...'

'In five years!' Beth exclaimed with a snort.

'Four, now they've started. And that's like four *sleeps* in Mummy-time,' Katie said with the finality of someone who had every ounce of logic on her side.

'OK, well, I'm going to try and let Jake find his own level a bit, at any rate. After all, no one was hovering over us the whole time, were they?'

'I don't know about your parents, Beth, but I wouldn't use my own as a great example,' said Katie.

Touché, thought Beth. Katie knew Wendy well enough to realise that she would have been hands-off enough as a mother to qualify as an honorary amputee. And she also knew that Beth would do almost anything to be an entirely different kind of mum.

'I take your point, Katie. But a couple of hours on the Alfie thing... that wouldn't do any harm? And it might stop you worrying so much about Charlie. An atmosphere of anxiety in the home isn't going to do him any good,' said Beth, hoping she sounded as though she was quoting from a respected childcare manual – one of the many that Katie still had piled up by her bedside and was even now prone to study like a scholar parsing the Rosetta Stone.

'You're right, I *am* fretting. It was partly the coffee morning,' Katie said.

'Oh, I forgot about that. How was it?'

There was a short, eloquent silence which made Beth glad that, despite her initial pangs, she had not made it onto Bloody Belinda's guest list.

'It was... interesting. Honestly, Beth, you would have hated it,' Katie finished in a rush.

'Go on, tell me everything. I'm dying to know.'

'Well, you know Belinda's house. Or rather, you don't any more. Did you realise she's had the whole ground floor redone?'

'No! How's she managed that? I haven't seen any vans near your place.' Being just a few doors down from Belinda, Katie was in a privileged, or accursed, position. On the upside, her house would go for a fortune if she ever put it on the market, thanks to Belinda's relentless campaign to persuade everyone that theirs was the best street in Dulwich. On the downside – she lived near Belinda.

'She must have been sneaking in the builders in the evenings, or something. Honestly, it was like one of those big reveals in the decorating shows. A real ta-dah moment. Except that most of the people she'd invited had never been there before, so it was lost on them. But I was pretty gobsmacked, I can tell you.'

Beth registered the blunt phrase, which was not usually in the sunny Katie lexicon. She frowned. 'What's it like then, this new look?'

'Well, it's all marble, kind of fresh grey paint, copper accents—'

Beth sat up straight on the sofa. 'Hang on a sec. That sounds like your house.'

'Yes,' said Katie. 'Honestly, it must be some sort of a coincidence, but I was taken aback...'

'I bet!' A situation which had Katie expressing mild surprise and disappointment would normally have Beth reaching for the nearest blunt instrument. 'Bloody, bloody Belinda! She's just basically nicked all your ideas.'

Katie sighed. 'Well, I suppose I don't own grey paint. And everyone's doing the copper thing now. I shouldn't get upset about it. It's a sort of compliment. Anyhow, that wasn't really the worst bit. It was more the whole, well, tenor of the coffee morning. It was just... embarrassing.'

'Really?'

'Yes. You know the way Belinda is...'

'Insufferable? Bossy? Intolerant?'

Katie giggled again. 'You are awful, Beth. I just felt really sorry for her. She was trying all the normal tactics, offering favours, suggesting she could open doors, you know, the usual...'

'What doors can she really open, though?'

'She has all the best tutors in her pocket. I mean, you know that yourself, Beth,' Katie said gently. 'Plus, the most tolerant and bulletproof music teachers, the best caterers, hairdressers...'

'Plastic surgeons? Therapists?'

Katie snorted this time. 'You said it. Today, though, I really felt for her. It all fell on deaf ears.'

'Wasn't anyone interested in joining the court of the sun queen?'

'Well, no. And it was sad. She's just got a bit... well, passé. People seemed to find her so obvious. I even caught a couple of the mums actually sniggering. I can see why. All these people's kids have already got into Wyatt's, so they're starting off on a level playing field. Why does Belinda think she's got some sort of special advantage that she can offer? She hasn't. But I can't help it, Beth, I felt so uncomfortable. I hope these people are going to be *nice*.'

'You can't blame them for finding Belinda absurd. That just means they're rational,' Beth countered. But it was a bit worrying. Their sons were going to spend so many waking hours with these new boys. She hoped their parents were the right sort, and by that, she knew she meant people who were exactly like her and Katie. Kind, considerate, pushed a bit too far by Belinda but still not willing to be nasty to her face. The odd giggle behind her back was absolutely fine, though, and perfectly healthy. Beth took a deep breath and made up her mind.

'You know what, Katie? I think you need the distraction of an investigation even more than I do at the moment. Stop worrying about Charlie and the new parents, and definitely stop worrying about Belinda, because she can look after herself. The one person in Dulwich who needs us to stick up for him at the moment is poor old Alfie Pole. Say my mother is right – it's a stretch, I grant you – but say he really *was* murdered. Who else, apart from us, is going to do even one single thing about it?'

There was silence at Katie's end for what seemed like ages. Then her voice came through, stronger than before, and more definite. 'All right then, Beth. You've talked me into it. What do we do next?'

NINE

Beth was going to pop into her office at Wyatt's, she really was. But maybe not today. She told herself that Jake needed space, to settle himself in. If he saw her lurking about in the playground (though why she would be lurking there instead of making straight for her office, she didn't clarify, even to herself), then that would surely embarrass him horribly, stunt any early buds of friendship he might be nurturing... No, she had... well, she couldn't call it a duty, but certainly she had very good reasons to steer clear for the immediate future. Luckily, no one was clamouring for her presence.

That was possibly both the bane and the boon of her job in the archives office. It was as little, or as much, as she made it herself. She'd started off with a terrible boss, and then acquired a powerful enemy in the school's admin department. One was permanently out of the picture; the other, the bursar Tom Seasons, was on sabbatical. True, she still had a line manager, but this was her friend and tireless supporter, Janice, who was married to the headmaster. And as Janice had a new baby who took up all her time and attention, Beth was left to her own devices.

She felt a familiar pang of guilt as she dropped Jake at the school gates and turned her back on what must surely be an in-tray mouldering away like an overripe Stilton. But catching up with Katie deflected that easily enough.

'So, tell me again what you've got in mind for today – and tell me why this isn't a completely mad idea?' Katie's broad and sunny smile took the sting out of her words, and Beth was soon explaining everything as they walked along the streets.

Calton Avenue was a reasonably wide thoroughfare, but the habitual double-parking of SUVs and the frequent knots of nannies shoving the latest go-faster buggies up the gentle hill meant it was hard for Katie and Beth to walk together, let alone talk, until they'd turned into the wider avenue of Dulwich Village proper.

Here, the shopfronts reflected the shining morning faces of the children plodding along to school, and the glinting cheek-bones of the glamorous mummies loping along in their long suede boots. The weather was only just starting to dip into cool-ness, but at the school gates everyone was keen to show off their new autumn/winter collections. As Beth and Katie passed, they caught a snatch of conversation. 'We've just booked our holi-days. Florida for half-term, because we promised the children, and then we've had to go for Bali at Christmas in the end. The dog-sitter won't take them for less than two weeks, so we really didn't have any choice. *Had* to be long-haul.'

Beth rolled her eyes at Katie so hard she nearly dislocated them from their sockets. 'Good to know that Belinda's already got competition for her throne at the Village Primary,' she said drily.

As usual, the dogs were as much a part of the parade as the owners. Once, Beth would have hardly noticed the pooches, but now, as the proud if still surprised owner of Colin, she ran a more experienced eye over the assortment, counting a schnoo-dle, a peekapoo, a poochon and a goldendoodle, as well as the usual porgis, chugs, and a rather sad-looking little pug that no one had bothered to cross with anything else. It was a shame she didn't have the old Lab with her; he would have loved to say hello to the gang. But Beth was relieved that Katie had left Teddy behind. Though the worst of his #MeToo days were now behind him, he still had a tendency to attempt to have his way with anything unwary and under fifty centimetres in height.

Soon they were crossing over the mini-roundabout near Dulwich's one remaining bank branch and making for Gallery Road.

On the left-hand side as they walked was one of Sir Thomas Wyatt's most flagrant acts of hypocrisy – a beautiful almshouse he had constructed for the poor of Dulwich. It had been financed by his oppression of the poor elsewhere – the slaves who had toiled on his plantations in the West Indies, piling up a fortune in the coffee which still kept Dulwich buzzing today. Next to the almshouse was a church, also built by Wyatt, whose stained windows looked out on to Beth and Katie as they passed, the petulant motto *For God's Sake* clearly visible. Next, was Wyatt's magnificent Museum of Art.

Beth shook her head mildly. It was extraordinary that three hundred-odd years after his death, one man still had such a stranglehold on Dulwich, in terms of culture, religion, education and charity. And that the man should have been such a flawed character. In many ways, it was typical of the place. He'd appeared so successful, outwardly, that for generations people had been more than happy to overlook and then forget the source of his wealth. Even now, his rehabilitation seemed suspiciously fast. It had been, what, a couple of years since Beth's discovery? She felt sure that the dust of amnesia was being heaped busily back onto Wyatt's reputation as fast as possible, so that the area could continue to enjoy the benefits of the man's bequests without worrying about their blood-soaked downside. Her conscience was pricked. If she didn't get round to writing her biography of the man, revealing all sides of his nature, then she would only have herself to blame if everyone persisted in seeing him as the closest thing Dulwich had to a saint.

She and Katie strolled onwards, the sharp scent of carefully mown grass giving way gradually to the fumes of traffic as they approached the perpetual snarl-up of the South Circular. Just before they saw their first glimpse of 4x4 tail-lights, usually stacked up as far as Lordship Lane in one direction and West Norwood in the other, they reached the sign for Belair House on the right-hand side.

Beth always thought the place looked like a child's drawing of a house – square front door slap bang in the middle, two windows on either side at the bottom, three across the top. She was pretty sure her attic was full of crayoned efforts just like this by Jake. The design had some embellishments that no four-year-old could have dreamt up, though. First there was a triangular pediment at the top of the building, with trompe l'oeil columns, inscribed with the date 1785. Then there was a circular carriage drive, which seemed to beg for every guest to sweep up in a coach-and-four. Beth and Katie were unable to oblige, and even their Shanks's ponies were a little puffed by the time they'd waded through the gravel to the front door.

Inside, the grandeur of the entrance hall was somewhat marred by the number of elderly people milling around. 'You weren't kidding when you said you'd be gathering them all,' Katie whispered admiringly to Beth.

'I think we'll have to give credit to Wendy for that,' Beth said, as her mother stepped forward, scarves aflutter.

'Now, everyone,' Wendy said, her tones a little quavery to start with but gathering strength as she went on. 'We've kindly been given permission by the house to reconstruct our meeting of, ahem, well, of last week. You'll all remember that's when poor Alfie, um, passed away. Not in the house, obviously,' she said quickly, glancing at a businesslike lady who'd just appeared from a door marked 'Office'. 'Let's all go upstairs and get out of everyone's way,' she said, leading the way towards the graceful winding staircase in the centre of the black and white chequer-board-tiled floor.

Just then, there was a slight commotion as an elderly woman dressed in a heavy tweedy jacket forced her way breath-lessly to the front. 'Now, just a minute everyone. As you all know, *I* am the chair of the Bridge Club. I'd just like to thank Wendy for her, er, contribution. And I'd like to ask everyone to make their way upstairs as quickly as possible.' She then clapped her hands briskly.

'Who on earth is that?' whispered Katie.

'I'm not sure, but I think it's probably Deidre MacBride. Do you remember, Mum mentioned her? Said Deirdre had asked her to deputise for her? It doesn't actually look as though she loves Mum taking charge, though,' Beth hissed back, wrinkling her brow.

Meanwhile, a steady stream of Bridge players was making its way up the stairs, while Wendy was waiting impatiently at the bottom for Beth and Katie. 'Hurry up, girls, do. We must get on.'

'Is that Deidre, Mum?' Beth asked.

Wendy pursed her lips and nodded briefly. 'Come on, we don't want to keep everyone waiting.' She turned on her heel and marched upwards, her small frame and flowing scarves disappearing into the mêlée.

As usual, thought Beth, there was very little logic to Wendy's statement. It was the rest of the Bridge players who were preventing them from getting up the stairs any more quickly; they meandered up, stopping to catch their breath whenever they felt like it, or just pausing to chat. It was clear that the Bridge Club, in various states of health, was going to take its own sweet time to reach the first floor, so there was not much point in Beth and Katie barging forward until the way was clear. Unlike Wendy, whose painstakingly sharpened elbows meant that she was finding a way through with apparent ease, Beth and Katie were much better off waiting patiently in the hall. They had ample time to look around and get their bearings.

'I haven't been here since Charlie's christening,' said Katie. 'I'd forgotten how beautiful it is.'

'Did you have it here? How grand,' said Beth.

Charlie's christening had taken place in the dim, distant and frankly rather grim period before she and Katie had first met at the playgroup in the strangely chalet-shaped St Barnabas parish hall in the village. At the time, Beth had been reeling from the double shocks of motherhood and widowhood, which had come hard on one another's heels and neither of which she'd been properly braced for.

'I'm leaving Jake's christening options open,' said Beth.

Katie smiled understandingly. They both knew it was never going to happen, due to Beth's perennial inability even to get round to prevaricating about anything that wasn't a total essential.

'Oh, wait a second, I actually did come to a fortieth birthday party here, a couple of years ago. One of Michael's friends,' Katie said. 'It was quite a do. Fireworks in the garden, a vodka luge. They know how to put on a party. I love it here. What an atmosphere.'

Beth looked around. With the Bridge Club still making its ascent of the stairs, like a rickety group of mountaineers, the place wasn't at its most seductive. But in the right circumstances, she realised it would have definite possibilities. And there was no question that the club was very lucky to be playing every week in such a beautiful place.

'We should probably make a move now,' Beth said, just as Wendy leant over the bannisters at the top of the stairs and waved her scarf at them like a semaphore signal. 'They all seem to have made it to the top.'

A couple of minutes later, Beth and Katie were at the entrance to a beautiful long room with parquet flooring of an even richer gold than the priciest manuka honey stocked in the village deli. Autumnal sunlight slanted in from floor-to-ceiling windows and bounced off the strange mother-of-pearl petals dangling from several modern chandeliers. To Beth's somewhat jaundiced eye, these looked like the bathing hats once sported by 1950s beauty contestants.

Here and there on the walls were oil paintings of stuffy-looking men in uniform and women who appeared to have been born ugly and gone downhill as the years piled on. She suspected these might have been bought as job lots at the auctioneer in West Norwood, to add a bit of atmosphere. Belinda McKenzie had similar canvases in her formal dining room, and no one in Dulwich had ever been able to spot a likeness between the paintings and their hostess, try as they might.

The large room was set up for Bridge, with five square tables laid out with green baize cloths, four spindly gold chairs around each one. On the cloths were strange brown plastic boxes, the size of a chunky old phone, and even odder flat red rectangular containers, the width of a pack of cards but four times the length. Beth and Katie shrugged shoulders at each other as the club members stood around in huddles.

Both Wendy and Deidre MacBride stepped forward at exactly the same moment. Deidre clapped her hands loudly, Wendy just waved her scarf, then saw Deidre's set face and took a quick pace backwards.

'Members. If I could have your attention, please?' It was framed as a question, but there was no doubt that Deidre expected instant obedience. She got it. Everyone fell silent and looked expectantly towards her.

'I've been asked to gather you all together today in order to, ahem, lay to rest some very odd ideas that seem to have developed about the very sad passing of one of our most popular players, Alf Pole.' There was a murmur as everyone said, 'Shocking, shocking', or 'good fellow', or just generally expressed their sadness. 'Alf is much missed, of course,' said Deidre, lowering her iron-grey head for a moment. Even her rough tweeds seemed to take on a mourning look. But it soon passed. 'The main thing, though, is to get us back to doing what we do best – playing Bridge. So we need to quash these silly rumours pronto.'

This seemed to be taking things a step too far for Wendy. She'd let the 'odd ideas' comment whistle past, but now that Deidre was openly condemning rumour-mongers, she burst into speech.

'Deidre, thank you so much for getting everyone together, so good of you to indulge us and help put these, er, stories to rest. Who among us has heard that something wasn't quite right about Alfie's death? Just put your hands up, please.'

There was a pause and then hand after hand went into the air. Beth looked on, unsurprised. When wasn't there a whisper doing the rounds in Dulwich? Some were big – over preferential treatment in the school entrance exams, or shenanigans amongst the estate agents. And some were small – over whose cat had been pooping in which garden, to name but one controversy in her own road alone. In a place like Dulwich, there would always be talk. And an unexplained death in broad daylight was bound to attract conspiracy theorists.

Wendy was now looking rather like Magpie when she'd managed to nab Colin's favourite spot on the sofa. 'So I expect I'm not the only one who'd like to get a bit of, erm, closure on the whole tragic situation,' she said, and heads nodded everywhere.

Deidre, who knew when she'd been outflanked, clapped her hands again.

'All right then, everyone. Take the seats you had last Tuesday, just before the break. And let's see if we can get this whole charade over with as quickly as possible. Then we might be able to play some *proper* Bridge.' There was a murmur of approval at this.

Beth hoped that Deidre hadn't locked too successfully into the Bridge Club's main preoccupation – playing the game they all loved. They were bound to prefer that to reconstructing a crime, but it was vital the procedure wasn't rushed. Wendy, on the other side of the room, raised her brows at Beth. It seemed she had the same doubts.

Everyone was milling around now, taking their seats. Beth and Katie stood by the ornate fireplace, looking on as people got settled. Once they were sitting down, they levered open the brown boxes, which displayed racks of cards marked with numbers and little hieroglyphs which, on closer inspection, turned out to be spades, hearts, clubs and diamonds. The red boxes were left in the centre of the tables in piles of three, like offerings on an altar, being worshipped by each quartet of players.

Wendy wandered over to join Beth and Katie, and started to explain in a low voice, 'The brown contraptions are bidding boxes. People use those so there's no ambiguity about what they're saying. And the red slabs in the middle, they contain the hands everyone's playing. Each set of thirteen cards goes into a different compartment, marked with North, South, East or West, so no one gets the hands mixed up. Then, once those three rounds of hands have been played, the cards are passed on to the next table. That way, everyone in the room plays the same hands of cards. That's why it's called *duplicate* Bridge, you see.'

Beth, who didn't see at all, nodded vaguely, hoping that a penny would drop at some point. But wait a minute. If every single person in the room had played the same cards, and someone here had been responsible for poisoning poor Alfie, then an anomaly in one performance might well indicate who was responsible. If this worked as she hoped, then finding the murderer might, for once, actually be easy.

But already she'd thought of a problem. 'How do you know these are the exact hands that were played last time?'

'Simple,' said Wendy. 'We write down all the cards on little slips of paper that are kept at the back of each of the red boards. That way we can refer easily to hands if someone brings up a problem later.'

'Does that happen? Doesn't everyone trust each other?' asked Katie, seeming astonished.

Wendy shrugged. This was Dulwich. This was Bridge.

'There's so much admin involved in this game. Is this normal? Or is this some kind of weird variant that suits people here, because so many people have run businesses or the civil service or whatever?' Beth asked.

'Don't be silly, dear,' said Wendy repressively. 'This is how Bridge is played all over the country. Well, we don't follow all the English Bridge Union ways; we have our Dulwich innovations. But it's all quite straightforward when you get the hang of it.'

Beth exchanged a glance with Katie. She wasn't sure, when she was retired, whether she'd have enough time to get used to the rules of Bridge before she finally turned up her toes. It all seemed a lot like hard work. The marvel was that it seemed to appeal so much to all these people. But then, they were a different generation. The one that hadn't had access to Netflix, iPlayer and the internet. They'd had to make their own entertainment – and endlessly arcane rules.

Another clap from Deidre MacBride broke into Beth's thoughts and cut effortlessly through the beginnings of chatter from the tables dotted around the room.

'Now then, everyone, if we're all quite set up for this whole little, erm, escapade? Yes? Well then, you may play,' she said magisterially, and as if by magic she produced a little golden hand bell from her capacious tweed pocket and rang it once.

As the sound died away, the groups at the tables leant forward, prised the clumps of cards out of the red boards and began sorting them into suits, all careful not to show their hands to their neighbours. There was a desultory hum of conversation. Deidre, standing near the door, looked hawkishly at any table where the murmurs threatened to break out into outright talking, and a couple of times the bell was heard to give the tiniest of tinkles. Immediately each time, silence fell. Bridge was a *very* serious matter.

Wendy watched, with Beth and Katie, as the first groups started ferreting in their bidding boxes and plopping thick wedges of cards down onto the tables. 'You see, the card on the top of the pile indicates the bid – one spade, one no trump, or whatever.'

Beth steepled her eyebrows at Katie. Yes, that was all as clear as mud.

'Wait a minute, Mum, shouldn't you be over there?' Beth asked, pointing to the only table where there were two people, not four. Wendy seemed rather reluctant to leave them and, once she'd finally taken her seat, Beth could guess why. There were now three at the table. Poor old Alfie had never seemed more absent from the scene.

TEN

Beth and Katie looked on, a little bemused, as all around the lofty ballroom, grown-ups ignored their beautiful surroundings and the gorgeous park outside, and concentrated feverishly on a few square inches of green. The cards were mounting up, but not in the middle of the table. Instead, the players placed the cards face up in front of them, then turned them over once each trick had been played and arranged them either vertically or horizontally. It seemed quite different from the way Beth had played as a child, when the cards had been heaped in the middle and then scooped up by the victor.

Beth sidled over to where Deidre was standing, little bell at the ready, and hissed to her, 'Why are they playing like that? Keeping all the cards separate?'

Deidre looked her up and down quickly, as though not quite believing anyone could be so ignorant. 'It's duplicate Bridge,' she whispered back, as though that explained everything.

'And that means...?' Beth said encouragingly. Deidre sighed, and drew Beth and Katie a little further from the tables, towards the door.

'We don't want to disturb them,' she said.

No, thought Beth. Because they're playing a game. Heaven forfend anyone should make a sound.

'Do you two know anything at all about Bridge?' Deirdre asked scathingly. 'There are rules, you know.'

'We're beginning to see that,' said Beth, with what she thought was commendable understatement.

Deidre raised her eyebrows but breezed on. 'The rules we follow make it easier to make sure there's no, ahem, sleight of hand. People only touch their own cards, the cards are always kept separate as they travel from table to table, and each pair of players has a chance to check scoring. That way, if there's a dispute, the director is able to step in quickly and sort things out. There shouldn't be doubt in any given situation.'

Beth was privately amazed. She'd thought Bridge was a pleasant pretext for her mother, set in her ways and living alone, to get together with friends a few times a week for a bit of mildly sociable mental stimulation. But all these preparations, which seemed to be exclusively preoccupied with heading off any possibility of cheating, or of accusing anyone else of cheating for that matter, suggested that Bridge was more like open warfare than a jolly pastime for elderly folk.

'Is this really necessary? These precautions?' Beth couldn't help asking.

Deidre gave her what could only be described as a dark look. 'Believe me, I wouldn't be running this group without them. It simply wouldn't be worth my while.'

'Do you really get a lot of cheating?' Katie piped up.

'No, we don't. For the simple reason that we apply all the rules. Rigorously. And that means that there is very little opportunity to, shall we say, manipulate the card play.'

'Are you playing for cash prizes or something? A car, maybe? Exotic holidays?'

Deidre's smile was a little wry. 'There's a cup, which is handed out once a year. But it's a century old now and requires a lot of polishing, so it's not that popular. Believe it or not, people just play for the kudos of winning.'

'But they're willing to cheat? All for an old, tarnished cup?' Beth was staggered.

'They don't cheat. Because we have rules,' said Deidre firmly. 'And they are obeyed.'

'By everyone?' Beth was remembering that there had been an issue on the day Alfie died. Wendy had been flustered because there'd been a dispute. It was one of the reasons the poor old man hadn't been discovered sooner.

'Well. Most people,' said Deidre, with an air of finality. 'Look, we really can't talk now. As you can see, the hands are in full swing.'

'Everyone's played these cards before, though, right?' Beth wanted to make sure she'd fully understood. 'In that case, why are they putting so much concentration into it?'

Deidre laughed softly, her stern face transformed for a few moments. Instantly, Beth was able to see the attractive girl (or probably 'gel', as she'd have said herself) the woman had been half a century ago. 'Half of them don't actually remember the cards. Well, it was, what, a week ago, now, wasn't it?'

'And the other half?' Katie put in.

'The other half are trying to improve on last time's scores. Of course.' Deirdre's mouth twisted back into its habitual lines, and the illusion of youth was gone. 'Look, we really can't be standing here chatting. We're putting people off. They're complaining.' With that, she marched away abruptly to the table at the far end, where spare bidding boxes, a folder of last week's scores and an attendance sheet were laid out.

Beth looked around. No one seemed to be complaining at all. Maybe Deidre just didn't want to explain things to them? Or maybe she actually had something to hide.

Everyone's heads were bent over the cards. Beth could see so many shades of grey. Maybe not fifty – this was SE21 – but a lot. In amongst them were a few women defying time with a dash of dye. And there was Wendy herself – one of the youngest present by at least a decade, though her hair had been white for as long as Beth could remember.

Beth had thought Bridge was just long-winded whist. But no. In Dulwich at least, it seemed as riven with rivalry and toxicity as the set of *Who Killed Baby Jane?* Was there a hobby in the area that couldn't get heated, though? she wondered. She'd heard in the past of tensions over allotments, jealousy at the Open Garden sessions, even passions rising at the annual Artists' Open House weekends. Was Bridge just another arena for this sort of intensity? Or had things really boiled over a week ago? And had murder really reared its ugly head?

Beth's musings were interrupted by Wendy scraping back her chair across the parquet floor, resettling her scarves importantly, and getting up from the table. Her opponents gave her a surprised glance but said nothing. As she passed, Wendy gave Beth a look full of meaning, then swept out through the door and was last seen trailing down the stairs, her scarves billowing in her wake. Never let it be said that Wendy couldn't do an exit.

'Where's Wendy off to?' hissed Katie. Beth waggled her eyebrows to suggest all would soon be revealed. Katie put her head on one side, as though to say, *Have you gone crazy?* Beth just gave her best enigmatic smile. She didn't want to have to explain everything yet.

Meanwhile, the cards were being played out all around them. 'Let's go and have a look, see what everyone's doing,' said Beth. They tiptoed off, gliding between the tables. Or rather, Katie glided, and Beth tried not to squeak too much as her cheap soles seemed to meld most unfortunately with the beautiful wax finish on the flooring while she trotted round.

It wasn't hard to tell which of the pairs took the game most seriously. Those who were social players weren't fazed when Katie and Beth popped up behind them. But those who considered that Bridge was much too important to be treated as a spectator sport started to shuffle in their seats, look round at the women, and otherwise show obvious signs of unease.

Of all the little quartets, Beth recognised surprisingly few, given the years that Wendy had devoted to the game. She spotted Jules and Miriam, of course, who were still sitting at the table that Wendy had just vacated, chatting together in very low voices and apparently quite happy to idle the time away. And next door to them were the Crofts, a couple she knew by sight. On the table one along was a serious-looking lady who could have been a retired teacher. She had half-moon spectacles perched on the end of her nose, attached to a string of rather pretty beads which Wendy no doubt envied. Her grey-blonde curls softened the effect of the shrewd eyes, glinting behind their glasses.

'That's Mrs Griffin, she used to teach Maths at the College School,' said Katie helpfully.

That explained a lot, thought Beth. Mrs Griffin's partner was a big man, his pale blue shirt at least a size smaller than its owner. Beth wouldn't like to be around when his buttons finally decided they'd had enough of this arrangement. Tall and over-spilling the spindly chair in all directions, he was frowning over his cards like a hippo scrutinising a matchbox.

'Who's he?' asked Beth.

'Mr Griffin,' whispered Katie. 'He taught at Wyatt's. History, I think.'

Playing opposite them were a brace of Miss Marple looka-likes, from their perms to their woolly outfits, sensible brogue shoes and battered shopping bags, lumpy with what could easily have been identical sets of knitting.

'You don't know them as well, do you?' Beth hissed.

Katie shrugged. 'Sorry. But they look very sweet.'

As they watched, one of the inoffensive old dears swooped down and dashed an ace onto the table. Mr and Mrs Griffin both looked chastened. Maybe not as sweet as they seemed, thought Beth.

They sidled over to the next table, and Katie sketched a little hello wave at the lady sitting in what Beth now knew was the North position.

'Yoga,' Katie explained. Indeed, despite being in her seventies at least, with age-mottled hands and a high neckline disguising the depredations of the years, the woman had the supple grace which Beth so envied in Katie – but which seemed to have eluded Beth herself when she'd had a go at yoga. Maybe you needed to do it more than once, said a small voice which she rapidly silenced.

The yoga lady was playing with a substantially less well-toned companion, who appeared younger and also looked quite smiley. For Beth, this was a welcome change. So far, all the players had appeared as grim-faced as converts to some joyless cult. This woman seemed to be having fun, at any rate. But maybe not for long. 'Moira,' tutted her partner, as the woman put down a card, and the opposition – two men in their sixties, both buttoned up in cardigans and hidden behind bifocal glasses – looked smug.

'I think she's trumped something she shouldn't have,' Beth said, glimmerings of those lessons years ago coming back to her. As soon as she spoke, the cardigan men gave her indignant glances, and Katie took her arm and ushered her on.

This time, they came to a stop near to a lady who looked familiar. She had what could only be described as a helmet of hair. It was as sugar-spun as Donald Trump's, though arranged in a more fetching style often seen on matrons of a certain age in the area. Beth was sure it was the product of many hours under a dryer in Dulwich Village's top salon. Looking round the room, she could see at least a couple more dead ringer 'dos. Add to that, perfect cerise nails, glinting as this particular lady held her cards, and an outfit which appeared to have leapt from the pages of a posh catalogue, and the woman seemed the archetypal SE21 scary gran.

Beth definitely had the disconcerting feeling that she'd met her before. Despite the careful grooming, there was something masculine about her regular features, the very prominent blue eyes... Did she remind Beth of a man she knew, or was she just too familiar with this whole look?

'Isn't that...?' Katie tailed off.

Beth, still racking her brains, turned to her, just as the woman raised her hand and said loudly, 'Deirdre, a moment, if you could?' It was framed as a question, but there was not much doubt that it was a command. She might as well have snapped her fingers.

Deidre plodded over the parquet and came to stand in front of the table. 'Yes, Mrs Hadley?'

Beth looked over. Now the lady had fixed her pale blue bullfrog eyes on Beth and was muttering to Deidre MacBride. Whatever she was saying, it looked pretty intense. Katie gave Beth a little smile.

Mrs Hadley was now looking right at Beth and yammering away into Deirdre MacBride's ear. Deidre was starting to look a little pained. She was having to bend down over Mrs Hadley's chair in a position that ill-suited her rigid, tweed-clad sausage of a torso. The others on the table were also starting to look restive. A thin, nervous-looking man was sitting in the West position, his dry wisps of hair clinging to a shiny pate like the last bits of seaweed trying to resist the tide. Opposite him in the East seat was a rather elegant woman, in an aubergine sweater that Beth quite fancied. Her face was serene, though she was nervously picking at her lower lip when she thought no one was looking. She had a great hand, or a terrible one, guessed Beth. Either way, she wanted to get on and play it.

In the end, it was Mrs Hadley's long-suffering partner who called time on her little confab with Deidre MacBride. One of the few women in the room under the age of sixty, and probably round about her own mother's age, Beth realised (though of course this woman looked much younger), she started off just by drumming her fingers restlessly on the green baize cloth, then cleared her throat a few times.

When even that didn't get Mrs Hadley's attention, she announced loudly, 'Rosemarie, I really feel we've held people up long enough. Maybe you could continue your little chat with Deidre during the break?'

The tones were dulcet, but the subtext was dripping with acid. Mrs Hadley raked her partner with a suspicious glance but turned to Deidre and dismissed her with a little nod of the head, which did not dislodge a single hair of her coiffure.

Deidre, whom Beth would never have marked down as meek, was surprisingly accepting of this high-handed behaviour, all but bobbing a little curtsey. She scurried back to where Beth and Katie were standing, seeming glad to have got away, Beth thought. And that was certainly fair enough.

'What was all that about?' Beth asked out of the corner of her mouth, but Rosemarie Hadley somehow heard her and raised her head, yet again, from the game. The bulbous blue eyes were not friendly. Her partner tutted loudly and Rosemarie played a card, but Beth sensed her ears were out on stalks.

'Is there somewhere we could go to talk?'

Deidre shook her head at Beth. 'I'm afraid not. I need to be here, in case of difficulties. And you can see how things can arise. By the way, where did your mother go?' She looked over at Wendy's table, where her opponents seemed to be managing fine without her mother's input, thanks to another player who'd stepped in and was sitting where poor Alfie must once have been.

'Oh, erm, she had to just step out... she said you'd be fine about it...' Beth began.

'She did say something a bit rude about someone being a,

um, dummy?' Katie added, seeming worried about giving offence.

But Deidre only chuckled drily. 'Ah, so Wendy would have been sitting out at this point last week, and Alfie must have played the contract – that means, played her cards for her. So the same will happen today. We allow dummies to move away from the table, unlike the English Bridge Union. We're lucky we've got Mrs Greaves to help out,' she added.

Beth looked more closely and realised that Alfie's replacement was the tiny and redoubtable Mrs Greaves whom she'd met yesterday in Belair Park.

Katie was a bit at sea. 'Isn't it rather mean to call someone "dummy"?'

'It might be frowned upon if they were actually playing at the time. Yes, that could be a little bit pointed,' said Deidre with a bark of a laugh. 'But in fact, they're only called that when they're *not* playing. They just lay out their hand on the table, and their partner plays the cards for them. Often, it's the partner who ends up being a bit of a dummy.' Deidre chuckled to herself again.

Bridge humour was an acquired taste, Beth decided.

But wait a minute. If whoever was playing dummy sat out the hand, then they would be in an ideal position to wander off and kill someone while everyone else was busy, wouldn't they?

'Can we work out who was dummy at the time that Alfie, ahem, died?' she asked Deidre.

'Of course,' said Deidre. 'But most people would be dummy at some point. And with six tables going, there'd be one from each table.'

For a moment, Beth was downcast. But then she perked up. Six potential suspects were a lot fewer than twenty-four. And in fact, it was only five, as one of the dummies had been Alfie himself. That was why he hadn't been missed more quickly when he'd wandered outside to the bench.

'Although...' Deirdre carried on inexorably. 'People play the hands at different speeds. Sometimes one table is much faster or slower than another. So there could be more than six dummies around, or there could be fewer.'

Beth was starting to feel that the first promising chink of light that had been shed on the mystery was on the verge of getting blotted out.

'All the same, Mrs MacBride. A list of all the dummies round about the crucial time would be brilliant.'

'I can't promise anything. But I'll do my best, I'll email it to you,' said the director, turning back to the rest of the room determinedly. She clearly felt she'd spent more than enough time chatting.

Beth's sense of unease was growing. Wendy had been gone for quite a while. *How long, exactly?* Beth struggled to think. She and Katie had been watching hands for what now seemed like ages. Bridge was a bit too soothing – if you were just looking on, at any rate. It was definitely time that she moved on to phase two of the plan.

'I'm a bit concerned about my mother. She's been away from her table for quite a while. Maybe some of us should go out and see what she's up to?' Beth spoke quite loudly.

A few heads bobbed up nearby, and Deidre immediately turned back to shush her. 'We don't want to disturb anyone. It's a game that requires a lot of concentration.' Even her tweed jacket seemed to bristle with disapproval.

'Well, I understand, but this could be an emergency...' Beth said. Their plan aside, it now really did feel like time they checked on Wendy.

Katie gave Beth a look that was full of misgivings, but she seconded her friend. 'Wendy's been gone ages...'

Deidre looked at her watch. 'People are taking forever to play this hand. Especially considering they've done it all before,' she conceded. 'But we can't just stop in the middle, you know. That would never do. You'll just have to wait for the break.'

'How long will that be?' asked Beth, no longer having to feign urgency. It had been at least twenty minutes since Wendy had slipped out. Maybe more.

Deidre pursed her lips, looking disconcertingly like a back view of Magpie. Beth looked away quickly. 'Just a few minutes more. But there's nothing stopping you from having a look around yourself, if you're really anxious.'

Beth didn't need telling twice. 'Come on,' she said to Katie, and they made for the door. They were surprised when Jules and Miriam abruptly pushed their chairs back and joined them. Mrs Greaves was left at the table, taking her time about moving as usual.

'Do you know where Wendy's gone?' Miriam asked, pushing her soft grey bob out of her eyes in a worried gesture. 'She just disappeared off, didn't even really say where she was going. I thought she was heading for a, you know, *loo break*,' she said in a discreetly lowered voice.

Heaven forfend a Dulwich lady might need the facilities, thought Beth.

'But then she didn't come back.' Miriam's faded blue eyes were wide and even Jules, her partner, looked concerned.

'We're just off to have a look. You're very welcome to join us,' said Beth. 'Do you know where she usually goes at break-time?' she asked cunningly.

'Well, only to get a cup of tea, of course,' said Miriam, as though Beth had taken leave of her senses.

Beth remembered. Wendy had been quite grumpy with poor old Alfie for breaking away from the mould. 'Um, yes. I wonder if she's... trying something different today,' Beth said. Everyone looked at her as though she'd grown an extra head. But when Katie popped into the loos to check, and came out shaking her head, they all trooped down the sweeping stairs thoughtfully. At the bottom, Beth clutched her forehead and said, 'I just wonder if she's gone to see where, *where Alfie was*, you know?'

Again, there came a suspicious little glance from Katie. But she said nothing and merely followed as the group trundled outside. The air was crisp, and Beth automatically did up the buttons on her jacket. The lunchtime traffic rolled by on South Circular, but the park was quiet.

'Now, where was Alfie exactly? You know, when he was... found?'

Jules and Miriam turned automatically towards Belair Park. Beyond the fence, there was a bench. And on the bench, as they could all see, was a small figure moving around.

'Is that her? Is it Wendy?' asked Jules, her deep voice just tinged with alarm.

'I think it is,' said Miriam, galloping off towards the little form. Beth looked on, her forehead pleated under her fringe.

Katie took her arm. 'What's going on?' she asked in a low voice. 'What are you up to?'

But there wasn't time to explain. Something about the way Wendy was moving was *wrong*. Her mother always fidgeted with her scarves and beads, and it drove Beth mad. But now she was positively throwing herself about on the bench. It was as though she was being plagued by a swarm of bees, and was trying to fend them off.

As Beth watched, her mother's arms jerked about. Beth felt terror shoot through her body, an adrenaline surge that had her racing past Jules and overtaking Miriam. Jake would have been astonished. Over the years, they'd both grown used to Beth being effortlessly outpaced by Belinda McKenzie every time there was a parents' egg-and-spoon race at sports day. Today, she would have left Belinda on the starting line. But when she reached the bench, she knew that, even at full pelt, she'd been too slow.

Wendy was now bolt upright. From behind, it looked as though she must be staring straight ahead. From the front, though, her eyes were half-shut, ominously glazed, while her mouth was slack. A string of saliva was unspooling horribly onto the front of her coat. Her upright posture was completely misleading. The lights weren't on, and Beth was terribly afraid there was no longer anyone at home.

'Mum! *Mum!*' she shouted, grabbing Wendy by the shoulders and shaking her.

To her horror, her action nearly lifted the slight woman from the bench. Wendy, who'd been so agitated only minutes before, was now rigid as a plank of wood. And her face still registered nothing.

Katie, who'd just caught up and was gasping for breath, already had her phone out. 'Emergency services? Send an ambulance. Now, right away. Dulwich. *Belair Park.*'

ELEVEN

It was a depressingly familiar scene for Beth. The faded blue coverlet, close in colour to Miriam the Bridge player's eyes. The still form lying beneath. The wall of dark windows, beyond which the trains whizzed unseen back and forth to Denmark Hill and Loughborough Junction. The cruelty of the neon lights, leaching all warmth from the room. And the reflection on those blank windows of the sad scene within.

Except that, thank God, all was not quite lost.

'You were in the nick of time, I don't mind telling you,' the tired-looking doctor had told Beth and Katie, his face as crumpled as yesterday's newspaper and about the same colour. 'If you'd got there any later, even five minutes...' he trailed off, and Beth grew pale at the thought of what might have been.

She reproached herself for the millionth time. She'd dangled herself as bait a few times in the course of her career as an accident-prone yet surprisingly effective sleuth. That was fair enough. But going along with her mother's batty suggestion? That had just been plain madness. Wendy wasn't fit to be walking the streets unaccompanied half the time, let alone trying to lure a killer into the open.

Beth didn't want to replay the grisly scene, but her head had other ideas. She was back in the park, peering at Wendy's still form, when suddenly her mother had started to twitch and flail again like a mannequin being electrocuted. It had been utterly terrifying. Beth had tried her best to get her arms around the semi-conscious but struggling Wendy, while Katie had looked on helplessly. God knew, the Haldane family were not big huggers. This was the closest she'd been to her mother for years, an irony which didn't escape her even as she sought to contain her mother's lashing arms.

As Wendy lurched and shivered, the familiarly cloying scent she used, Je Reviens, rose up around them. Ironically, Belinda McKenzie sometimes used it too, though lately she'd started opting for the even more appropriate Poison by Dior. Usually, Beth found Je Reviens a threat rather than a promise – from the perfume itself to the menacing name, which always reminded her of Arnold Schwarzenegger's ponderous line, 'I'll be back.' This time, she could only hope fervently that her mother would stop throwing herself around and would, indeed, return to her. Any of even the most annoying Wendyisms – her fluttering scarves, her jingling beads, her constant put-downs, the mean asides about Beth's cooking, or the way Jake was shaping up; anything, anything at all – would have been so welcome then.

Just as she was despairing that help would ever come, she'd caught sight of activity at the perimeter of the park. Thank God, it was a police car in its garish livery of blue and yellow rectangles on white, like a Battenberg cake concocted by a blind chef with a grudge against his customers. It was quickly joined by another and, at last, an ambulance. It wasn't until the sirens had been cut off and peace had briefly descended that Beth realised how hard her heart had been beating.

Wendy had quietened in her embrace, but Beth hadn't been sure that was a good sign. Thank goodness there were people pelting towards her now. And amongst them, the familiar figure of someone who instantly made her feel simultaneously calmer, and braced for a blistering row.

It was Harry, striding across the grass. He came to a stop right in front of her, seeming to take the situation in at a glance. Instantly, he was directing paramedics, getting a PC to unwind incident tape, directing another to start combing the area, though for what, Beth wasn't quite sure. All she did know was that, within seconds of his arrival, everything had started coming back into focus. Nightmare and panic began to recede.

The paramedics approached the bench quite gingerly. Beth's arms were prised gently from around her mother, a sedative was briskly administered, and Wendy's limbs stopped their last bits of twitching and thrashing.

As her mother was lifted onto a stretcher, Beth, to her own horror and astonishment, had burst into noisy sobs and had buried them, not for the first time, in the rough and familiar texture of Harry's navy blue peacoat. Even as she'd wiped her nose surreptitiously on his sleeve, she'd thought that it was high time she bought him another jacket. He'd had this one for maybe an adventure too long.

But after the high of being saved by her knight in shining armour, as usual there was a corresponding low. Harry saved his anger until Wendy was safely admitted to a ward at King's College Hospital, and Katie had been despatched to fetch both the boys from Wyatt's and take them home with her.

Beth shivered slightly as she remembered the long look he'd directed at her, as they sat on either side of Wendy's bed. Beth dreaded to think what she'd looked like. First, she'd run full pelt to Wendy's side, then she'd been battered by her mother's involuntary jerks and lurches, and finally she'd been tossed into the back of the ambulance. None of it was calculated to make her feel at her most soignée. Harry, of course, looked as ruggedly gorgeous as ever. If his blond hair ever got ruffled, it just enhanced his blue, blue eyes, the uncompromising lines of his face and the impressive width of his shoulders. And his Aran jumper and chinos could take all sorts of rough stuff without looking any the worse for it.

Under his gaze, she'd tried to rebundle her recalcitrant hair into its scrunchy and had shoved her fringe out of her eyes, but it had swung back as inexorably as a pendulum. She quailed slightly as she remembered his cold tones.

'I suppose it's no use my asking what the hell is going on?'

She'd been grateful, for the first time, that her mother was so poorly. At least it meant he couldn't give in to what was clearly his greatest desire and shout his head off at her.

'Well, Mum was on the bench—'

'Listen, Beth. You may think I was born yesterday, but actually I bloody well wasn't. This little caper has all the hallmarks of one of your crazy ideas. I've got used to you putting yourself in danger – I don't like it, but I know you can't help yourself because you've got a bit missing in your brain. But dragging your old mum into it?'

It was just as well Wendy had been unconscious, Beth thought, a tiny, tiny smile tugging at the corners of her mouth. Though Wendy always did her best, for reasons no one understood, to appear at least two decades older than she was, she would still be horrified to be described as 'old'. There was no logic to human behaviour, and absolutely none at all to her mother, thought Beth.

'It was her idea!' Beth had remonstrated, knowing it was a very weak retort – the kind of response that even Jake would have examined and discarded when being told off for one of his little transgressions. Mind you, Jake as an only child usually didn't have anyone handy to blame things on, apart from Magpie and Colin, of course.

'Look, I can explain,' she'd tried again, but it seemed Harry had run out of either time or patience. He'd looked at his watch, grunted and stood up abruptly.

'It'll just have to wait,' he'd said, turning on his heel.

Beth had bowed her head and shrunk into herself. But then Harry had relented, and on his way out had done a little detour to kiss her quickly on the top of her head, put a warm, heavy hand on her drooping shoulder and whisper, 'They said she'll be fine. Don't worry. See you later.'

But Beth, alone now in the quiet room, had nothing to do but worry. Harry, for once, was right. She should never have put her mother in this position. Yes, it had been Wendy's plan. But Beth had years of resisting her mother under her belt. She shouldn't have gone along with it. And now Wendy was paying the price.

For the thousandth time, Beth wondered why she'd ever said yes. But she'd been so surprised when Wendy had rung, excited and full of the wheeze she'd dreamt up.

'Listen, when you come along to the reconstruction at the Bridge Club, I'll slip out just before breaktime and I'll sit on the same bench as Alfie – and pretend to be dead! You watch everyone's reactions, and the murderer will give themselves away,' she'd trilled.

Beth, to be fair, had been full of doubts. 'Mum, I'm not sure something like that will work, outside the pages of an Agatha Christie. Anyway, I bet the murderer will just keep a poker face, or maybe a Bridge one – if that's a thing.'

'It isn't a thing, actually, Beth. And I think you should take this idea seriously. This will save us loads of time. If we don't do this, then we'll have to check on the whereabouts and motives of all the people in the room at the time that Alfie might have been poisoned. Not to mention anyone who might have been passing in the park and could have slipped him something then.'

'Surely he wouldn't just take something offered to him by a random stranger?' Beth had remonstrated.

'Ah, but it might not have been a stranger. It was probably someone who knew him – and hated him. Anyway, Beth, they always do reconstructions on *Crimewatch*. And then they catch the crook.'

Wendy had been so bubbly, Beth hadn't had the heart to tell her that *Crimewatch* had been cancelled quite a few years ago, and had only solved a handful of cases, even in its heyday. And anyway, the chances of the miscreant blushing beetroot or fainting or shrieking or helpfully announcing their guilt by some other means, were negligible, in her considered opinion.

No, Beth had stupidly agreed because it had actually felt good, being involved in a conspiracy with her mum. They hadn't even told Katie, which had made it feel even more special. She couldn't remember ever having had a little plan like this with Wendy. Even when, years ago, they'd planned birthday surprises for her dad, it had always been her brother Josh who'd been roped into helping. Beth had stood on the sidelines, as astonished as her father when a fully lit birthday cake was produced from the kitchen or a wrapped present materialised on his seat in front of the telly.

Wendy's excuse then had been that Beth was too young and couldn't be trusted to keep a secret. It was a stance that was hard to keep up now that Beth was in her mid-thirties. Beth did wonder if things would have been different if Josh had been in the country, and had shared her own terrier-like interest in worrying away at puzzles. Would she have been left out in the cold yet again? As it was, she felt guilty that she hadn't confided in Katie – especially as things had gone so badly wrong.

Oh well, that was just another parcel of remorse to add to the mountain she had on her conscience. And Katie was even now doing her another favour, looking after Jake while she sat at Wendy's bedside. Her friend had already popped into the house on Pickwick Road to check that Magpie's bowl was brimming with her priceless cat food, and a very surprised Colin had been marched off to spend the night with his on-off doggy chum Teddy.

Beth texted Katie quickly to get an update on supper, and a reply pinged back immediately telling her not to worry, that all the homework had been done (What homework? thought Beth with another ramping-up of her guilt levels), and that they were all watching *Cats and Dogs* on the big telly in perfect harmony. She smiled at the picture and then sighed. At least Jake and Colin were having a good evening. And Magpie would be perfectly happy having a free run of the sofa without her rival butting his cold wet nose in.

She thought for a second then, before she chickened out, she rushed off a message to Harry. *Thanks for everything today. You were wonderful. Miss you xxxx*

It was probably the soppiest text she'd ever sent. But as soon as it disappeared from her screen, she somehow knew that it had plopped into the great abyss where half her missives to Harry ended up. He was not a believer in replying politely to everything. She sometimes had to wait days for an acknowledgement, and he often appeared in person long before a text was returned. She'd got used to it, but as she sat in the bleak, neon-lit room, by her mother's ominously still form, she couldn't pretend she liked it.

TWELVE

Harry York's legs dangled uncomfortably off the edge of his lumpy couch as he tried to find a comfortable reading position. He knew of old it wasn't a simple matter. Every time he tried to get himself settled with a good book, it was a case of beating the sofa into submission first, like a recalcitrant suspect in a windowless interview room. Not that he'd ever use his fists to get a conviction. He'd grown up watching cop shows like *The Sweeney* and *Prime Suspect*, where bruises bloomed on interviewees' cheeks shortly after the arrest and just before a full confession, but nowadays such tactics were beneath contempt. And even if they did cross anyone's minds, there was too much surveillance, from CCTV cameras in the custody area to meticulous recording of every interview.

Being too big for the furniture wasn't a new problem. He'd reached six foot four inches in his teenage years, but then he'd dreamt of the day when he'd buy his own couch and all the dangling would cease. He'd reckoned without a world of titches, though, and furniture designed accordingly. He sighed and shifted a leg across so that it reached the small table bearing his cooling cup of truckers' tea. None of that fancy-nancy Earl Grey dishwater Beth was constantly plying him with.

Thinking of Beth caused an automatic twinge, like putting weight on a pulled muscle. He'd received her text over an hour ago. For her, he was well aware that it was fulsome, mushy even. His fingers had hovered over the keys, thinking up replies. He'd even typed a couple. But what could he say? He knew she was in need of comfort. Her mother was lying in a hospital bed, for God's sake. What kind of man was he that he couldn't reach out to her with sympathy at a time like this?

But the trouble was that, as usual, it was Beth's own fault that she and Wendy were in this predicament. He wasn't a parent, he didn't even have a pet (unless you counted his step status with Jake, Magpie and Colin, which he didn't), but he knew that training was important. If you kept letting people get away with stuff you didn't like, wouldn't they keep on making the same mistakes? The ones that drove you mad.

Why in a million years would Beth think it was a great idea to go along with a clearly cracked stunt like the one she and her mother had pulled today? She could blame it on Wendy as much as she liked, but in all the time he'd known the older woman, she'd shown less of a tendency to put herself in the line of fire than almost anyone he knew, whether the task was as simple as making a cup of tea or as onerous (relatively speaking) as picking up young Jake after school.

Harry wasn't saying he approved of it, not at all. Much though he liked Wendy, he could see that she was lazy and self-centred, and therefore not particularly helpful as a parent. But for Beth to suggest that she'd go from this lackadaisical attitude to her daughter and only grandchild, right to the other extreme of offering herself as a guinea pig – no, a crash-test dummy – for a frankly insane scheme on behalf of a, what, a Bridge partner? A sort-of collaborator in a part-time hobby? Well, he didn't buy it, not for a minute. And the plan itself was so ridiculous it could only have been of Beth's devising.

Just thinking about it all was raising his blood pressure again, when he was trying to get comfy and finish off *The Unpleasantness at the Bellona Club*. There was something so relaxing, so reassuring, about other sleuths' problems. For a start, they were finite. There might be twists and turns along the way, but all the reader needed to do, if they weren't in the mood to work, was to carry on turning the pages until the problem obediently unravelled itself. In this, Dorothy L Sayers' fourth whodunit, the mystery surrounded the onset of rigor mortis and the setting was a reassuringly posh gentleman's club, of the type Harry had never once visited and didn't expect to be invited to any time soon. It was all pleasantly removed from real life and washing over him like a warm bath.

He even loved Lord Peter Wimsey's central problem, which was never to do with the corpse in hand but more a question of disguising his razor-sharp mind, in a time when being seen to be a hard-working aristo was to risk becoming horribly déclassé. Would that Harry had such troubles.

He moved his foot an inch, still searching for the sofa's sweet spot, and disaster struck. He nudged the table a tad too hard and cooling tea slopped everywhere, soaking into his sock and dripping relentlessly onto the floorboards. If he didn't get up and stop it, he knew from experience it would eventually soak through and stain his downstairs neighbour's ceiling.

Harry leapt to his feet, and there was an ominous crack from the sofa. As he watched, the armrest sagged like a drunk on a Saturday night.

Bugger. That's all I need. Now it was either a trip to Ikea – where he always confidently expected to bump into Sisyphus rolling a rock up the part of the maze that connected dining chairs to children's furniture – or the simpler option.

Moving in with Beth.

He sat down again heavily, wet socks, broken couch and puddle of tea notwithstanding. Had that time really come?

There was a jumper on the back of the sofa that could probably do with a wash. He dropped it onto the beige lake on the floor and swished it around with an already-sopping foot, while his mind worked overtime.

It was a big decision. One of the biggest he'd ever make. Was he ready? Was it the moment? Was he mature enough? And, more to the point, was she?

It never occurred to him for a second that Beth might say no.

THIRTEEN

Beth Haldane wasn't the only person in south London who could prevaricate, Harry realised the next day. He'd remained rooted to his sad old sofa for quite a while last night. Even the clammy state of his socks hadn't been quite depressing enough to drive him to move – until he'd surprised himself by finally shooting to his feet.

The turn of speed hadn't come because he'd made up his mind about Beth and Pickwick Road. Far from it. He'd simply changed course, and put the dilemma away on a really, really high shelf at the back of his consciousness. Because, if Wendy had been poisoned, then most likely, so had Alfred Pole. That meant an investigation should be instigated. Right now.

It was yet another victory for Beth. For a rank amateur, she had a surprising hit rate when it came to odd goings-on in her vicinity. This time, she had her mother to thank. Wendy had been convinced there'd been something suspicious about the old man's death from the off. Now they'd both be smug that he was cottoning on at last.

He hated to be playing catch-up to his Beth. She was like a tiny but razor-sharp thorn in his side – when she wasn't the woman of his dreams, that was. But despite the fact he'd be making her day by opening up the Alfie Pole business, it would be a relief to get going on the case. If there was one thing he and Beth always seemed to agree on, it was that there was nothing like a nice juicy murder.

* * *

Is there anything worse than murder, Beth thought, sitting by her sleeping mother's bedside. Though she had now widened her net of recriminations to include Wendy, for having thought up this crazy idea in the first place, Beth was still cursing herself roundly – and of course the killer, whoever they were, for making it all necessary.

Wendy hadn't stirred for hours. In a way, it was one of the most peaceful times they had ever spent together. The little figure in the bed had lain still and silent all night long while Beth, upright, watched the black rectangles of the windows turn gradually to iron grey and then become sludgy with the dawn, like milk stirred into mushroom soup. She'd be good for nothing today, that was for sure.

When her phone pinged at 8 a.m., she knew it must be Harry at last. Her heart leapt. She dragged it out of her bag and pored over the screen. But no, it was Katie, with the strange news that the Bridge Club had been asked to gather at Belair House again, this time by the police. Katie seemed to have got herself on the email list, which was definitely a plus. But what on earth was Harry up to? And why hadn't he told her about it himself?

The frown under her fringe was deepening into a groove by the time a frayed doctor burst through the door. He wasn't the one who'd seen Wendy initially, but had a competent if self-important look about him. His dark eyes were all but obscured by large, heavy-rimmed glasses, and his thick black hair was slicked down with enough gel to keep a boy band going for weeks. For once, there was no gaggle of students in tow. Either Wendy's case was considered too serious to be a teaching opportunity, or Harry had asked the hospital to be discreet. Beth hoped fervently it was the latter.

The doctor, who reassuringly looked a year or two older than her, examined Wendy briefly, held her limp wrist, bent over the bed, and then said very loudly into her ear, 'Wake up, Wendy!'

Beth squawked in alarm. Surely this was no way to treat a very sick woman. But then, to her astonishment, Wendy blinked a couple of times, opened both eyes, smiled widely at the man and batted her eyelashes at him.

'Good morning, doctor,' she said coquettishly, and levered herself into a more upright position.

Beth, who'd sat on the edge of her seat all night, not getting a wink of sleep and imagining Wendy was hovering between life and death, felt all her usual exasperation with her mother rushing back in to fill the space which had been hollowed out by remorse.

'You're feeling much better. You'll be home soon,' the doctor said, delivering both statements in a clipped voice that brooked no argument.

At this, Wendy instantly wilted. 'But, doctor...' she quavered.

Even Beth, who was rapidly beginning to suspect her mother was up to her usual tricks, was a little stunned. 'Surely, doctor, she's been very sick...'

'Yes, she has, but she's fine now. No lingering after-effects after atropine poisoning. Right as rain now, I expect.'

'Hang on a minute... atropine poisoning? Is that definitely what it was?'

'Definitely. There are characteristic symptoms. "Hot as a

hare, blind as a bat, dry as a bone, red as a beet, and mad as a hatter." I'm told you had all those, Wendy?'

Both Wendy and Beth nodded, Beth remembering all too clearly the terrible scene on the bench when Wendy had lurched around like a maniac.

'Are you saying it was deliberately administered?' Beth asked the doctor.

'Must have been. Unless you took it yourself, Wendy?' The doctor raised his voice slightly when addressing her.

Beth's opinion of the man instantly took a dive. Doctors shouldn't patronise the elderly. And Wendy wasn't even that far gone in years.

'I'm not hard of hearing, young man. And no, I most certainly did not take the stuff myself,' said Wendy with what Beth had to admit was understandable asperity. Perhaps this was where she got her own occasional feistiness from, she recognised. If so, then she owed Wendy. It was definitely useful to have an aversion to being talked down to. Though, if you were Beth and Wendy's height, it was an occupational hazard.

'Can you tell us any more about atropine poisoning? Where would you even find atropine?' Beth asked.

'I wouldn't go looking for it, young lady,' the doctor said severely, peering over his glasses and losing even more points.

For a second, Beth wondered if she should say, 'I'm not actually that stupid, young man,' but it would sound ridiculous. And wouldn't get them better treatment for Wendy, if she did have to stay in for longer. She contented herself with giving him her most malevolent glare instead. Unfortunately, he seemed to have the sort of armour-plated ego that was impervious even to a Beth death-ray stare. He simply adjusted his glasses and carried on talking very loudly to Wendy.

'The discharge nurse will be round later and will talk you through anything you'll need to watch out for. We'll let you go tomorrow morning. Of course, come back if you feel any onset of your symptoms,' he said.

'All right then, doctor,' Wendy shouted back.

'And maybe we should get your hearing tested. I find people speak loudly when they can't hear,' the doctor said, walking away with a stiff back.

'Or when they can't make themselves heard,' Beth muttered.

Wendy gave her a complicit smile and they shared a rare moment of unspoken accord.

'So, atropine. Have you heard of that before?' Beth asked. 'Anyone you know taking it?'

Wendy shook her head, lying back on the pillows. Was she paler, or was she just making the most of her moment in hospital? Hard to know. Beth had a go at googling atropine, but her phone reception was slower than Jake tidying his room under duress. And any attempts to connect herself to the hospital's wifi involved filling out a questionnaire about everything from her inside leg measurement to her earliest memories, all of which she was pretty sure would be sold to the highest bidder to keep the hospital's consultants in free parking spaces. She gave up crossly. It was something she'd have to do when she was home.

'You don't need to stay,' quavered Wendy with her eyes shut. 'You've been so good, but you must have things that you need to be getting on with...'

Just a bit, thought Beth, trying not to picture the in-tray at work, which must by now be like a relief map of the Himalayas. Not to mention Jake (though he'd actually be more than fine going off to school with Charlie); Colin, who'd be cluttering up poor Katie's house; and Magpie, no doubt simmering with rage at being left home alone.

'No, that's fine, Mum. It's important that you've got everything sorted out to go home,' Beth said with resignation. As she knew from personal experience, leaving hospital was strangely difficult these days. Yes, you could sign a form saying you were flouting medical advice and taking yourself off, but to do that you had to find someone with the form in the first place, and then someone else to hand it back to. No easy matter, when nurses were thin on the ground and doctors were so over-stretched that you hesitated to buttonhole one lest a patient somewhere else died of neglect. And waiting for the discharge sister was like trying to spot a wild rhino on the African plain.

She sighed a little. 'Shall I go and get you a cup of coffee or something?'

'No, no, sit here and we'll have a nice chat. When do we get the opportunity for that nowadays? You're always so busy, rushing around with all your hobbies. I hardly get a look in,' Wendy said with one of her tinkling laughs.

Beth gathered up her bag, all of a sudden too angry to speak. Her major 'hobby' was making enough money to feed herself and her child, not to mention the four-footed dependents they had acquired along the way. Once she'd got her voice under enough control, she said tersely, 'I'll pop to the canteen. Back soon.'

She walked along the corridor, her rubber soles squeaking painfully on the lino like tortured mice. Wendy had been supported by her husband all her married life, then cushioned by his plethora of delicious insurance policies after his death. She'd never had to tangle for a moment with the hell of grocery receipts that unfurled like streamers to a depth unmatched by her pockets. Not to mention all the other bills that jostled for a place in Beth's nightmares. And that was without the self-inflicted agony of the looming Wyatt's school fees.

If only James had insured himself up to the hilt, as her father had. If only she'd taken out a couple of policies on him herself... but she hadn't. It had seemed absurd to worry about lightning striking twice, and James had been young and fit. And, frankly, they'd both been stupid.

Never mind, thought Beth, squeaking along frantically now. If the worst came to the worst, they could always eat Colin. No, they couldn't, she thought immediately, not even able to joke in a tiny corner of her mind about sacrificing that pure soul. Magpie, maybe? Beth smiled crookedly. They'd never catch her, even if they were brave enough to try. That cat had a sixth sense about human needs and emotions. Very much unlike Beth's own mother.

Once she'd got to the canteen – optimistically rechristened a café but still producing the same lacklustre fare – Beth calmed down a lot. There was something about seeing all the hard-working NHS staff in their variously coloured scrubs that instantly made her certain she was leading a charmed life compared to the people who had to battle, day in day out, with the crumbling edifice that tried its best to keep them all in one piece.

She fetched a cup of tea and scanned the place for a vacant seat, eventually spotting one in the far corner. She wedged herself in, with her back to two women in lovely purple scrubs. At the other end of her own six-seater table was another woman, in pale blue. Not knowing the code, Beth tried to work out what everyone did. Sometimes, when you had a massive puzzle on your mind (and she could choose here between the murder of Alfie Pole, the attempted murder of her mother, or where the school fees were going to come from), it could be quite therapeutic to pick away at a lesser conundrum. The women in purple obligingly struck up a conversation.

'So I said to him, no one's ever going to believe you're single, if you keep that dirty great wedding ring on.'

'You didn't!'

The pair collapsed in giggles.

Meanwhile, the slender woman in blue picked up her buzzing phone.

'No, it's your time to collect her. No, I did say so. Yes, I'm sure.'

Easy-peasy, thought Beth. The purples were nurses, the blue was a surgeon. Next question. But then the girls in purple spoke up again.

'So, we'd better get to it. I'm assisting with a thoracotomy, how about you?'

'Appendectomy. But I'm flying solo today, Mrs Chung said.'

Beth hastily revised her judgements, especially when the woman in blue slid her phone into a handbag almost as exhausted as Beth's own.

For a moment, she imagined a Dulwich in which everyone was colour-coded according to their income – or ambitions. Belinda McKenzie would be in gold, with go-faster stripes; Katie in sunny yellow. What would she be in? Probably the same dingy grey she was wearing now, she thought, looking down at her uniform of sweater, jeans and boots. Time to turn her thoughts back to crime.

FOURTEEN

Harry York was standing in the thick of what seemed to be a huge milling crowd of elderly folk. The autumn sunlight poured through the windows of the former ballroom, glancing off silvery heads, a Zimmer frame and a walking stick. He was starting to feel uncomfortably hot in his navy jacket.

He'd thought all this would only take a moment. He'd reckoned without the complications of getting everyone up the stairs quickly, gathering them here, and now, the final step which seemed to be beyond him, getting their attention. This was ridiculous. He'd quelled full-blown riots in less time than this was taking.

He strode to the front of the room and cleared his throat. The din around him rose up a notch. He tried again. Nothing. He clapped his hands together, and one or two of the people in front misunderstood and joined in, giving him a spontaneous, if unearned, round of applause. When it died away, he finally had silence. He leapt in before anything else could go wrong.

'Thank you all so much for arriving early today. I understand you'll be playing Bridge later...' There was a bit of a murmur as a few of the audience looked yearningly towards the bidding boxes and cards already on the tables. Harry hurried on before he lost them again.

'Well, as you know, we've had one or two very serious, erm, incidents within the Bridge Club recently. Now, I'm going to need your help to sort this lot out,' he said, beaming down expectantly at his audience like a progressive headteacher begging the pupils not to vandalise the premises.

'Do you mean the murders?' said a dry voice at the back of the room.

The audience shuffled a little to either side, parting like a rather slow-mo Red Sea, eventually giving Harry a glimpse of his heckler. He was a man in his later years, wearing a very correct check jacket and tie, with white hair collected into two tufts over his ears, like a cartoon professor.

'Well, erm, it's one murder so far...' Harry said, then kicked himself and came to an abrupt halt. *Damn.* He tried again. 'That is to say, we're not making any announcements yet on that, erm, extremely regrettable happening. I'd just like to appeal for your assistance on some issues that could help us with our enquiries pertaining to the matter,' he said, painfully aware that he was using appalling management-speak jargon and, even worse, that a pleading note had entered his voice. This was definitely a tough crowd. He coughed a little and started afresh in a deeper tone which, he hoped, brooked no argument.

'I'd like to ask you all to show any medications you have to my officer stationed by the door here,' he said, indicating Narinda Khan, the DC he was trying to train up. She looked at him with an unquestionable spark of fear as the crowd began to advance inexorably towards her.

'Now, if you could form an orderly queue, please. One at a time, there, one at a time,' said Harry, but it was to no avail, as a press of pensioners, rattling pill bottles, pushed forward.

* * *

'Well, that was a disaster, wasn't it?' Harry pushed his hand through his rough blond hair and looked ruefully at Narinda Khan, who in turn was surveying a table mounded high with drugs. They'd moved to a small side room when it had seemed clear that the volume of medications was much more than one DC could reasonably be expected to stuff into her pockets.

The Bridge Club was now back in the ballroom, thank goodness, tranquillised by Deidre MacBride who'd popped up just in time to announce that play was starting. It was amazing how the cards calmed them. There was barely a murmur now, and when Harry had last poked his head round the door, every table with its green baize cloth had had a peaceful quartet arranged around it, scrutinising their hands as though their lives depended on them.

Harry certainly hadn't been able to think of a good reason to delay proceedings. He just hoped he didn't get lynched by a roomful of angry pensioners when they realised the drugs were hopelessly mixed up. 'Did you even manage to note down whose stuff was whose?'

Narinda shook her head infinitesimally and could barely meet Harry's eyes. 'But they'll know which bottles are theirs, won't they, when they come and collect it all?'

'Will they?' Harry asked heavily. If they were anything like his mother, who was still a lot younger than this bunch, they wouldn't remember which room to come to, let alone be capable of collecting their own prescriptions. But he was probably being silly. If they were all sharp enough to play Bridge so well, they'd be able to recognise their own medications. Surely? He ran a hand over the brown bottles, packets of pills and phials of drops. Some of them did have names on, which was a blessing. But not all.

'Do you think there's even any atropine here?' Narinda asked diffidently.

'Nothing's marked atropine, that's for sure. But we'd need to google all these different prescriptions, I suppose, to check whether any contain it. We could basically be here forever.'

'Unless you found a helpful retired doctor who could give you a hand?' said a voice from the doorway. 'I was going to knock, but I didn't want to interrupt your chat.' It was the elderly chap with the tufts of hair, which were now accessorised with a rather merry smile.

Harry stepped forward. 'Of course, sir, do come in. So, you're a doctor?'

'That's right, Dr John Brett. GP of this parish for forty-odd years. Only retired a couple of years ago; my nephew's got the practice now. I know most of the Bridge group, treated them or their children – or grandchildren – over the years. And I know which drugs contain atropine.'

They were the magic words.

'Come in, sit down.' Harry looked around wildly. The room was small and evidently rarely used. Other than the cluttered table, there was nothing else there, apart from a couple of stands in the corner for displaying large floral arrangements for wedding receptions. 'Khan, fetch a chair for the doctor, please. If you wouldn't mind having a look at this little lot, sir, you could really help us out.'

'Got a bit more than you bargained for, didn't you?'

'You could say that,' Harry admitted ruefully, surveying the huge pile of pills.

'Seventy-five per cent of people over fifty are on medication. And of those, fifty per cent take four or more types of drug,' the doctor said and smiled.

'Wow. In that case, perhaps I should have expected even more than this little lot?'

'I'd say so. In the general population, we are heavily medicated at the best of times. But of course, in Dulwich, you're dealing with a high median level of fitness. People here live longer, healthier lives than in, well, outlying areas,' the doctor added, with a sympathetic wince at what those outside this charmed postcode might need to swill down to sustain normal life.

Narinda came back in with one of the spindly chairs from the ballroom, and the doctor sat gratefully and started to pick away at the pill mountain. Moving a bottle at the foothills caused a small avalanche, but after quite a while he seemed to have found what he was looking for. He withdrew both hands from the table, each clasped around something. His hands were large and capable.

Like a magician putting the final touches to his favourite trick, he opened both fists with a flourish. Lying on each palm was a small vial. One was white plastic and was the sort you'd buy over the counter at Boots. The other was a more traditional, brown glass bottle, the type Harry could imagine an old-school apothecary dishing out.

'Which of these do you think contains the deadly poison atropine?' said the doctor, twinkling again. Harry looked at him severely. This was no joking matter. But he was willing to humour the man. To an extent.

'I'd say the brown one, sir. But enlighten me.'

'You're wrong. This one is just common or garden saline. Probably used to ease nasal congestion. We give it to mothers to help their babies with snuffles, and it's good in the later stages of life, too, to, ah, soften things up.'

Harry blanched but his searching glance didn't falter. The man was obviously enjoying his time in the spotlight. Doctors were by no means infallible, but they got used to having all the answers and being treated with plenty of awed respect by their patients. Presumably, opportunities to command such attention grew a lot sparser when one was retired. Harry allowed him his moment.

'So, it's the bog standard one that's the potential killer. Who'd have thought it?' he said obligingly, glancing at Khan with a raised eyebrow. She looked appropriately impressed.

'Of course, it's not sold as a poison. It's just plain old eye drops. For those little irritations,' the doctor explained. 'A lot of people suffer from hay fever around here. We have quite a few plane trees in the area, they're a terrible nuisance. I don't know if you're a sufferer?'

Harry was tempted to say he didn't have time for hay fever. There were so many other major irritations ready to get under his skin, pollen was the least of his problems. But he knew that for those prone to it, it was a blight which ruined the summer months.

'So, does atropine do the job then, for hay fever? And how come it's sold over the counter?'

'Well, it's a case of what you don't know won't hurt you. A lot of common compounds can be deadly, if used in the wrong way. But who would know that adding a dash of that or a teaspoon of the other could result in death? If we don't advertise the fact, then usually we don't have a problem. We must be dealing with someone who has a modicum of medical knowledge.'

'Someone like yourself, then, sir?' asked Harry, raising an eyebrow.

'Rather more than a modicum, in my case. And wouldn't it make me a rather obvious suspect? Besides, I think you'll find that I wasn't actually at the gathering when the lamentable incident occurred.'

'Which lamentable incident might that be, then?' Harry's blue eyes were at their most piercing.

'The murder, of course. Of Alfred Pole.' For the first time, the doctor looked a little less sure of his ground. 'That is what we're talking about, isn't it?'

'Thank you so much for your help, doctor. I'll just take this, if I may,' said Harry, holding out an empty plastic evidence bag so that the doctor could drop the phial into it. After a moment's hesitation, when the elderly man seemed to realise for the first time that his fingerprints were now all over a potential murder weapon, he let go of the little bottle and it plopped into the bag, which Harry then sealed.

He held out one hand to Khan, who obligingly passed him a biro, and he marked a few quick hieroglyphs on the blank space that were as hard to decipher as any prescription the doctor himself could have written. Then he slipped the package into his pocket, patting it rather ominously. The doctor looked at him, suddenly seeming smaller and more frail.

'Well, if that's all, I might return to the game...'

'Of course,' said Harry, genial again. 'I imagine your table will be getting impatient?'

'Oh no,' said the doctor. 'I was the dummy. That's why I could slip out to, er, assist you.' He gave another smile, but it was rather tentative, as though he was on the brink of saying something else. Whatever it was, he thought better of it. Then he turned on his heel and made his way out of the room, walking with a slight limp now.

Harry stared after him. For a moment, he wondered what the doctor had been about to say. But then all speculation was banished. He gazed straight ahead, unseeing, at the closed door. Narinda Khan stood on the sidelines, looking at him strangely, but Harry York's expression was completely blank and then, as though a mist had cleared, he started to smile. He'd had an idea.

FIFTEEN

Beth sat in her little office in the archives institute at Wyatt's. She'd had an idea.

Naturally, it wasn't about the outline for a life history of Sir Thomas Wyatt – the project she'd been working on, in a desultory sort of way, for so long. It was about her mother, about Bridge, and above all about poor old Alfie Pole. Beth took an exasperated look at her in-tray, looming like a tatty sort of south London Matterhorn over her entire office.

Colin, lying at her side with his head peacefully upon his two folded paws, gazed up at the teetering collection of school notices, play programmes, copies of the head's speeches and timetables of rugby fixtures, with a slightly wary expression in his soft brown eyes. He seemed to hate filing almost as much as Beth did. Plus, he probably didn't want that little lot cascading down about his silky ears. But he banged his tail on the floor encouragingly when Beth peered at him, and gave a tiny little snort, which could have been contentment or impatience, depending on how you read it. Beth, who'd got much better over the months in decoding Labrador, decided it was impatience. Perhaps he needed to avail himself of the facilities?

She scrabbled in her drawer for the cache of plastic bags she now squirrelled away all over the place for Colin's doings, and got to her feet.

'All right then, boy, you've talked me into it. Walkies.'

Colin, a little surprised but never one to look a gift perambulation in the mouth, got stiffly to his hind legs. He was getting a bit rheumaticky in the back quarters these days, but he wasn't one to grumble. He gave Beth's hand a grateful lick and submitted to the lead being clipped onto his collar. He gave his tail an experimental wag or two before settling into the steady rhythm of an outboard motor and, thus propelled, followed Beth out into the fresh air.

Beth's motives in taking this unscheduled break were many and various, but there were few she wanted to acknowledge openly, either to herself, to the ever-patient Colin, or to anyone else. She happened to know that the bell was about to ring for break and that Jake had Latin at second period, so he would be walking across this particular corner of the asphalt playground just about – ah, there he was. Swinging his bag, lagging at the back of a gaggle of boys, walking along with, yes, there was Charlie. But there were a couple of others too. Laughing and joshing with these new friends, Jake was also casually scuffing the shoes which had cost her a fortune – and so much angst – only a few days ago.

Beth felt a smile tugging at the corners of her mouth. Jake, never voluble about school even when he'd been in the cosy Village Primary, now seemed to have taken some sort of Trappist vow about what went on between the hours of 8.45 a.m. and 3.30 p.m. Sneaking the occasional glance, like this, did so much to reassure her that everything was going as well as could be expected at this point. And she could give some feedback to Katie too. She'd be really interested to know that Jake and Charlie had both got to Latin on time without any undue incidents.

Yes, she was actually doing this for Katie, Beth told herself as she dodged behind the Science block, hoping Jake hadn't caught sight of Colin's distinctive chocolatey coat. Although she had a perfect right to be strolling the grounds of Wyatt's. And she wasn't spying on her boy, oh no.

'Beth!' said a loud voice at her elbow. She hadn't seen Janice coming up, so intent had she been on the little group on the edge of her sightline.

'Ah, I was just looking for you, Janice,' she said, flustered.

'Hmm, were you? Because I almost never hang out with the boys doing Year 7 Latin,' said the imperturbable school secretary with a fond smile. 'Come on, Beth. You know Jake's doing fine. I'd tell you if he wasn't.'

'Yes, but what if even you don't really know what's going on, Janice?' Beth burst out. 'It's not like he tells anyone anything. It would be much easier to get a full life story out of a clam than to get a simple hello from Jake these days.'

'Listen, Beth, I hear you, you're an anxious mother, that's fine. We've all been there,' said Janice patronisingly, seeming to forget she had recently called Beth up at 2 a.m. because her baby had 'looked a bit funny'. She took a breath and carried on. 'But Jake's absolutely fine. Don't you think I've got the whole cohort of teachers primed and ready to report back to me if there's the slightest problem? And why on earth should there be? He's a lovely boy. You've got nothing to worry about,' she said firmly.

Beth felt silly. 'You're right. I'm being ridiculous. Colin, don't do that,' she said, pulling at the dog as he advanced inexorably on Janice. 'I'm sorry. You know he's got a fixation,' she said, as Janice swung her shoulder bag across her body to protect herself from Colin's probing nose.

'I take it as a weird compliment. A *very* weird one,' said Janice.

Beth wasn't sure she should be so accepting – Colin was not

particularly discriminating; for him, it was any crotch in a storm – but it was very sporting of Janice. Beth had tried to cure him of his obsession, and luckily he didn't do it to her, but he was nothing short of an old perv sometimes.

'Shall we go and have a coffee in the canteen? Take your mind off it all? And how's Wendy? She'll be out soon, won't she?'

Beth wasn't surprised that Janice had heard all about her mother's travails. If there was a hamster sneezing anywhere amongst the Wyatt's pet population, Janice had made a vet's appointment by the afternoon.

She sighed. 'Yes. I'm not sure when exactly, but if they don't discharge her the minute she's OK, there's a danger that she'll milk the whole situation and take root in that bed. You know what she's like. She just loves the attention.'

'But it must have been so awful when you found her!' Janice's eyebrows were raised, and Beth immediately felt a pang that she'd switched so quickly from terror that her mother would die to irritation that her mother was very much alive.

'Oh God, yes, yes, it was terrible. I really thought she'd... For a minute I was so sure... It was really grim.' Beth's hand went to her heart at the memory, and she was transfixed for a moment. She should be more patient. So what if Wendy wanted to block an NHS bed for a bit? She'd had a ghastly experience. She probably needed a rest. And if whoever it was who'd done this had genuinely meant to bump her off, then she was certainly safer in hospital than out on the streets of Dulwich where, Beth realised with a frisson of horror, it would be the easiest thing in the world to have another pop at her.

'Mothers and daughters, eh?' sighed Janice with the smugness of someone whose own daughter was currently kitted out every day in a Babygro with bunny ears attached, and was entirely unable to remove the outfit or exert any sort of freedom of choice, sartorial or otherwise. It was quite clear Janice could never envisage a time when the dynamics between them might be more complicated.

Beth smiled inwardly. Long may her situation remain so blissful.

'Do you have any idea yet who'd want to try and kill Wendy? Or her friend, for that matter?' Janice asked earnestly.

'It's still a complete mystery. Well, maybe not so much with Mum. I can't be the only one who's tempted every now and again.' Beth said it lightly, but Janice gave her a bit of a look. Beth recalibrated mentally. Even joking about matricide was not really on, she supposed, when they'd just had such a narrow escape.

To her surprise, Janice then pressed her arm for a moment. 'It's been rough on you, I bet. And just when you want to be concentrating on Jake. Well, to reassure you again, he's settling in brilliantly. I wish I could say the same for all the boys.'

Instantly, Beth banished Wendy to the back of her mind – for now – as she scented a chunk of gossip. 'Wait, it's not Charlie, is it? Katie's son.'

'What? No, no, he's another duck to water, that one. No, it's someone quite unexpected, really. Well, it's a big transition, isn't it? Primary to secondary. And I have to say, the ones that have been tutored extensively to get in sometimes relax a bit when they're over the finishing line, so to speak. And that really isn't a great idea. If they need that much help to pass the exams, then they probably shouldn't be here, or they should continue with the tuition to keep up. We move along pretty fast, even at the Year 7 level.'

Beth was beginning to wonder if she could make an educated, or *tutored*, guess at the boy who was struggling. The extra lessons part certainly rang a bell – a large, glitzy, Belinda McKenzie-sized klaxon. But she suddenly felt it was a bit unfair to tattle about Billy, if it was indeed the poor lad. She couldn't exactly say she'd grown fond of him in the brief time when she'd caved in to her own worst fears (and Belinda's bossy urgings) and occasionally driven him, his brother and Jake to Camberwell for a bit of cramming. He was too loud, too sporty, too *confident* to win, or even to seem to need, a place in her heart. But there was no malice in the lad. What you saw was what you got, and there was plenty of it, if you liked that sort of thing. And it definitely wasn't his fault that he was Belinda McKenzie's son.

'Will you be, er, having a word with his mum?' asked Beth.

'For sure. Unless he picks up very soon. It doesn't take much to get left behind, believe me. This first phase is pretty crucial. Of course, the teachers do pile on the homework a bit, just to test the boys' nerves. But there are also a few little exercises done in class, where no one else can "help", and that can really separate the sheep from the goats.'

'I've never totally understood that phrase,' Beth murmured, immediately worried about how Jake might be coping with any impromptu quizzes. They were among the many, many things he hadn't mentioned to her.

Janice looked at her sharply, then smiled. 'You're right, I shouldn't really be discussing it with you. Bit close to home. Let's go and grab that coffee.'

'What shall I do with Colin?' Beth asked. The old boy had been suspiciously quiet as they'd walked and talked. Sometimes, she got the impression that he was actually eavesdropping. His head would nod when Beth was chatting with friends, he'd even pant wisely at times, but he'd always hold his own counsel. Not for the first time, she wondered what on earth he'd say if he could only talk. But they probably both preferred it this way, she thought, patting his velvet head.

'He can't come into the canteen, but everyone's in classes for half an hour, so you can just loop up his lead here, outside, and I'll get one of the catering staff to bring him a bowl of water.

Everyone loves Colin,' said Janice, who'd obviously forgiven him for his earlier probing.

A short while later, Beth was having a very unusual sensation. She was rather wishing Janice would shut up. Her friend normally talked nothing but sense but, having just had a baby, she was now understandably obsessed with everything pertaining to tiny little Elizabeth Grover. It did not make her the most fascinating company. Beth thought back to her early days with Jake, and inwardly sympathised with everyone who'd had to listen to her droning on about nappies and feeds and sleeps and rashes and teething and... But Beth was devoted to Elizabeth. Not just because Janice had paid her the enormous compliment of borrowing her name and making her godmother, but also because the baby was a chip off the old block, the snuggliest and most gorgeous creature Beth had ever seen. Nevertheless, hearing endless details about the state of the child's buttocks was doing her head in.

Janice was halfway through a tale about Elizabeth regurgitating a feed, when Beth could take no more. 'Can I just ask you, because you know everything, can you think of anyone in the Bridge Club who'd actually have a grudge against Alfie Pole? Or my mother?' she said desperately.

'Oh! Well, I don't know... and isn't that the sort of thing that you're supposed to be working out? You're the detective, after all,' said Janice.

'Oh, I'm not,' said Beth. 'I've just had a few lucky guesses in the past...'

'More than that. Don't be modest,' said Janice over the rim of her coffee cup. 'Now does it mean anything that there were specks of spinach in—?'

'It's just that you do know everyone in Dulwich,' Beth blurted. 'If there was some ancient grudge in the Bridge Club, well, you'd be the one who'd have heard all about it.'

Janice halted again, reluctantly, but thought a little bit

longer this time. She shook her head. 'No. The Bridge Club always seems fine, runs like clockwork, thanks to Deirdre MacBride. I've heard the odd dispute does break out when she's not around for any reason...' She tailed off with a little cough when she remembered who she was talking to, while Beth stored the information away for later but said nothing. 'But it's not like the allotments, is it?' Janice continued. 'Or the gardening people? I mean, they're really crazy.'

'Are they? Truly? I've heard talk before, but no one ever seems to know any details. And is this the allotments down by the side of the school playing fields?'

Janice sighed. 'We might need some more coffee. This could take some time.'

'I'll grab refills, and some sandwiches, and we'll take them back to my office, shall we?' said Beth, delighted they were on the right track at last.

A few minutes later, they were back in the archives institute, getting settled, with Colin lying at their feet.

'So, tell me all about these crazy gardeners,' said Beth, leaning forward over her desk.

'Oh yes,' said Janice. 'Well, let's see. Suppose I start with the Open Gardens set, then. They're all lovely, they really are, but there are one or two... You see, what you've got to understand about Dulwich and gardens is that it's...' She tailed off, thoughtfully.

Beth, on the edge of her seat, couldn't hide her impatience. 'Yes? It's like what?'

Janice shook herself. 'I'm so sorry. I'm so tired with Elizabeth waking up three times a night. I'm doing it all, letting Tommy sleep, as he's got to do a full day...'

As usual, Beth's own mind went blank for a second as she computed the fact that the great Dr Grover, the head who had brought Wyatt's on in leaps and bounds, was just plain old Tommy to Janice, and now talked about in faintly dismissive terms. Janice had little time for anything that wasn't wearing pale pink accessorised with pureed apple at the moment.

'Did Jake do that?' Janice was still speaking.

'Do what? Wake up? Oh, they all do. It's standard issue. Breaks you in for everything to come,' Beth said with a shrug. To tell the truth, she couldn't really remember those early days. Mind you, she didn't try. It had been a fog of weariness and confusion. She sympathised with Janice, she really did, but she didn't want to go back there. Especially as they seemed to have hit on a promising line of enquiry at last. But she could see that her friend's head was drooping like a tulip in need of water. The poor girl was shattered.

Beth quickly made a little pillow with Janice's cashmere cardi, plumped it up on the desk and then coaxed her head down onto it. She left the sandwich and one steaming coffee just out of elbow-jogging range, in case Janice had a nightmare about little Elizabeth.

As she tiptoed over to her conference table, she was thinking furiously. Not about sleep deprivation and the delightful, precious menace of tiny babies, but of gardening clubs and allotments.

By half-past three, Colin was also sound asleep and Beth herself was in danger of nodding off. She had scaled a couple of faces of her own personal Matterhorn of post, and had silently filed the essentials in her archive – nowadays, a sleek and efficient record of the school's doings, a million miles from the tatty collection of dog-eared play programmes from the 1940s that she had inherited from her unlamented predecessor.

She'd also downloaded Deirdre MacBride's very efficient list of people who'd been dummy during the fateful hand of Bridge when Alfie Pole had met the great director in the sky. Beth crossed off Alfie's own name rather sadly. That left five.

Some were a little surprising. *R. Joyce* – that definitely rang some sort of bell. *Rosemarie Hadley* – oh yes, the woman with the blonde helmet of hair. *Peter Tilling* – Beth had never heard of him. *Dr John Brett* – if he was a medical doctor, and not a PhD (you could never tell in Dulwich), he might well be au fait with poisons. And finally, *Christina Smith*. Again, Beth didn't know her.

Was she just giving herself a lot more work with this little lot, or could it really crack the case? She wasn't sure. Before she could talk herself out of it, she decided to email a copy off to Harry at his Met Police address. Checking a whole bunch of alibis was much more the traditional police bag than her sort of thing. She liked to make intuitive leaps, she decided. Plus, she really didn't have the time to do all that gumshoe stuff, trekking round and making herself unpopular by asking too many questions. I'll let my boy in blue do that, she thought, and smiled as she hit send.

She hadn't quite got round to her book outline, but she wasn't going to reproach herself, for once. She'd made good progress. Tomorrow she'd be able to get straight down to it.

For some reason, this sparked a twinge of doubt. She'd been prevaricating for so long on the whole issue that she wasn't even sure she could remember what to write. But she shushed the little voice. She'd leave Wyatt kicking his elegant high red heels – as depicted in the astonishing full-length portrait that looked down on them from the wall of the magnificent assembly hall – for yet another day. There was stuff to get on with now.

She gently woke Janice and packed her off home, then picked up Jake, or rather, lurked outside the gates and almost caught up with him as he pottered back with Charlie and a couple of others – the same boys he'd been with earlier. When they got to the crossing near the chemist, she strode forward and tapped her son on the shoulder. He spun round, then saw

Colin, and introduced him to everyone while she stood around feeling ridiculously like a gooseberry.

The boys all stooped to pet Colin, who obliged them with plenty of tail wags and a goodly portion of drool. Beth, tiring of her role as Colin's silent walker, reminded Jake they had to go and visit his granny in the hospital. With hastily concealed reluctance, he said goodbye to his friends, and they picked up the little green Fiat and sped off. Or tried to; it was, of course, bumper to bumper through the village at this time of day.

It wasn't until they'd edged down East Dulwich Grove and passed the Goose Green roundabout, where more kids probably went to the state school and so didn't require intensive ferrying from one congested street to the next, that the traffic eased up. Beth tried a bright bit of chatter to while away the journey.

'How was school?' she tried.

'Good,' came the response, with the decided downward inflection that told her there'd be no more to the sentence, and that any other conversational gambits would meet an equally high brick wall. Nevertheless, she ploughed on.

'How's Billy McKenzie doing? Is he in your class?'

Jake looked at her. They were at a red light, so she gave him a quick smiley glance, hoping to appear as innocent as the enquiry. Jake's face, by contrast, was as carefully shuttered as Katie's new holiday home in off-season.

'Why do you want to know? Is this about what happened?'

Instantly, Beth was agog. She just about managed to stop herself from saying, 'No, what happened?' in a high-pitched squeak. She paused a beat, then said, 'Might be.' Two could play at monosyllables.

'Because it wasn't a major thing. Stuff like that goes on all the time. No biggie.'

'Of course not,' said Beth with a reassuring smile, as she pushed the car into gear and drove off. *Damn.* She wasn't going to get anywhere by asking more questions. So how on earth was she going to find out what was going on? And what was this non-biggie, exactly? Her mind boggled quietly. She'd have to ask Katie; maybe she was a more efficient interrogator. The thought was a little depressing. How had things come to this, so rapidly?

Surely it wasn't more than a few months ago that Jake would come to her, unbidden, with all his problems, every little event from the playground, and would enjoy telling her about them. But maybe she was deluding herself. There were always filters between parent and child, there had to be. But now these filters seemed to be as big and as wide as the car. Well, her Fiat was titchy. Maybe the car next to them, which was, inevitably, a Volvo SUV. She sighed.

'OK?' asked Jake.

Beth smiled, her shoulders sagging with relief. His little question was exactly the reassurance she'd needed that he was still her sweet boy, however grown-up he was suddenly getting.

'Just thinking about Granny,' she lied. Well, it wasn't entirely a fib. She'd been worrying, off and on, about her mother all day. Particularly about why Wendy hadn't quite made it out of the hospital yet. She suspected Wendy was clinging onto that bed for dear life, but it was always possible that she was taking longer to get over the whole, deeply unpleasant, incident than Beth had imagined. She sighed again. *Terrible daughter, terrible mother.*

At least she was doing OK with Colin. He was safely in the back of the car, having another little snooze. He wouldn't love staying in the car park at the hospital, but they couldn't spend too long with Wendy, even if they'd wanted to. Jake would have homework. Probably. Though no doubt he'd rather die than tell her about it.

As it turned out, Jake was happy enough to settle down in the corner with his books once they were in Wendy's room, and once he'd hugged her and seen for himself that she was pretty

much fine. Getting his homework out meant that he was behind
a useful screen of paper and could safely get out of too much
family interaction.

Honestly, where does this male desire to escape come from,
wondered Beth. She twitchily tried to look at her watch while
Wendy told her, for the umpteenth time, how she'd been on the
verge of being discharged when her temperature had suddenly shot
up and they'd insisted she stay in for a while longer. Beth peered at
her mother through half-closed lids, wondering if Wendy was
capable of performing that old trick of warming up the thermometer
on a handy hot drink, then realised to her chagrin that these days the
nurses probably had fancy digital devices that they waved over the
patients' foreheads or popped into their ears. Wendy must
genuinely have had a turn. But she really seemed fine now.

'Well, since you're in for a bit, I wondered if you could help
me on some background. I was hearing about the allotments...'

'Oh, you know I'm not interested in gardening,' said
Wendy, lying back against her pillows like an eighteenth-
century heroine about to expire.

Beth did indeed know it, as Wendy had passed on her lack
of skill and general apathy to her daughter and she was very
much afraid that Jake had inherited it, too. The whole lot of
them seemed destined to have horrible scrubby gardens, which
was a terrible shame when you saw what could be done, even
with a small plot. Most of Dulwich was a treasure trove of
delightful shrubs and fragrant blossoms. Apart from the bits
inhabited by Haldanes. Beth did love listening to *Gardeners'
Question Time* but had no idea how to put anything she heard
into practice. She'd once been amused to hear that the climbing
rose named Eleanor Roosevelt had been described as 'good in a
bed, but better up against a wall', and had made the mistake of
relaying this to Harry. She smiled reminiscently.

Her brother Josh was rubbish on the gardening front, too –

not that he was in the country long enough to acquire a spade these days, let alone deploy it. Beth wasn't even sure if he had a flat with any outside space. He'd always kept a pied-à-terre in the area, but these days wouldn't have time to dip even a toe into it even if he'd wanted to.

'What about your next-door neighbours, though?'

'Mrs Pink? I think she's ill, you know, *women's problems*,' said Wendy in a stage whisper. 'Shame, as she used to be lovely about taking in parcels. Her late husband was in insurance. Told me that your father had made wonderful arrangements,' she added smugly.

Beth thought with irritation that they all knew that much. Not for the first time, she wished her dad had lasted long enough to encourage her own poor James to sign up for some policy or other. Things could have been very different.

'Should you be discussing financial things like that with people?' she asked. 'But isn't the lady on the other side a gardener?'

'Mrs Hills? Well, I suppose she's keen,' sniffed Wendy unenthusiastically.

'Come on, Mum, she's got a waterfall in her back garden. And doesn't she have those fish?'

'The carp,' said Wendy darkly. 'They give me the willies, those blighters.'

'Why?' Beth asked.

'Ugh, they're just so huge. And the way they glide about that huge tank of theirs. They're like sharks. But quieter.'

Beth didn't point out that sharks were hardly known for the loudness of their banter. 'At least they don't bite.'

'You think? Rather you than me, sticking a finger in that pool,' said Wendy with a theatrical shudder.

'Are they like piranhas, then? Cool,' said Jake from his corner.

Beth looked over sharply. You never knew, these days, when he'd tune into a conversation. It was quite disconcerting.

'I wouldn't put it past them, let's say,' Wendy said with a smile.

Despite herself, Beth was pleased to see grandmother and grandson enjoying a little moment of accord, even if it was totally wrong-headed. Carp surely just ate fish food. But maybe lots of it.

'How's the homework?' she couldn't stop herself from saying, and instantly Jake was back behind his wall of books and folders.

'Yeah, good.'

Good. That was all he said these days. It wasn't *good* at all, she thought crossly.

'How about if I give you some money for a snack, bag of crisps or something? You must be getting peckish?' she said to Jake, while eyeing Wendy. Her mother still had her eyes closed and Beth was keen to ask her a few more questions before they had to leave.

'Nah. I'm good,' said Jake, behind his Latin textbook.

It was a terrible shame to interrupt him while he was actually getting down to some work, but it had to be done. 'Chocolate bar?'

''S'OK.'

'Can of Coke?' asked Beth in a shrill voice.

'All right, all right, Mum. You must be desperate to get rid of me. I'll get you a tea as well, shall I? It must be ten minutes since you had one,' said Jake, uncurling himself from the chair.

She realised with a shock that he was now almost the same height as her, and not only that but he had a much clearer grasp of what was going on than she had hoped. She was going to have to seriously up her game if she wanted to carry on outwitting him. She pressed a ten-pound note into his hand and smiled up into those eyes, so like James's. 'Get a tea for Granny as well, could you? Two sugars.'

Wendy, from the bed, protested for a moment. She liked to pretend she only took one sugar, but always added in a second. She seemed too tired to insist on the charade today. 'Thank you, darling boy,' she said.

The door closed behind him and Beth got down to it. 'Listen, Mum. I'm trying to find out who else might have had a motive to bump off poor old Alfie and try to poison you as well. There's the Bridge lot, sure, but Janice at the school was saying the gardens people are even worse. Your neighbour, Mrs Hills, opens her garden up in the summer, doesn't she?'

'Mmm, yes. She's part of the Open House mafia,' Wendy agreed.

'There must be a reason why people call them a *mafia*,' said Beth. 'How well do you know her? What about the rest of them? What are they like? And is there a big crossover with the Bridge lot?'

'That's a lot of questions,' said Wendy weakly.

'While I'm at it, there are a few people who were dummy at the same time as Alfie that day. They'd have the best chance of killing him. I need to go through them with you.'

Wendy shuddered, and Beth wished for a moment that she'd been a bit more euphemistic. After all, this group of people had all been dummy again yesterday, and therefore had probably tried to kill Wendy too.

'It's urgent, Mum. Let's just rattle through the list and you can tell me what you think,' Beth said more gently. 'So, how about Dr John Brett?'

'Johnny? Are you mad? He was our doctor for years; your father played golf with him.'

Beth thought darkly that he couldn't have been that brilliant a medical man if he hadn't noticed her father was about to make a sudden one-way trip to the great clubhouse in heaven, but she moved on. 'Christina Smith?'

'Ha! She couldn't kill anyone to save her life,' said Wendy. 'She's got a bad leg. Did something to her knee ages ago. I think she fell, or did too much of something. Anyway, she won't have got up from the table the whole time, mark my words.'

'Rosemarie Hadley?'

'No, she was sitting down all the time Alfie was out. I saw the back of her head, you know, that hairdo. It's unmistakable. I don't know about the attempt on me, of course.'

'I'm pretty sure I saw her,' said Beth, squinting to remember. That blonde coronet... she'd seen the light glinting off it... hadn't she? Beth mentally crossed her off too. 'R. Joyce?'

'Well, you'd know her better than me. Isn't Regina Joyce a teacher at Wyatt's? Part time, I suppose, or she wouldn't be able to come to Bridge. But she's very scatty, I doubt if she could finish anyone off even if she started.'

Beth put her head on one side. She remembered the beleaguered-looking former English head. It was true, she was always dropping things. Did being a klutz rule you out as a killer, though?

'How about Peter Tilling?'

Now Wendy laughed aloud. 'His arm is in a sling, didn't you see? He broke it on his allotment.'

That reminded Beth about gardening. 'Alfie had an allotment, too, but paid other people to keep it up for him. Do you think it's something to do with that?'

'I told you, I have nothing to do with that whole gardening set,' said Wendy faintly. 'Frankly, as soon as they start talking about pruning their petunias, I tune out. I know there was a bit of a hoo-ha over something last year, though. Alfie mentioned it to me, but he would always start chatting when we had a difficult hand. I often had to shush him, you know.'

Beth bit her lip. Her mother wasn't a multi-tasker at the best of times. And the more she found out about Wendy's Bridge playing, the more she suspected her mother only hung onto her status as a good player by dint of sheer bloody-mindedness.

'So Alfie really *was* into gardening?'

'Oh yes, darling. Have you not seen his place? It'll go to that daughter of his now, I suppose, though she never did a thing for him. Honestly, *I* did more to look after him than she ever did.'

And that was really saying something, Beth thought, given that Wendy had just more or less admitted she had a habit of shutting the poor man up every time he opened his mouth. Beth hoped Wendy wasn't expecting to be remembered in Alfie's will. It was potentially a fertile source of motives that she needed to investigate, though, she thought with a gleam of hope. Maybe they were getting somewhere at last?

'Did he have a lot to leave, then, would you say?'

Wendy pursed her lips and considered. 'Well, not much,' she said at length. 'Just the house in Dulwich, I suppose.'

Beth nearly tutted in exasperation. She wasn't sure if Wendy was being faux-naïve or not. A house in Dulwich never went for under a million pounds, and they often changed hands for far more. 'Where did he live again?'

'Oh, you know, Pond Cottages, over that way. His was the house with the enormous hollyhocks outside.'

Immediately, Beth knew just the place her mother meant. It was a charming, not to say absurdly idyllic, little house, not dissimilar to the one that Katie had just spent a fortune on in Cornwall, except that you didn't need to drive for six hours to get to Alfie's place. Other than at school pick-up time, of course.

On a private road still owned by Sir Thomas Wyatt's estate, nestling close to the wide-open spaces of his endowment schools' emerald green playing fields, and opposite Dulwich's original millpond, it was as close as you could get to rural living without leaving London. Although the little row of Grade Two listed gems was called Pond Cottages, and the houses did look tiny from the outside, they were Tardis-like – deceptively spacious and mostly with at least three bedrooms. Many had had garden rooms, studios and summerhouses tacked on at the back to extend their footprints over the years, in times when Southwark Council and the Wyatt's estate had been less picky about architectural integrity. In fact, most of the houses would be quite familiar to anyone who'd caught even a glimpse of a costume drama on TV or at the cinema, as they were frequently hired out to film companies for location shoots.

So, that was a cast-iron motive right there. Alfie Pole's gorgeous south London 'cottage' was no doubt worth a very fair sum, and probably had its own lucrative career as a backdrop to everything from *Great Expectations* to *Vanity Fair*. His sitting room alone, which was bound to come complete with attractive original Georgian panelling, mantlepiece and shutters, no doubt earned more in a day than Beth did in a term at Wyatt's.

'Oh, does he hire it to film companies, then?'

'Absolutely not,' said Wendy, in scandalised tones. Her voice was still quiet, but she was vehement as she explained. 'No, Alfie had quite a thing about all that. He was always complaining about the way the neighbours rented out their places. "Prostituting their homes," he called it. Said he'd never, ever do it himself. He loved the peace and quiet of his little place. And to be fair, when they make a film round there, it does fill the whole row up with vans and people and stuff.'

Beth immediately wondered. Alfie had been sitting on a little goldmine but refusing to dig. Was that reason enough, she wondered, for his neglectful daughter to want to bump him off? Stranger things had happened. Beth put the woman straight at the top of her list of suspects. Next should come anyone who intersected between the Bridge and gardening worlds, as Alfie would have had the opportunity to annoy them in either, or perhaps even both, spheres.

'I don't suppose Alfie ever told you he'd fallen out with

someone, did he?' Beth hazarded, without much hope of a useful response.

'Well, only that thing that he kept harping on about... what was it? So hard to concentrate when one's working on a complicated bid. And Alfie would keep introducing new conventions, you know.'

'Conventions?' Beth knew she'd probably regret asking, but she couldn't let it go.

'Yes, you know, when you bid two diamonds after one no trump but that actually means hearts... come on, darling. I've told you all about this time and again,' said Wendy in tones of quiet exasperation.

'Yes, but fifteen, no, probably twenty years ago... and I wasn't listening then,' said Beth mulishly. She was conscious that time was ticking away, and Jake would be back any minute with his haul of junk food and tea. She definitely couldn't afford to get sidetracked into a discussion of weird Bridge stuff now. 'You must have been thinking about this, Mum. Who do you think would poison Alfie, and then have a go at you? You *must* have a suspicion.'

Beth looked closely at her mother, who still lay with her head back on the pillows. Wendy looked straight at Beth, with those eyes that sometimes looked exactly the same changeable shade as her son's.

'Do you know, I really don't like to think about it?' Wendy said, at her most maddening.

There was silence in the little room. The daylight had leached away, the windows reflecting back the navy blue of the Denmark Hill sky, twinkling with what looked like and passed for stars in south-east London, but was really an amalgam of street and car lights piercing the night. It was beautiful if you didn't look too closely.

Beth thought for the umpteenth time about the case and had to admit that she was stumped. There were too many suspects, or too few, depending on the way you looked at it. And there were rumours of motives, but nothing that one could put one's finger on. Alfie's daughter, for instance, presumably already had a home of her own somewhere, because she didn't live here. Would she really kill to get her hands on a Dulwich cottage, even one which could bring in a healthy income? Mmm, that was tricky. Beth herself had often passed the little row of houses on her way to see her mother, and had always imagined how lovely it would be to live there. She'd stop short at murder to get her dream, of course. But there were lots of people in Dulwich who were much more determined than her, and at this point in her career as an accidental sleuth, she'd frankly got people arrested on far wispier motives.

Beth needed to get a look at this daughter, and as soon as possible.

'Do you know when Alfie's funeral is?' she asked, turning to her mother again.

Wendy shut her eyes firmly in response to the question. 'What makes you think that I'd have the faintest idea, cooped up in here?' she whispered.

Beth immediately felt terrible. Wendy had been at death's door; of course she'd be none the wiser.

'Sorry, Mum, I don't know what I was thinking of,' she said in a softer voice, peering over at her mother's still-wan complexion. She'd thought that Wendy was over the poisoning, but maybe it had more serious after-effects than she'd thought?

For a moment or two, there was silence in the room and Beth could hear Wendy's breathing; regular, if a little shallow.

Then her mother said softly, 'Tuesday after next.'

'What?' Beth was startled.

'The funeral's on the Tuesday after next. You did ask,' Wendy said crossly, opening one eye and squinting at her daughter.

'But how do you know? Who told you?'

'Deidre, of course. There are such things as mobile phones, you know,' Wendy said with dignity, looking towards her bedside table, which had now acquired a thick layer of essentials, from a rainbow of scarves to a selection of hand creams, lipsticks and necklaces, and, Beth could just about see under the detritus, Wendy's phone.

'Why didn't you say so? Oh, really.' There was no point remonstrating with Wendy. And anyway, here was Jake, bursting back in with two teas, a suspicious white paper bag and, bringing up the rear, Harry York.

'Look who I found in the canteen!' the boy said, delighted, as he settled back in his chair at the back of the room and dragged out his phone to show the big policeman something. 'Here it is, Harry, the game I was telling you about.'

Harry sidled in, his bulk immediately making the spacious room seem the size of a full-to-capacity lift, about to judder to a halt between floors. He raised his eyebrows at Jake's game, greeted Wendy with a kiss on the cheek, which she sat up effortlessly to receive in queenly fashion, and then leant over to ruffle Beth's hair. She batted it back down quickly.

'I didn't know you were here?'

'Oh, you know. Enquiries and all,' he said laconically.

'Have you found out anything? Like what Mum was given?' Beth scanned Harry's face. Immediately, it was as firmly closed as one of those boarded-up shops along the South Circular that wasn't even going to bother turning into a charity store. She'd get no information there. Her shoulders sagged a little. How on earth was she supposed to make any progress, when her mother couldn't help, and her boyfriend wouldn't?

'I sent you an email earlier,' she said to him with a challenge in her voice. 'Did you get it? Any thoughts?'

'Mmm,' he said, at his most maddeningly non-committal.

'You'll let me know how you get on with it?' Beth asked.

'Yup,' he said, in the way that she now knew meant a most definite no. Great.

She gathered up her handbag crossly and looked over at Jake, who was scarfing an illicit doughnut. 'Time to get home so you can finish off that homework properly. And have something sensible to eat.' She raised an eyebrow at Harry. 'Are you coming with us, or...?' She hated having to ask in front of her mother and Jake, but with an arrangement as loose as theirs, nothing was a given.

Harry favoured her with the sort of on-off smile he'd bestow on a member of the public who'd stopped to ask him the time in the middle of an armed pursuit. 'I'll just be chatting to your mum for a while,' he said.

She paused. Did that mean five minutes, so they should wait outside; or two hours, so they should go home without him? She looked at him again, willing him to be more specific, but just got that smile again. She gave Wendy a perfunctory peck, thought better of it and leant over for the sort of awkward hug that made her feel all elbows, then avoided kissing Harry and grabbed Jake's bag and coat.

'Off we go, then,' she said to her son, her tone making it clear that this was a three-line whip, no arguments.

As soon as they were outside, Beth dropped Jake's bag to the floor and pressed her ear against the closed door. Nothing. The NHS might be on its knees, but apparently it was still lavishing good money on sturdy doors. She got up on tiptoe to peer through the small square pane of glass high in the frame, and then plummeted down, having met Harry's steady-but-amused gaze. He'd obviously been waiting for her to try that.

'Mum, honestly. Spying?' said Jake, as he pressed buttons on his game, not even looking up.

'Come along now, Jake.' She tutted as though she hadn't heard. 'And by the way, what's happened to your new shoes?'

Jake looked down at the white half-moons scarring both

toecaps and bit his lip. They clattered down the stairs without exchanging another word. At the bottom, Beth relented. The canteen was sort of on their way out, and they did exactly the sort of overcooked nursery food that Jake loved. Plus, eating there would mean Beth didn't have to cook.

'Want to get supper here?'

'I thought we had to rush back for homework?' Jake said a mite frostily, but seconds later he'd realised which side his bread was buttered on. Or, in this case, deep-fried. 'Yeah, let's do that.'

He seemed a much happier bunny as they walked towards the smell of saturated fats. Surveying the menu, Beth wondered if the hospital was trying to ensure its supply of patients never dried up. It was chips with everything, including the chips themselves. Jake was in heaven. Even after a doughnut, he had a growing boy's bottomless appetite.

She took two plates loaded high with delicious crispy beige food to one of the tables by the windows, which were now showing velvet black squares of night outside. She had a pang of doubt about the car. Colin would be in his default setting of deep unconsciousness; an extra half-hour wouldn't hurt him. But was her parking ticket still valid? Fishing out her phone and blessing all these apps that did everything bar the washing-up, she extended her time by paying roughly enough to buy the hospital a new defibrillator. There, all done. Now she could eat.

'Where's the ketchup, Mum?'

With a sigh, Beth got up and searched around. As she scanned the tables for a lurking sauce bottle, she did a double-take. Who was that, over there? That piled-up salt and pepper coiffure, like a tsunami of hair about to break free of the spindly moorings of its hairpins? That scarf, rivalling Beth's own mother's in the way it looped and trailed? That worried look, directed now at the woman who sat beside her and was holding her hand so tightly? It must be, mustn't it?

'Regina? Dr Joyce?' Beth said, placing the woman. 'My mother was just saying that you're a Bridge player,' she said.

Dr Joyce looked up, and immediately a hank of hair fell to her shoulders like a starling felled by an archer.

'Oh! Oh, yes, it's um, Bella, isn't it? From the school?'

'Beth, Beth Haldane from the archives. Haven't seen you around all term.'

'Oh, well, I've been, erm, busy...' said Dr Joyce vaguely, darting a look at her companion.

The woman next to her, Beth noticed, looked distinctly peaky. And also, a little familiar.

'Ah,' she said in a quiet voice. 'So, you're Wendy's daughter?'

'I am. And you're... her next-door neighbour, Mrs Pink, isn't it? I'm sorry, I didn't recognise you out of context,' Beth said with a broader smile.

'And, of course, Wendy and I haven't exactly been the best of friends over the years,' said the woman with a wry smile. 'When her fence blew over for the third time and she didn't get it fixed, well...'

Beth tried to look as neutral as possible. She didn't know the ins and outs of the matter (though she'd heard Wendy fulminating at length about how unreasonable her neighbour was), but nor did she think it was good form to badmouth her mum while she was upstairs getting over an assassination attempt. And Jake was not far away, eavesdropping again for all she knew.

'Mum's never been much of a one for gardens. Yours is lovely, though, Mrs Pink.'

It was the right thing to say. The woman visibly swelled with pride, a little of her missing colour coming back at the compliment.

'Do call me Helen...'

'Anyway, we mustn't keep you,' Regina Joyce broke in. 'You'll be getting tired, Helen,' she added sternly.

'And I think my son is going to waste away if I don't find some ketchup for his chips,' said Beth, looking over to where Jake was staring at her a little crossly.

'Here, take ours,' said Regina, and Beth felt rather as though the woman was trying to fob her off with the scarlet bottle and get rid of her.

'Thanks. Well, see you soon,' she said. The women looked at her, Helen Pink with a smile, Dr Joyce with an enigmatic stare.

Beth wandered off, deep in thought, and plonked the bottle down on the table in front of Jake. 'Eat up. We need to go and see how Colin is getting on soon. He'll be so bored, we've been gone nearly two hours,' she said, glancing at her watch. She didn't have to tell Jake twice. He was shovelling in chips as though there was no tomorrow.

'Can we eat here every night?' he mumbled.

'Definitely not,' said Beth. His enthusiasm was hardly a compliment to her own cooking, or even the ambience of their home. The harsh neon lighting, clatter and pungent smell of the canteen were not exactly cosy. But still, novelty counted for a lot with boys, she comforted herself.

Later, at home and with a mildly put-out Colin having been thoroughly aired round the block and even up and down the main drag of Dulwich Village as a treat after his long incarceration, Beth was hunched over her laptop, desperately trying to collate her rambling thoughts on the Alfie Pole case, if she could even dignify it with that title.

What did she have so far?

One dead pensioner. Alfred Pole, in his later years, widely liked, in possession of a lovely home. Hobbies: Bridge, gardening. Some sort of dispute with the allotment society? Daughter keen to inherit?

One attempted murder. Wendy, in her fifties though you wouldn't have guessed it, also with a lovely home, but with a neglected garden that was a source of conflict with at least one neighbour. Hobbies: Bridge, not gardening. Son and daughter wouldn't mind inheriting but not inclined to hasten the day. Son with cast-iron alibi, as he was perpetually out of the country, and the daughter had no murderous inclinations. Or none that she was willing to put into practice.

Other suspects: the entire Bridge Club, the entire Dulwich gardening world. More specifically, there were the people who'd been dummy at the time of Alfie's murder, and therefore also at the time of Wendy and Beth's ill-advised reconstruction which had led to the second poisoning. Regina Joyce looked too cack-handed; Peter Tilley had a broken arm; Dr Brett was, well, a doctor. Though he was retired, the Hippocratic oath still stood, didn't it? Beth made a mental note to google that. Christina Smith had done something to her leg. Could she have injured it gardening? And there was someone else, too, though Beth couldn't think for the life of her who it was. She scrolled to the 'sent' file of her email account, hoping to chase up the email she'd sent Harry, but it wasn't there. Damn. She must have used her school account.

It was all so frustrating. Beth stared at her laptop with increasing irritation. Even Colin's regular snores, usually an oddly comforting sound, were tonight a jarring distraction. Why did she feel as if there was something she was missing? Had someone said something to her that she ought to have written down here? She replayed snatches of conversation in her head.

It was all very mysterious, and seemed to be getting more so the more she worked away at it. Surely this hadn't happened before. In retrospect, it seemed that every previous case she'd been involved in – or more accurately, stumbled into – had unfurled obligingly like a brand-new umbrella. This time, the more she fumbled with it, the more the enigma refused to budge, instead looping itself around her like one of her mother's maddening scarves. And why did that image stick in her mind particularly?

Beth flipped down the lid of her laptop in fury, then immediately reopened it to make sure she'd done it no damage. She put it aside on the sofa and wandered into the kitchen to make herself a mint tea. Sometimes this soothing process helped calm her mind and drag some useful idea to the fore. But when she returned to the sitting room, she found that Magpie had settled her capacious fluffy body right on top of the still-warm computer and was not at all willing to shift. It seemed to be the universe's way of telling her to abandon her quest for the night. She gave Magpie a hard stare, which was returned with interest. Then she snapped off the light and went upstairs to bed.

Passing Jake's room, she peeped in quickly and saw her son sprawled on top of his duvet. She'd always loved the way his sleeping face harked back to the blankness of babyhood. Now, in the light from the landing, she could see that his nose was sharpening and his cheekbones were taking shape. It was as though the man he would one day be was already peering at her from inside the child she'd known and loved. It was disconcerting. She gently put a blanket over him.

In her own room, with the comfort of her flowery duvet pulled over her nose, she had space for a final brace of questions before sleep claimed her. Would Harry be coming over? And, if he did, would he tell her what, exactly, he'd discussed with Wendy?

SIXTEEN

Beth got her answers the next morning. No, and no. She woke up with Harry's side of the bed unrumpled and her own stock of certainties still as scanty as ever. And as soon as Jake was downstairs at the breakfast table, the negatives continued to rain down on her. No, he didn't want toast. No, he hated that cereal. No, he hadn't finished his homework last night. And no, he wasn't going to explain why.

Beth had a sudden feeling of dread. Years ago, she'd watched a comedy sketch where a delightful twelve-year-old boy had turned, on the stroke of midnight, into a ghastly mono-syllabic teenager – spotty, uncooperative, a nightmare in every way. Was this now being re-enacted in her own home?

She had a stalled investigation, a job she could never quite get down to, a book idea she for some reason wasn't able to commit to paper, an on-off boyfriend who now seemed defi-nitely off, and, on top of everything, a horrible son. Could things get any worse?

She pushed up from the table, intending on shoving her bowl and mug into the sink, and immediately stood in something squishy and warm. She didn't want to look down. 'Magpie! What have you been eating?'

Ten minutes she could ill-afford later, she'd cleaned the cat sick off the floor, changed her socks and jeans, and scrabbled everything into her bag. Jake was long gone, having loped off on his own, not bothering to conceal his glee at having evaded a parental escort this morning.

'Colin, you're staying here today, I can't cope with anything else,' said Beth sternly as the old Labrador advanced slowly towards the front door, his tail banging into one side of the narrow hall and then the other. But as she wrestled herself into her coat and met his liquid chocolate eyes, full of trust, hope and expectation, her heart melted. Magpie had been known to pay her back for even *thinking* about buying cheaper cat food, but Colin wasn't holding even the tiniest bit of a grudge against her for leaving him in the hospital car park for far too long last night.

In a tricky world, there was something about the love of a chap like Colin that helped her keep on believing everything would turn out for the best in the end. 'All right, then. You win. But just don't tell anyone what a ridiculous softy I am,' she sighed, clipping on his lead and ushering him out of the door. As he passed, he brushed her hand gently with his cold wet nose, and it felt like a benediction.

Janice pounced on her as soon as she arrived at the school. 'Beth, I just need to talk to you right away, it's really urgent,' she said, her voice squeaky with what sounded like panic.

'Is it Jake?' Beth asked immediately, tying Colin's lead around the railings guarding the pristine lawn, and allowing Janice to draw her quickly past the heavy brass-trimmed front door and into the plush reception area.

'No, no,' Janice said. 'Nothing like that.'

Beth breathed out but noticed shadows like violet thumbprints under her friend's eyes. And, even more worryingly, the buttons on her trademark cashmere cardigan were done up all wrong.

'What is it, then?' Under her fringe, Beth's forehead wrinkled. Was there something amiss with her tiny goddaughter?

'It's this. It's very important that you answer me honestly. I feel that everyone's been lying to me for so long,' said Janice, tears trembling on her long eyelashes.

'Look, let's sit down,' Beth said, steering Janice to one of the wonderfully squishy sofas designed to cosset anxious parents while their offspring were being interviewed. 'Now, just ask me and I'll help if I can,' she said slowly and gently.

'Do babies, well, do they... do they *ever fucking sleep through the night?*'

Despite her friend's wail of anguish, Beth couldn't help laughing. 'Oh, Janice.' Then she looked again at the mortified, exhausted face. It wasn't just the dark circles. Janice's pretty milkmaid features had taken on a pinched quality which Beth was only just noticing. It seemed cruel to giggle, but Beth was too relieved not to. She couldn't have borne it if there'd really been anything seriously wrong with the scrap of gorgeousness that was little Elizabeth.

'Believe me. You'll look back on this as one of the happiest times with your daughter. Enjoy her while she's tiny. Yes, she may not sleep, but she's all yours and she stays where you put her, and she doesn't answer back, and eats what you cook and... oh, she's your lovely tiny little baby.'

Janice, looking a bit shocked that there might even be a time when all that would change, mumbled something about having a lot to do. Beth immediately felt terrible. She reached out tentatively, then touched her friend's arm.

'Listen, I've been there. It's just a long time ago. But I do remember how awful it was, never getting enough sleep, being woken through the night, and worrying all the time... Well, some things never change, hey?' She smiled but realised she was hardly being reassuring.

'Just try a few things – later feeds, a different bedtime routine – and something will work. But chances are, it will just be coincidence and she'll have decided of her own accord to try sleeping better,' Beth said.

'The other thing is, don't believe anyone who says they have all the answers. Other mums might try and tell you they've cracked it, but there'll be something down the line that they can't do and you can, so don't measure yourself against anyone else.'

Beth rooted in her bag for a clean tissue, found one eventually and handed it to Janice. Then she pointed to the offending cardi buttons. 'You might want to, erm...' she hinted.

Janice flushed and sorted things out. 'Honestly, I'm a mess at the moment,' the girl said, bottom lip wobbling perilously.

'You're just tired. The short answer is yes, they do sleep through the night. It might take Elizabeth a while, but she'll get there, and so will you. Do you have anyone who can babysit, let you get out for an hour or two after work?'

'Magenta would stay later if I asked her to, if Tommy and I wanted to go out... but we don't.'

'Are you sure? It might do you some good just to have a dinner together, see a film... get a break,' said Beth, feeling for poor old Dr Grover. He'd had such an ordered life, and a perfect wife... If Janice was reeling, he must be feeling his whole world had fallen apart.

'I don't know...' said Janice, looking as though the idea of leaving Elizabeth, even for a short while, was a terrible betrayal.

'Listen, I'm happy to have her for an evening. She is my goddaughter. It would be a pleasure,' Beth found herself saying, then immediately kicked herself. What was she talking about? She was stretched to the limit already with a job she wasn't doing, a son who was growing away from her, a mother in danger, and a boyfriend who was far too free range for her liking. Adding a newborn into the mix was just completely bonkers.

'Are you sure?' asked Janice, delight lighting up her eyes like the dawn returning to a post-apocalyptic land.

Beth's heart sank. That was the face of someone who was definitely going to take her up on her half-witted offer.

'Can I let you know when?'

'Of course,' said Beth, inwardly cursing herself. Great. The only thing she remembered about babies Elizabeth's age was that they were even harder work than the Maths assignments Jake wasn't showing her. But never mind. Janice's smile made it all worth it. Almost.

'If you want to have a peaceful forty winks now, why don't you take Colin along to my office and just have a snooze on my desk again? I don't think anyone will bother you,' Beth said, knowing full well that the chances of anyone bursting into her domain with urgent archiving that needed doing were less than zilch.

'But I'd be stopping you from getting on with your work. What will you do?' said Janice, getting to her feet immediately.

Beth tried to look as if being prevented from making headway with her book outline was going to be a real problem, but gave it up as a bad job. 'Don't worry about me, I've got a lead I could follow up... erm, on some details about Sir Thomas Wyatt,' she added unconvincingly.

Janice gave her a quick look but seemed too sleepy to pursue it.

Outside the building, Beth handed over her keys and Colin's lead. Colin goosed Janice quickly, as though going through the motions, getting an inconvenient social ritual out of the way for both their sakes. Janice crossed her legs briefly and exchanged glances with Beth, but then patted the old boy on the head.

Beth watched as they plodded off to the archive institute together. Janice was so exhausted that her normally sprightly pace perfectly matched the old dog's.

Pausing for a moment as they disappeared out of sight, Beth wondered if there was really any merit in her latest wild scheme. But she pushed all such doubts aside and set off herself at a trot that would have had Colin's tongue unrolling like an old pink carpet.

Ten minutes later, she was on the little patch of grass that separated Pond Cottages from the wide private road hemming the edge of the Wyatt estate. It was as tranquil a spot as you'd ever find within a stone's throw of the South Circular. Somewhere, the traffic poured on relentlessly, cars and trucks in their endless game of tag. Here, though, the sound was subdued to the level of a rough purr, like big cats playing out of sight – apart from a succession of clangs and clatters. They were coming from a pantechnicon parked at a rakish angle on the grass outside the little houses. From inside it, Beth heard the familiar vinegary tones of south-east London workmen dropping stuff on their feet. Outside, a woman with a clipboard looked very cross.

'Can you get that last rig out? We're running way behind,' she shouted into the depths of the van.

Beth took advantage of her distraction to nip past, into the front garden of the late Alfie Pole's bijou home. Though the hollyhocks had faded, the well-stocked flowerbed was still boasting a regiment of late-blooming dark purple and blood red dahlias. Beth loathed dahlias. They were one of the few flowers she actually recognised, but only because the fleshy petals and unnaturally round blooms always looked like three-dimensional bruises to her, particularly in these colours. But they stood as a silent testament to the green fingers of their late owner. His fingers would be very green by now, she thought with a shiver of macabre disgust as she hurried past. To her surprise, the door was open, solving her dilemma about whether to ring or not. She sauntered on in.

Expecting the dark, cool interior of a house designed two hundred years ago, when keeping sunlight from one's precious embroideries was the biggest design craze going, she was surprised to find that the house was in fact flooded with crisp autumnal light. The back of the place, at the end of the narrow hall she stood in, seemed to be a wall of glass. The passageway led her past a tiny panelled parlour and a slightly larger book-lined study, both gorgeous rooms she'd love to poke around in if she had the time. She'd decided to make for what had to be the kitchen, where all the noise was coming from, when she was hailed by someone coming down the narrow stairs.

Beautiful, tetchy-looking, incredibly thin, and dressed in a virtually transparent floor-length dress, a young woman was waving a wad of papers at her. 'Hey, you. This scene, yeah?' she drawled in an accent so American that Beth could almost taste the milkshake and fries. The empire line of her gown was jacking up meagre breasts and exposing a wealth of gooseflesh as she leant over the banister. 'So, my motivation here, I mean, you've got to be kidding, right? She turns this guy *down*? Have you seen his house?'

A page fluttered over the newel post and Beth bent to pick it up, scanning it before handing it back. It was a scene which looked strangely familiar. '...*the concern I might have felt at refusing you, had you behaved in a more gentlemanlike manner...*'

Wait a minute, *Pride and Prejudice*! It was only being made – or remade, for the umpteenth time – right here. Beth could hardly believe it.

'Mr Darcy? He's coming? He's on his way?' she asked breathlessly.

The woman stared at her, then rolled her eyes contemptuously. 'You're not the writer. Who the hell are you? Where's the runner?' she grumbled, stomping rudely past, picking up her muslin skirts and revealing Doc Marten boots and stripy fleece socks.

Beth paused for a beat, inwardly thrilled at having been mistaken, however absurdly, for Jane Austen, then followed. At the end of the corridor, Alfie Pole's house opened up into a beautiful modern kitchen with glazed double doors to quite a spacious garden, in which more workmen were rigging up spotlights, while a woman in jeans was being harangued by a fat middle-aged man, now joined by the rake-thin actress. She detected a flurry of movement on the other side of the fence – was that a rapidly retreating form, heading towards the house next door?

Beth was torn between waiting for Mr Darcy to turn up, primed and ready for his proposal – surely, like most women in Britain, she had waited a lifetime for this moment – and finding out what the hell was going on in Alfie's house.

She dithered, the seconds lengthening and Pemberley passing before her eyes for the third time, before she stepped forward. On the fringes of the group in the garden was a woman in her mid-thirties looking almost as out of place as Beth, with a mug of tea in each hand, evidently waiting for a pause in the argument so she could pass over her offerings.

Beth closed in on her. 'Miss, er, Pole?' she said tentatively.

Immediately, the woman's head whipped round. 'Who are you?'

It was the second time Beth had dodged that question in as many minutes. 'I thought your father swore blind he'd never have films made here?' she countered, an accusatory tone in her voice.

The woman took a step back, sloshing tea on her hands and wincing. 'How dare you question my right? This is my house now. And what's it got to do with you, anyway?'

These were all fair queries, Beth couldn't help admitting to herself. But something told her to plough on, for Alfie's sake. 'He's not even cold in his grave. What would he have said about all this?'

'That's absolutely none of your business. And how dare you breeze in here and have a go at me? I'll report you to the police. This is trespassing. And harassment.'

'The door was open. And I'm not harassing you,' said Beth, mentally adding a *yet*. Whatever relations between the Poles had been while Alfie was alive, his daughter was showing no signs at all of sorrow after his untimely passing. In fact, throwing open his house to a production company so soon seemed almost an obscene act, in view of poor Alfie's steadfast refusal to 'prostitute' the house himself. This woman was going right down in Beth's estimation – but rapidly ascending her list of possible suspects.

'Well, close the door *on your way out*. What I choose to do with my own property is my business,' Alfie Pole's daughter hissed.

The large man and the harassed woman broke off from their intense discussion and looked over at her.

'Everything OK there, Venetia?' the woman asked in a high-pitched voice.

The scrawny actress piped up, 'That's the woman I was telling you about,' and the fat man took a step towards Beth.

Just then, there was a squawk from the woman's earpiece. 'What's that? He's parking? He's early. Get him to go round the block. I don't care if he's dying for a pee! We're not ready for him...'

Just as Beth was hoping against hope that she'd soon be meeting Mr Darcy, although perhaps not quite in the propitious circumstances she'd always dreamt of, he was there. Bursting through the front door, striding up the passageway towards them, his face in darkness until, suddenly, there he was, the shards of weak September sun glinting off the high shine on his chestnut riding boots and caressing the unfortunately rather obvious highlights in his mane of painstakingly tousled hair.

She gasped, and so did Venetia Pole. He was magnificent. Then, as she took in the tidemark of foundation around his neck, the petulant curl of his lip, and the fact that not a hair on his head moved as he shook his head this way and that, Beth's dreams curled up and died. Yes, he was terribly famous – he'd been the star of last year's massive Netflix hit, *Blame the Drones* – but somehow he was just, well, a bit meh in the flesh. His bony co-star was welcome to him.

Beth exchanged a surprisingly sympathetic glance with Venetia, then they both remembered that she was distinctly *de trop* here, and she withdrew, thinking this Mr Darcy was definitely one of the last men in the world she could ever be prevailed upon to marry.

Where did it leave her investigation? That was the question. Venetia Pole's motive had become three-dimensional, certainly. Each day of filming would be netting her a tidy sum, and the house itself was a substantial asset even without its day job as a backdrop. Did Venetia actively need the money, though?

And was that a glimpse of Alfie's neighbour she had got while they'd been in the garden?

Once she was outside again and contemplating the fierce cannonball dahlias, Beth hesitated, taking a peek at her watch. Hmm, she just about had time. Janice and Colin would no doubt be fine. Both would be in the land of Nod by this stage, she was willing to bet. And when would she next be around this way?

She marched back down the path towards the pantechnicon, which was disgorging still more lights, cables and large black boxes of trickery, no doubt essential for magicking the pair of unappealing actors within into celluloid gorgeousness. Pausing to click Alfie's gate shut, she opened the one next door, and strode up to that house before she had time to think better of her actions.

Rapping sharply and looking from left to right to see if anyone was watching, she wasn't surprised when nothing happened immediately. From what she'd seen, Alfie's neighbour was too busy spying on the filming to pay much attention to her own morning callers.

The workmen didn't seem remotely interested in her actions, and Venetia Pole was too busy kowtowing to her clients to keep tabs on her. She had nothing to lose by checking a theory.

Just as she was giving up hope, the door cracked open a chink. She could just about see a woman inside, crouched over, her eyes gleaming faintly in the shadowy depths. Raising her index finger, she beckoned Beth in.

On the threshold, Beth took a last look around behind her, then stepped forward, to be swallowed up by the darkness.

SEVENTEEN

If Alfie Pole's house had astonished her with its light, his neighbour had gone firmly in the opposite direction. The walls were painted in a blue-black so intense that it seemed to suck the life out of the day, though it made the Japanese plates displayed on them glow as vividly as Alfie's dahlias.

'You'll be from the Council. Come away in,' said the woman.

Beth couldn't get a fix on her; she didn't seem to be a typical Dulwich type at all. For a start, she was Scottish. Then she was short, but with a slight figure, dressed in clothes that Beth recognised with a shock were both boring, and familiar. Well-worn jeans, a jumper bobbling a bit around the arms, feet in plain dark socks. By the front door there was a sorry little line of down-at-heel suede boots. She wore no jewellery, no watch and was middle-aged. This, at least, was a comfort. She had at least ten years on Beth, if not fifteen.

'You'll be wanting to know what's going on, I take it?' The woman was fixing her with a surprisingly intense stare from eyes that were midway between blue and green.

'Um, absolutely,' said Beth truthfully, then thought she'd

better qualify that, in case impersonating a Council officer was an offence of some sort. 'That is to say, I'm not from Southwark—'

'You'll be from the Wyatt's estate then. Aha, I thought so,' the woman said, nodding.

'Aha,' echoed Beth, feeling as though she'd strayed somehow into Alan Partridge territory. 'Although, not quite in the way you might think...' she added, about to clarify that she did work for Wyatt's, just not for the estates.

'It's complicated,' the woman said, nodding. Beth nodded along, knowing she was getting deeper and deeper into what she'd like to describe as subterfuge, but which she knew others – principally big, grumpy policemen of her acquaintance – would call plain lies and deception.

'Um, what seems to be the trouble?' Beth asked, crossing her fingers behind her back in the vain hope that this would somehow cover her against any charges of fraud.

'Well, let me just show you. Probably easier, isn't it?' the woman said, ushering Beth down the corridor.

Thus far, it was a mirror of Alfie Pole's floorplan. But, at the end, where Alfie's hall opened up into that magnificent all-mod-cons kitchen with its wall of glass, this one finished in a small door which, when opened, gave on to a room that was still straight out of the 1950s. Poky and as dark as the corridor they'd left behind, this little kitchen was clean and tidy but utterly uninspiring. There was frosted glass in the back door – the type that was thick and swirly and stopped you seeing out. But a very small window over the old aluminium sink showed a tiny rectangle of the garden.

Immediately Beth stepped forward, drawn to the picture it made. It was simply beautiful, even this late in the season. A weeping willow tree cascaded onto the lawn, neat beds boasted drifts of purple and yellow pansies behind star-like pink flowers that Beth had never seen before. Nearer to the house, she recognised clusters of cheerful cyclamens, chiefly because she usually managed to kill at least one of these every September.

'You see? You see the problem?' the woman urged, leaning on the side of the sink but craning towards Alfie Pole's fence.

Beth turned her attention and noticed straight away that the huge arc lights were very close to the boundary, while the garden itself was now bursting with people – some of them shivering girls in frocks who were clearly meant to be Bennet sisters, and a mass of gophers who, Beth decided, must be all the mysterious 'dolly grips' and 'best boys' she'd seen flashing past in movie credits and had always wondered about.

'Hmm. Must be really noisy.'

'Noisy? *Noisy?*' said the woman incredulously, her delicate brows scampering up her forehead and making her look suddenly like Coco the Clown. 'Is that supposed to be a joke?'

'Erm, no,' said Beth. 'What am I looking for exactly?'

'Plastic! It's all plastic,' shrieked Alfie's neighbour.

Beth was astounded. 'Really?' She took another look at Alfie's patch of garden. The bright flowers, the neat shrubs, even the ivy covering his fences. 'All of it?'

The neighbour nodded dourly. 'Even the lawn. Astroturf,' she shuddered.

'I can't believe it. Really realistic, isn't it?' said Beth with a smile.

The neighbour looked at her in disgust.

'And what about those ghastly dahlias in the front, they really are the pits,' Beth said with a shudder, putting unmistakable feeling into her words.

The woman looked her up and down. 'They're real,' she said with contempt.

'I think it's time I was leaving,' said Beth brightly.

Before she knew it, she was at the gate and waving a tentative goodbye to the woman, who still looked furious as she slammed the door. So, Alfie wasn't such a great gardener after all. What have I stumbled into now, she thought, as she retraced her steps back to the school.

As she'd hoped, when she pushed the archives door gently open, she was rewarded with the sight of Janice, face-down and fast asleep on the desk. Her head was pillowed by something that looked, most unfortunately, like Colin's favourite blanket which he drooled on and chewed incessantly and which Beth hadn't got round to washing for months. It seemed he hadn't begrudged his new friend, though, as he was snoozing by her feet, paws neatly crossed like a debutant on very best behaviour, glossy brown head lolling to one side.

It was such a peaceful scene that she was quite tempted to tiptoe away, except that guilt about her neglected duties would keep stabbing her with its long, accusing finger. She gave the pair a wide berth and slid out one of the chairs at her conference table again. She'd never yet seen fit to convene an archives conference – long may that state of affairs continue – and she could easily get through some of her tasks sitting here, as she had yesterday.

It was one of the most tranquil afternoons Beth could remember. She plodded on with her work, while Colin, on the floor, intermittently chased Magpie in his dreams, and Janice, slumped across the desk, let out the occasional soft snore. Spending time with those she loved, especially when they were being absolutely no trouble at all, was really rather blissful, though Beth did wonder what it said about her that she preferred her companions deeply unconscious.

It was too good to last, though. The daylight started to fade. Beth realised she'd have to scoot along to pick up Jake or, more realistically, follow him home at a discreet distance pretending they weren't related, which was how he preferred it these days. Then her phone suddenly shrilled.

She got up and lunged for her handbag, slung as usual on the coat hook near the desk, hoping to cut the call off before it woke her sleeping beauties. But the tune 'Bridge over Troubled Water' warbled out for far too long, while Beth scrabbled amongst the forest of Haribo packets and school notices that she habitually dragged from place to place. Eventually, she found the phone and answered it in a whisper, only to find both Janice and Colin peering at her with strangely similar sleepy expressions.

'Hi, Mum, I can't really talk now...' Beth started, realising this was how she began most conversations with her mother.

But Janice was already getting to her feet, smoothing down her cardigan and rubbing at her cheek where it had come into contact with the blanket. She patted Colin, who obligingly moved in for a goose. Janice dodged him, waved goodbye and mouthed a big *thank you* to Beth, then was out of the door.

'Sorry, Mum, it's OK now, go ahead,' said Beth, sliding into the chair Janice had just vacated and hurling the blanket off her desk. Colin, with a grateful pant, got on top of it again and chewed the edge thoughtfully, apparently very much enjoying the addition of Janice's unique flavour to the old familiar mix.

'I was just saying,' said Wendy with that slightly querulous edge she often used in conversations with Beth, 'that he'll be coming over a week on Sunday. I'm hoping that's convenient.'

'What? I think I've missed a bit. Who's coming over, and where will they be going on Sunday?'

'Your brother, Beth. Don't you ever listen to a word I say? And he's coming to lunch. I knew you'd want to see him. It's been so long.'

'Josh? And he's having lunch where? Not at—'

'Well, of course, if you can't be bothered to have your brother round, when you haven't seen him for at least a year...'

'It's not that,' said Beth, feeling defensive, but also furious with her mother for inviting herself and Josh over without any sort of consultation. 'But I might have plans...'

'Well? Do you?'

'Do I what?' Beth was rapidly wondering if she was as muzzy-headed as Janice.

'Do you have *plans*?' Wendy asked, managing suddenly to make her voice sound very frail.

Immediately, Beth remembered her mother had just been through a terrible ordeal. And she had sworn to treat her differently from now on. She sighed.

'No, that would be, um, great. Is it just the two of you coming, or is there anything else I should know about?' She couldn't resist adding that. Just to show she wasn't going to be a pushover.

'Josh will be bringing his girlfriend. Isn't that lovely?' trilled Wendy. Now she'd got her way, she was sounding a lot stronger already.

'The same girlfriend as last time?' Beth asked, knowing full well what the answer would be.

'I shouldn't think so, dear. But actually, he didn't say,' said Wendy.

I bet he didn't, thought Beth. Josh changed his girlfriends more regularly than he changed his sheets. They were all lovely, but she'd almost got to the point where she'd stopped listening to the names, as there wasn't really much point trying to remember them. Their ages were frozen, though, in a sort of mid-twenties zone, while Josh himself was now pushing forty. It was a pattern that Beth really wished she didn't have to expose her son to.

'Bless Joshy. He's so worried about me,' Wendy was continuing.

Honestly, thought Beth. When had Josh last worried about anyone but himself? And if he's so worried, why isn't he on a plane right now? But then she realised it was quite obvious that this had been coming. Wendy was always trying to get Josh to come home, and preferably get a nice sensible job like his late father's while he was at it. No doubt she had been giving him the works about her brush with death. Even Josh couldn't help but be horrified at the thought of a murderous attempt on his mum's life. Beth knew when she was beaten.

'What time will you be coming?' she said, resigned to her fate.

'Well, Beth. What a question. Any time that suits *you*, of course. You're the hostess!' said Wendy blithely, much too far away to hear the sound of Beth grinding her teeth.

When she was slumped in front of the telly later, after an unsatisfactory evening of chivvying Jake about his homework, getting no further with details about Billy McKenzie, and then opening the door to Harry, who'd forgotten his keys, Beth realised that the looming lunch party was at least a safe topic of conversation. Harry had already headed off her attempts to cross-question him about the substance used to poison Wendy, not to mention her emailed list of suspects. Though she was pretty sure it was the same atropine that had seen Alfie off this mortal coil, it would have been nice to have had that confirmed. Then any discussion of Venetia Pole, the cottage or gardening was met with stonewalling.

'So, are you going to come to this lunch?' she finally asked.

'With your brother and your mum? Wouldn't miss it for the world,' said Harry heartily, before gluing his eyes back to the screen where DI Perez was gazing moodily out to sea in *Shetland*. Beth sighed and gave up. Perhaps next week would be easier.

EIGHTEEN

After quite a restful weekend, for a change, with Harry doing the footballing honours, Beth had high hopes for Monday. But as soon as she looked out of the window she sighed. There was a nasty thin rain falling, the type that seemed expressly designed to make everyone in Britain question their motives for living on a bleak little rock in the middle of a cold sea. There were people right now, thought Beth, who were getting ready to spend their days on golden beaches. Why was she having to muster a recalcitrant boy and a Labrador who was going to smell to high heaven after five minutes in this downpour? Harry was no help. He was long gone, having grabbed a coffee and a piece of toast in the early hours and rushed off to tend his cache of secrets down at the Camberwell police station.

As they set off, the sun broke through the scudding clouds and the rain finally stopped. Once upon a time, Jake would have splashed in the puddles that now studded Dulwich Village, shiny as the rhinestones on a leather jacket. These days, Beth noted sadly, he was old and wise enough to step carefully round their edges, not because he was at all interested in protecting his expensive shoes, but because he didn't want soggy trousers all day. They intersected with Charlie and Katie at the junction with Court Lane and, once the boys had done a bit of jousting with their gym bags, they ran off down the road. Beth and Katie were left looking at each other and shrugging.

Katie linked her arm through Beth's. 'How's it all going? How's your mum?'

'Oh, she's fine. I'm picking her up later. She's well enough to be inviting everyone round to mine for lunch at the weekend, anyway,' said Beth, rolling her eyes.

'Bet you're glad, though,' said Katie, not fooled.

'Yeah, it's such a relief. No Teddy today?'

'Don't judge, Beth, but I've hired a dog-walker,' said Katie, looking embarrassed.

'There's no shame in that,' said Beth bracingly. Privately, she was surprised it had taken Katie this long. Teddy needed walking for about twelve hours a day. 'And it'll give you more time for the investigation. I'm getting nowhere fast with finding stuff out... I could do with your input.'

Katie didn't reply.

'Listen, are you still on the case with me?' Beth asked.

Katie looked even more shamefaced. 'The thing is, Beth, I don't think I can spare the time. I've got some, um, concerns...' Her eyes flicked nervously from side to side.

'What's up? Are you leaving me in the lurch?' Beth said, as light-heartedly as she could.

'I hoped you wouldn't take it like that,' Katie said sadly.

'I was joking,' said Beth quickly. 'If you've got other things to do...' she tailed off, not quite seeing what could possibly be as urgent as chasing a murderer. Hovering over Charlie's home-work like an Apache assault helicopter? Going to coffee mornings? Katie must be able to see they were just peripheral activities, not serious work at all.

'Look, I'm a bit worried about Charlie,' said Katie, her voice dropping even though the boys were now far ahead of them, nearly at the school gates and paying them no attention at all.

'What's going on?' said Beth, feeling a clutch of alarm. Whatever it was, she selfishly hoped it didn't involve Jake. Was that awful? No, she reasoned. It was human. And it didn't mean she wouldn't help her friend as much as possible.

'It's... well, it's... Billy McKenzie,' said Katie in a small voice. Instantly, Beth relaxed. This wasn't what she'd been imagining at all. Her thoughts were always darker and wilder than they needed to be, she told herself. Anything involving the McKenzies was basically silly, and usually concerned some sort of social jostling. Nothing real. Nothing serious.

'What's up with him? He's a nice enough kid, but...'

'I think he's been having a go at Charlie. *Really* having a go,' said Katie, unmistakably upset now.

'Oh my gosh, you mean Billy's been bullying him?' Beth said, concerned. No wonder her friend had been off the radar for a bit. 'I asked Jake about Billy just the other day and he was really evasive,' she said. 'I'm surprised he didn't say anything. You know he loves Charlie and would always stick up for him,' she added.

'I think Billy's being cleverer than that. It's very... insidious. He's just said some snide things, quite a few times now, to Charlie. Implied that he's a bit rubbish at Latin, for instance. Or that he wasn't going to get great marks for Maths. You know my Charlie, he's quite suggestible. All of a sudden, he seems to have a problem with the work. And this is behind it.'

Beth sighed. It didn't take much; just a tiny bit of poison, dripped here and there. Sometimes words were every bit as toxic as whatever had done for Alfie and carried Wendy to the hospital. She placed a hand tentatively on Katie's arm. 'That bloody Belinda! All the pressure she's put on that kid... and now he's taking it out on Charlie. I could wring her neck.'

Katie smiled. 'Not sure you could reach.'

'I'd get a ladder,' said Beth through gritted teeth. They both looked at each other and laughed. It was the lessening of tension they'd needed. 'Seriously, Katie, I'm going to ask Jake again—'

'Don't,' Katie broke in quickly. 'I don't want anyone to treat Charlie any differently, not now, and especially not Jake. I'm thinking of just talking to the teachers. Or even going to Belinda. I bet she'd be mortified if she knew.'

'Mmm.' Beth wasn't so sure. Belinda might easily veer the other way, go full tiger mother and refuse to hear a word against her son. It was a horrible situation for Katie. And, of course, for Charlie. 'Can you stop him hanging out with Billy? Just nip that whole situation in the bud?'

'How can I?' said Katie, gesturing to the school gates. Right in front of their eyes, they saw the ponderous figure of William McKenzie bound up to Charlie and Jake. He launched himself at Charlie and yanked his gym bag, so it fell to the ground and bounced into a puddle. It was more or less the jousting that Jake and Charlie now used as a greeting – just ratcheted up a notch too far. Katie gripped the iron railings so hard her knuckles showed white.

Beth put a hand up to pat her friend's shoulder for a second. 'We need to have a coffee. Sort out a strategy. But not today. I've got to pick up Mum from the hospital now.'

Katie nodded. Beth was alarmed to see her blue eyes were glassy with unshed tears. *Bloody Belinda McKenzie. And bloody Billy.* She turned away and trudged back to Pickwick Road alone to fetch her little car.

Two frustrating hours later, Wendy was back in the comfort of her own home. As usual, leaving hospital had felt like breaking out of a benign but bonkers prison camp, but finally Beth had achieved it, signing a pile of forms and dutifully collecting a huge paper bag of painkillers that she could have purchased in a quarter of the time (and probably for half the price) at the Superdrug in West Norwood.

The lady of the house was installed in her favourite armchair, with innumerable cushions and throws protecting her from the merest whisper of a draught. A dainty bone china cup of tea, plastered with blowsy cabbage roses, teetered on one of Wendy's spindly occasional tables. If Jake – or Beth – had lived here, her mother's entire china collection would have ended up in small bits before the week was out.

'Are you sure I can't get you anything else?' asked Beth, her eyes beseeching her mother to let her go. But Wendy seemed unable to stop milking the situation – quite literally.

'Well, if you insist, dear, you could just top up the jug – semi-skimmed, we must watch our figures, mustn't we?' Wendy raised her eyebrows at her daughter and her glance rested for a moment too long on Beth's sturdy, jean-clad thighs.

Beth tossed her ponytail, immediately feeling a surge of the boiling rage that had fuelled her teenage years, and stomped off to the kitchen. Just like the sitting room – and, in fact, the rest of the whole blinking house – it was infested with the knick-knacks Wendy found so 'adorable' and which Beth could have hurled into a skip with the greatest of pleasure. There were wilfully naïve pottery bowls from Brittany on the shelves; there were tea towels embroidered with winsome mottos tacked onto the walls; there were cute little ceramic kittens (real pets were too much trouble) peering at her from the windowsills. Even the washing-up liquid dispenser – Wendy couldn't possibly have a plastic bottle of Fairy on display – was garlanded with hectic floral patterns. The washing-up gloves, too, were emblazoned with large fake cornflowers. Where did Wendy find this stuff?

Beth felt a sudden sympathy with Venetia Pole. There must, indeed, be a satisfaction in taking over a property from a parent and blatantly flouting their dearest wishes. Then, imme-diately, she felt the stab of familiar guilt which came so often when she was around her mother. Only a few days ago, she had sent up her silent prayer to the heavens, begging for Wendy's life and pledging to be a better daughter. Where was that resolve now?

She went to the fridge. For a moment, she was tempted to use full-fat instead of semi-skimmed, but she curbed the impulse and slopped a little of the thin bluish milk into the preposterous daisy-splattered jug. The shelves were all but empty. She should really organise an Ocado shop to make sure Wendy didn't go hungry, but a quick peek in the freezer below showed her enough of Marks & Spencer's finest posh ready meals stacked up to take her mother through the nuclear winter if necessary.

'Right, I'll be off then,' she said firmly, gathering up her bag, dropping a kiss onto Wendy's white hair and shutting the front door behind her before her mother had time to dream up any more tasks. She was thoughtfully retracing her steps to her car when she was hailed by a querulous voice. She stood stock-still for a horrible moment, but it was only the next-door neighbour. Beth trotted over with a smile pinned to her face.

'Hi, Mrs Hills, how are you?'

'Fine, dear, but *how's your mother?*' said the stout middle-aged lady, lowering her voice in that way people do when they speak of the terminally ill.

'Oh, she's fighting fit.' Beth smiled.

Was that the slightest twinge of disappointment flitting across June Hills' face? Beth had never been sure about Wendy's neighbour. The two women, both widows and roughly the same age, had lived in a state of armed neutrality since Wendy had moved there after her husband's untimely death. While, in Beth's opinion, Wendy had devoted herself to frilly inconsequentialities, Mrs Hills had ploughed on very much as she had when her husband had been alive, for the first ten years or so at least. A top civil servant, she had run various govern-

ment departments with one hand apparently tied behind her
back. Having recently taken early retirement on a massive
pension, she had turned her attention to her garden. From the
front gate, Beth gazed at the serried ranks of shrubs, all neatly
pruned into balls of various sizes, like green marbles which had
rolled into position after some celestial game of solitaire. At
regular intervals, chrysanthemums exploded upwards in bursts
of acid yellow. After a moment's thought, Beth decided she
preferred Alfie Pole's fleshy dahlias to these aggressive blooms,
but it was a close-run thing.

'Garden's looking amazing,' she said, carefully selecting an
adjective that could cover the good, the bad and the ugly. The
transformation in June Hills' manner was immediate. She had
asked after Wendy as a matter of form; her years of discreetly
manipulating the levers of power meant she was nothing if not
diplomatic. But the garden was her baby; was, indeed, her
entire family, as her husband's death had left her without any
close relatives.

'Would you like to see what I've done with the back?' she
asked, girlishly shy all of a sudden. 'It's a new planting scheme.'

Beth, realising she was probably the worst person to ask as
she knew so little about gardens and cared even less, couldn't
turn down the invitation. From everything she'd heard, gardens
might well be the clue to Alfie's death, and even her mother's
poisoning. If the Bridge Club seemed to be yielding a disap-
pointing no-bid so far as potential suspects were concerned,
Beth needed to turn her attention to one of Alfie's other
obsessions.

'Love to,' she said, trying to look as enthusiastic as possible.

June Hills ushered her in through a hallway that was as
minimalist and airy as her mother's was cluttered. Everything
was painted an uninspiring but inoffensive beige. They didn't
pause, but trekked straight to the sitting room at the rear of the
house. In Wendy's place, next door, this had been made into a

kitchen, but June Hills had kept to the original floorplan and a large book-lined room, in shades of wheat, corn and biscuit, acted as a neutral frame to the real drama, which was all going on outside.

A drift of tall acer trees spread across the back of Mrs Hills' garden like a wall of flames, their vibrant oranges, reds and purples all but crackling in the mellow autumn sun. Beth was astonished she'd never appreciated their true beauty before, but June Hills had erected a high fence almost as soon as Wendy had moved in and Beth, like her mother, had rarely bothered venturing into the neglected back garden. Wendy had muttered about complaining to the Wyatt's estate, which had strong views on correct fence heights, but inertia and her hectic Bridge schedule had got the better of her.

The rest of the garden was as beautiful as the trees: a lush expanse of grass, the first that Beth had ever seen that could rival the Wyatt's lawn, then more of the close-clipped shrubs, and a staggering variety of flowering things whose names Beth couldn't even guess at. There was even a large pond in the centre with the waterfall Beth had remembered glimpsing before the fence went up. And as she watched, she could see the sleek, strangely muscular-looking bodies of giant white and orange fish flashing up and down. They must be the carp that gave Wendy the 'willies'. The whole thing looked like one of those pictures of perfect gardens you got on the sort of vintage biscuit tins that Wendy no doubt had in profusion next door.

'Wow! It's astonishing.' Beth sighed. It was no struggle to pick the right word this time. The garden really was a labour of love, and it had paid off handsomely.

'I'm so glad you think so,' said Mrs Hills. Her voice was as monotone as ever, but there was a wash of pink in her cheeks now. 'If you don't mind, I'd like to show you something else.'

There was no mistaking it; June Hills was decidedly tentative. Beth gave her a surprised look, but the woman avoided her eyes, led her out into the corridor again and then up the stairs. This was a bit odd. People didn't normally take you to the upper regions of their homes, unless the only loo was up there, for instance. In this case, Beth was pretty sure they'd passed a small bathroom downstairs. But she trotted obediently behind her hostess, up the cream-of-mushroom carpet, passing several anodyne prints which managed to be both terribly tasteful and instantly forgettable. The landing was another sea of beige.

Then Mrs Hills flung open the door to a large, square room. It was evidently a spare bedroom, and looked as though it had been hoovered to within an inch of its life moments before. Even Beth, who was no fan of clutter, balked at the relentless blankness of the décor – magnolia again, with long pale taupe velvet curtains and a matching bedspread. There was one personal touch, a rather battered old teddy lying on the pillows, but the poor old thing was pretty beige, too. The only splash of colour came from the acers outside.

June Hills tiptoed through the lush pile of the squeaky-clean carpet, and Beth had a passing pang at the thought of her own floors at home. She really must give them a good going-over, and soon. Then Mrs Hills brought her over to the window. They looked down on the spectacular garden again. June Hills sighed in pleasure and clutched her hand to her chest. Beth looked at her capable, sausage-like fingers and square-cut nails with slight misgivings.

'Lovely,' Beth muttered, feeling that however fabulous this garden was, she had probably praised it enough at this stage.

Impatiently, Mrs Hills shook her head. 'Look, over there. See what I mean?' she asked, gesturing now with the stubby hand. Beth obligingly craned over to her left – and then immediately guessed what the problem was.

From here, one had a perfect view of Wendy's back garden next door. If June Hills had worked to make hers a blessed plot, then it seemed Wendy had done just the opposite. Weeds, the rank, dark green of spinach past its prime, choked what had once been a perfectly acceptable lawn. A nasty old patio was riven with cracked paving stones. Between them, more weeds burst out exuberantly, like mischievous tufts evading a swimsuit. Meanwhile, a rusting barbeque was propped against the fence like a sozzled guest at a drinks party, compounding the disreputable scene. Somewhere at the bottom of the garden lurked a shed, its window cracked and its door sagging on ancient hinges. Perhaps Wendy had a mower in there. Perhaps she didn't. But it was abundantly clear that she was never going to use it, even if it did exist.

'Do you know what that is?' said Mrs Hills, pointing to the far side of Wendy's patch.

'Er, no,' admitted Beth, though that was hardly surprising – there was so much in both gardens that was a mystery to her.

'Japanese knotweed,' said June Hills, through closed eyes and painfully pursed lips.

'Aha,' said Beth, none the wiser. 'Do you want me to ask my mother for a cutting?' she asked helpfully.

'No!' shouted Mrs Hills. 'No, no, no! It must all be burnt. It must be reported to the Council. It's a pest, it's going to bring our houses down. Destroying my garden will only be the first step,' she said, staring at Beth with true venom.

'Really? Are you sure?' asked Beth, scrutinising the boring-looking weed again, squinting down at it and trying to see it as the villain that Mrs Hills was surveying with equal parts anger and terror.

'Of course I'm sure,' she said blisteringly. 'I ought to have your mother prosecuted for this, you know.'

'Gosh, that's going a bit far, isn't it?' Beth remonstrated.

'I've told her time and time again. I first noticed it months ago. And she's done nothing. It's *Japanese knotweed*, for God's sake. Don't any of you know the first thing about gardens? It'll spread. Spread like wildfire!' Mrs Hills said, raising her hands to the beige ceiling like a gospel preacher bringing the word of the Lord to an extraordinarily bland congregation.

Beth looked at her in alarm. Either the woman was one daff short of a window box, or Wendy had been very remiss. She thought for a moment and decided it was quite clear which was which.

'It undermines the foundations. It strangles other plants. It's like having a, a, a *serial killer* loose in your back garden, and doing nothing about it. I can't let it get at my acers,' Mrs Hills continued with a high-pitched wail.

'Of course not,' said Beth. She almost patted Mrs Hills on the arm, but held back at the last moment, not sure if it would help or tip the poor woman right over the edge. 'I can't believe my mother hasn't dealt with this. Did she realise how serious it was?'

'You know Wendy,' said Mrs Hills bitterly. 'If I've explained it to her once, I've said it a thousand times. I've even taken photocopies of the advice from the Royal Horticultural Society itself and stuck it through her door,' she added.

Beth could just imagine how much her mother had loved that – and could almost calculate the number of seconds she'd spent glancing at the information before shoving it in the bin.

'She goes at her own pace, your mother,' Mrs Hills said bitterly.

Or didn't shift at all. Whatever suited her best, thought Beth.

'She did say her son would soon be over and would sort it all out, but that was ages ago and there's been no sign of him. She said you were always much too busy,' she added with a sideways glance.

Beth was silent. It was true, she had a lot on her plate. But she could have found time for something serious – and Wendy wouldn't have hesitated to ask. She'd also have loved to drag Harry into the whole thing, getting him to pull down or dig out or burn or whatever you did with this stuff. Her mother just hadn't taken this seriously enough.

'Look, leave it to me,' said Beth, trying her best to mollify Mrs Hills. The last thing they wanted was to get the Wyatt's estate involved in this. Or Southwark Council either.

Beth left the house feeling a bit shaken. It was partly the realisation that, yet again, Wendy was refusing to act her age. This time, though, she had apparently gone back in time to some sort of reckless teenage abdication of responsibility. But there was another reason for the new pleat etched into Beth's forehead, beneath the sheltering curtain of her fringe.

There was no mistaking it. Mrs Hills was very, very angry with her mother. Was she furious enough to have reached the dead-heading stage?

NINETEEN

Beth woke up the next morning feeling as though all the cares of the world were pressing down on her slight shoulders. There were the usual worries – Wyatt's, Jake, Harry, even the succession of coffee mornings she seemed to be left out of. Then on top of that, there was the death of poor old Alfie, and the ghastly attempt on her own mother's life. As if that wasn't enough, the whole lot had now been garlanded by Mrs Hills with a lavish portion of Japanese knotweed.

Thank goodness Josh was coming over soon – a phrase she never thought she'd hear herself say. He didn't yet know it, but she had a busy schedule of root and branch weed removal sorted out for him, after she'd spent last night researching ways to kill the terrible blight lurking in her mother's back garden.

Today, though, there was another ordeal to face. Not work. Not even trying to find out from Katie what was going on with the McKenzies. No, for her sins, she'd agreed to go to the Bridge Club with Wendy, and act as her partner.

In a way, it was a quid pro quo. Wendy had agreed, reluctantly, to take the knotweed removal seriously, if Beth would just come to Bridge with her.

Beth felt slightly sorry for her mother. She'd lost a lot when Alfie Pole had shuffled off into the big card game in the sky. Not having a regular partner meant missing out on her great passion, and also on a lot of her social life.

After her weed discussion with Wendy, Beth had said she'd step into the breach this once, but she'd made it clear it wasn't going to be a regular thing. Her mother had readily agreed, but in a way which suggested she was inwardly listening to a different tune, and one which pleased her more. Beth hoped fervently that they'd both be singing from the same song sheet by the time today's session was over.

Some aspects of Beth's morning were a lot easier now that Jake was older. While she was dragging herself from her bed and readying herself for the coming ordeal, Jake was showering and dressing without any parental intervention at all. By the time she'd made it downstairs, he was already plopping his cereal bowl in the sink, gathering up his expensive blazer, its motto *For God's Sake* winking up at her with all its golden threads, and tugging on his battered, equally expensive shoes. She was amused to see he'd already found a hack for the laces – by squashing down the back of each shoe, he could slip his feet in and out without undoing the bow at all. She winced at the damage this was causing, but couldn't help feeling a little burst of pride that he was so good at problem-solving. She wondered if it would catch on with his peers.

'How's it going in the class? Any boys you like? Anyone you want to invite over?' she said to his back as he walked rapidly down the hall.

'Just Charlie,' he said with a smile as he turned and let himself out.

She was left contemplating the door as it slammed, and thinking for the umpteenth time how like his father he was when he grinned in a certain way.

Under the kitchen table, Colin had finished his morning

chore of mopping up any spillages and looked at her expectantly. 'Oh, Colin,' she said, smoothing the warm velvet of his
head. 'I'm not sure about you and Bridge. I don't think Belair
House is that dog-friendly. And, though you'd be a brilliant
guide dog, I'd have to be blind, which would probably mean I'd
be even worse at Bridge than I actually am. You might have to
be very brave today and stay and look after Magpie. What do
you think, boy?'

Colin gave her a deeply reproachful glance. Magpie,
stalking past to check on the nugget situation in her bowl, shot
her a much more vicious look, altered her course abruptly, and
dived out of her cat flap as though the hounds of hell were
pursuing her, instead of one tired old Labrador who'd probably
appreciate the company.

'Tell you what, Col, I'll have another cup of tea with you,
shall I? I've got a bit of time before I have to go off to the Bridge
Club. How's about that?'

Colin batted his tail against the cool kitchen tiles and
opened his mouth to pant. It looked exactly as though the old
dog was smiling a wide, happy smile, and Beth decided she'd
take it as that and ignore the drool dangling perilously near her
foot. 'Good boy,' she said.

Later, Beth would look back on these few moments of
shared companionship with Colin as a quiet beacon of hope in
an increasingly violent and disordered world.

TWENTY

Beth surreptitiously looked at her watch. It was past ten o'clock, but everywhere the room was still full of people chatting aimlessly. Opposite, she could feel Wendy's gathering frustration. She'd been ready to play since they'd taken their seats ten minutes ago. She'd had far too long away from the game, what with one thing and another. The fact that one of these things had been poison, probably administered right here in this very room, was a terrifying truth that didn't really seem to have struck Wendy properly, Beth thought, as she looked sideways at the people clustering around the room. Was one of these apparently innocent old dears responsible for her mother's agonies? And, even worse, were they the person who had sent Alfie to his grave?

It didn't bear thinking about, yet that was exactly what she needed to do. And, she reminded herself sternly, she needed to come up with an explanation before the culprit had another go. At the moment, their motive was obscure and whatever purpose had propelled the first two crimes might still be driving them now.

Was it the Japanese knotweed? she wondered. Although, as

Mrs Hills didn't play Bridge, Beth probably couldn't lay the crime at her door. Was it something to do with the allotments? But as Alfie had only been a gardener for show, after all, it seemed unlikely. Was it a simpler motive – his own daughter's wish to turn his house into a movie location? But then, why would she have had a go at Wendy? That would only draw attention to her crime, and Wendy had nothing to do with Alfie's house. It was all quite baffling.

While Beth had been thinking, the others had finally taken their seats. The tinkle of Deirdre MacBride's little golden hand bell interrupted a dozen murmured conversations, and everyone bent to the red boards containing the cards. Beth struggled to prise her set out of the funny little aperture, and almost dropped the lot. Wendy gave her a stare and she clutched the little fan more carefully. Now, how did you do this again? What were the cards worth? Each of the picture cards had a value – four points for an ace; three for a king; two for queens; and a single point for a jack.

She scrutinised her hand. Well, that was easy. *Null points*, as they always said to the UK these days in the Eurovision Song Contest. She rapidly moved a card or two from suit to suit and, hey presto, she was organised. She looked up, pleased with her work, only to find three sets of eyes focused on her expectantly.

'What?' she asked, raising her eyebrows at her mother.

'You're the dealer,' Wendy hissed.

'Eh?' said Beth.

'That means you bid first.'

'Oh.' That was easy, Beth thought, contemplating her duff hand. 'No bid.'

'Use the cards.' Wendy gestured at the box at Beth's elbow.

With difficulty, Beth fished out a little green no-bid marker and put it on the table in front of her. But Wendy obviously either had a great hand or was desperate to play, and ended up pledging to make ten tricks out of the total of thirteen. Beth was dummy.

As soon as the player on her right led a card, Beth put down her hand for Wendy to use as best she could. As the deeply unimpressive twos, threes and fours appeared, one after another, Wendy's expression got more and more thunderous, though she said nothing but a very clipped, 'Thank you, partner.'

Even a novice like Beth could see that the resultant play was nothing short of a massacre. She wondered why on earth Wendy had decided to bid on, with no support from her partner. But it turned out that Beth's hand had been quite unusual.

'Only you could have a Yarborough, Beth,' Wendy snapped, when they were tallying up the points after the rout.

Beth looked all around her. 'A what? Where?'

Wendy tutted. 'That's what they call a hand without a single point. Not even a ten.'

The man on Beth's right explained kindly, 'It's named after the second Earl of Yarborough, in the nineteenth century. It's said that he placed a constant bet so that, when he had a hand with any points in it, he'd win one pound, but when he got a point-free hand, he would pay out one thousand. Over the years, he made a fortune.'

'So it's lucky then, really?' asked Beth brightly.

'Depends whether you actually want to do well at Bridge or not,' said Wendy drily.

Beth, feeling chastened, wondered again why she'd ever agreed to do this for her mother. There were more useful ways she could spend her time. Though, she admitted to herself, this might be her only route to finding the poisoner. She looked over her shoulder. They were sitting at Wendy's usual table, which meant Beth had her back to the room. She couldn't spend the session peering behind her, but she was determined to try and get a good look at her fellow competitors when she could.

There was a sea of ashy heads at the six, no, seven little green-covered tables. Blue rinses seemed to be out these days. Beth remembered when she'd been young that old ladies had often had blue, pink or even purple coiffures, making their curls look like candyfloss. Today, there were just a couple of unlikely blonde hairdos shining out against the muted white walls and toning with the beautiful honey-coloured parquet.

Twenty-eight people, almost half of them men, and they all looked very unlikely poisoners, mused Beth. Just then came a dry cough. It was Wendy. Everyone was waiting for her to put down her card.

Honestly, there was another mad rule every time you turned round in Bridge, thought Beth with a mental shrug. It was almost as if those playing had nothing to do with their time but make up arcane conventions just to catch out unwary newbies.

But, watching Wendy a little later, when she seemed to be making all the tricks for a change, Beth realised her mother looked a lot perkier than she had for ages. Since Alfie had died, in fact. Whoever had done for him had really knocked the wind out of Wendy's sails – even before trying to bump her off as well. Losing her Bridge partner, when all the other pairings in the room seemed so settled, was a blow which had hit Wendy really hard. You could ask for someone to bid for you, if you had no regular arrangement, but that meant relying on other people to help out all the time. Beth could see why Wendy would prefer a partner – even her daughter.

And that, Beth suddenly realised, was as good a motive as any. Yes, people usually killed for what she thought of as the three 'S's – silver, sex or silence. Silver meant any kind of money; not just weird collections of five-pence pieces, though they'd do if there were enough. Sex also covered a multitude of sins – adultery, abuse, even avarice in the sense of coveting a neighbour's ass. Silence spoke for itself – or rather, it didn't. But would anyone kill just to spoil someone else's fun?

'*Beth?* Honestly, I'm so sorry,' Wendy apologised to her neighbours on either side. It was time to bid again. Wendy would have been a lot crosser, but having snatched victory from the jaws of defeat despite Beth's consistently terrible cards (which Wendy seemed to see as a personal affront rather than a random selection which her daughter had had nothing to do with choosing), her mood was buoyant.

Beth picked her cards up with very low expectations, but the first one she saw was an ace. She fanned them all out and was confronted by a rogue's gallery of kings, jacks and aces, and even a winking queen. She started counting points, but her head was soon swimming. Twenty-three? Could that be right? And what on earth was she supposed to do now? This felt like an onerous responsibility, as though she'd been asked to babysit a royal family and prevent, single-handedly, any sort of coup seeking to curtail its power or, even worse, chop off all these crowned heads.

Twenty minutes later, she'd made all the tricks but one, and was hoping for high praise from Wendy. But as the tables all around them broke up for much-needed tea, Beth sensed that she'd let her mother down badly in some obscure way.

'Wasn't that great? Twelve tricks!' she couldn't help chirping.

'Mmm,' Wendy said repressively, and then spent the entire break filling her in on where she'd gone wrong. It turned out her mother did actually know a surprising amount about Bridge, no matter what other members of the club might say. How much went above or below the line, what you got for extra tricks, who was vulnerable and who wasn't... It seemed there was a separate rule for every minute you were playing, and lots left over to cogitate on afterwards. No wonder it took up so much of Wendy's life.

Beth was pretty sure it wasn't going to encroach on her own free time. She couldn't deny that she'd felt a thrill when fanning out that marvellous hand of colourful faces. That, she imagined, was what kept Bridge players ploughing on through the mediocre scores and lost rubbers, the dodgy bids and the misplayed cards. Chance was, indeed, a fine thing – when it came to call.

Through Wendy's breaktime pep talk, Beth kept an eye on the other players. Was one of them even now plotting more devilry? Or should she be digging around on the allotments for answers? Now that Alfie had been revealed as a much more lacklustre gardener than people had thought, with his shameful plastic secret, she was pretty sure that the answer didn't lie with the Open Garden brigade.

And everyone here seemed benign, too, she thought, her eye sweeping over the nodding heads of the players. Her gaze rested on the back of a very well-coiffed lady, one of the couple of blondes. Not a hair was out of place, and her outfit of Chanel-like jacket and skirt was very smart indeed – maybe a little too formal for something like this? But it was a social event as much as anything, Beth realised, as the chatting reached cocktail party levels of intensity and snippets of conversation swirled around her. 'She'll be going to the College School next year – assuming she gets in, the exams are ferocious now, not like they were in my day...' 'Of course, my son is so employable, it won't take him a moment to find something else. How they'll manage without him, I can't imagine. Ridiculous, but he felt he had to do the decent thing...'

Soon they were all trooping back to their seats. Beth was, by this time, frankly exhausted. The effort required to keep counting to thirteen – to make sure she didn't lose track of the trumps – sounded like something any schoolchild could manage, but in practice it took more concentration than she'd used for quite a while. After this, it would be a great relief to get back to any of her own work – even the filing.

If Bridge, like football, could ever be said to be a game of two halves, the second part of Beth's session was a complete fiasco. And in the final round, she made the unpardonable error of revoking.

Wendy threw up her hands in horror. Their opponents, while icily polite, insisted on calling over Deidre MacBride as director, to give the judgement of Solomon on the matter. And Beth found herself having to concede two extra tricks to the other side, as well as all those that she'd already lost through ordinary incompetence. It was no real surprise when their contract ended up floundering like the *Titanic* shortly after meeting the iceberg.

'Well! That was... quite something,' said her mother, as Beth reached for her handbag. Their opponents had already thanked them courteously for the thousand or so points Beth had handed them on a platter, and taken their leave.

'Sorry, Mum,' Beth mumbled, thinking that at least she'd never be asked to fill in again.

'Don't worry, darling,' Wendy said, quite brightly under the circumstances. 'I'm sure you'll do much better next time.'

Beth's heart sank like a stone, but some good had come of the afternoon. Wendy left Belair House as though she was walking on air, the last traces of her poor-me poisoning persona wiped away by an afternoon doing what she loved most. She'd wafted round saying her goodbyes, fixing up more games and generally acting as though she owned the Bridge world again.

If nothing else, Beth was definitely helping with her rehabilitation. Was it at too great a cost to her *amour propre*? she wondered. Or would she actually get the Bridge bug herself? Stranger things had happened. Occasionally.

TWENTY-ONE

After her drubbing at the Bridge Club, Beth spent the rest of the week blamelessly in her archives – thinking almost exclusively about the poisoning, and getting nowhere. She woke up on Saturday morning, overjoyed that it was the weekend at last. Jake had been looking a little grey about the gills – the punishing new routine at Wyatt's was taking a toll. At his age, he was used to school hours. But there must be quite a difference in what was now going on in his lessons. The Village Primary had been all about inclusiveness, the growth mindset and gentle encouragement. Beth had a suspicion that had gone right out of the window, to be replaced by a first-past-the-post mentality which, although a bit depressing, was probably more aligned with the realities of life in modern Dulwich.

So, Jake would be at his leisure – but she realised, with a stab of anxiety, she would be scurrying about just as much as ever. Thanks to her mother, Beth would be hosting quite a complex lunch party tomorrow. She was looking forward to seeing her brother, but the dynamic between him and Harry was a tad strange. They had hardly met, thanks to Harry's work schedule and Josh's rigorous avoidance of Britain. But on the few occasions when they had coincided, there had been an odd jostling for Beth's attention which, though it amused her a little, she was pretty sure she was going to find tiresome if it spread over too many hours of her precious off-duty time.

There was also the fact that she had to cobble together a menu and source the ingredients. Normally, Beth was a lot more sanguine than most Dulwich residents about the strange lack of a Waitrose in SE21. But when she actually had people coming round, she felt it every bit as acutely as Katie, and even Belinda. As per usual, she had not been organised enough to sort out an online delivery instead.

With a sigh, she heaved herself out of the warm snugness of the bed, where Harry was taking up the lion's share of the duvet but at least generating enough heat to compensate, and got herself down to the kitchen table to plan her campaign. As soon as she was settled with a piece of A4 and a hot cup of tea, her mobile shrilled. 'Bridge over Troubled Water'. That was all she needed. Once upon a time, she would have blithely ignored her mother's call. Now, after that hospital bedside pledge, she was a reformed character – or trying to be.

'Hi, Mum,' she said as brightly as possible.

'Just making sure you've got everything sorted out for tomorrow,' said Wendy cheerfully.

'Of course,' said Beth, crossing her fingers and trying not to look at the bare kitchen cupboards. 'All under control.'

'Well, that's great, because I've got one or two little things you could do for me,' Wendy said, a wheedling note entering her voice. 'Just at the garden centre, you know...'

Beth immediately thought of Mrs Hills and her, what was it, Korean tangleweed? 'Yes, we've got to get on the case with clearing your garden before the Council gets notified...'

'What? Oh yes, I'm getting Joshy to do all that. But if you could get some bits and bobs, make things look a bit prettier. Well, you'll have the time as you're sorted for tomorrow. And you've got the car, whereas I'm, well, I don't like to complain, but I am still feeling a little weak...'

Beth gritted her teeth, well and truly hoisted by her own petard. Why had she tried to pretend she was ready for the lunch? Her mother surely knew her better than that. And now she was just plain taking advantage. But Beth couldn't admit she'd lied. She was reduced to mouthing curses as her mother dictated a list of plants on the pristine sheet of paper that was supposed to feature tomorrow's menu. Beth knew Wendy was only trying to make her garden look a little better to impress Josh and whatever girl he had in tow. But at least, she supposed, it would mean that this troublesome weed was going to get its comeuppance at last – and they'd avoid Mrs Hills' wrath and a possible summons from Wyatt's estate and Southwark Council.

'While we're on the subject of Josh, I don't suppose you know if his girlfriend has any dietary requirements or anything?'

'What on earth do you mean, dear? Why would she be on a diet?' asked Wendy, in Beth's view wilfully misunderstanding her. 'And in any case, if you've already shopped it's a little late to ask now. Looking forward to seeing you in a short while,' Wendy said, signing off abruptly.

Deflated, Beth scribbled down a few things that she was pretty sure she should cook, looked at her watch, grabbed her bag and jacket, and made for the door. 'Bye!' she shouted up, to total silence from two sleepy males. She was pretty sure things shouldn't be like this. Where were her helpers, when she needed them? But it was too late to waste time worrying about that now.

Just as she was about to slam the door, the one male who was always willing to lend a paw padded up to her, all beseeching eyes. 'Oh, all right then,' she said, clipping on Colin's lead.

. . .

By going to the small Tesco on the Croxted Road, Beth managed to get everything on her food list, and although it wasn't the corn-fed, lovingly coddled produce a Waitrose would have provided, it didn't leave her bankrupt either. She stuffed the bags in the boot, got Colin out of the car, and then they nipped across the road, past one of her favourite bookshops, and dived behind the parade of shops to find one of the area's hidden gems – a little garden centre, tucked away.

This is definitely the place to do a little, ahem, digging, thought Beth, as she wandered past tables stocked with beautiful plants that she knew full well would last only moments if she ever got them home. She could only hope that, against all the evidence, Wendy was turning over a new leaf and would remember to water this stuff once it was in her back garden.

She'd just about stopped Colin from cocking his leg against a very fine miniature tree in a pot, when an assistant bustled over, wearing a long green apron with the garden centre's logo on the bib.

'Can I help?' he said politely. 'And would your dog like some water?' He diplomatically pointed over to a bowl in the far corner. As well as being a kind offer, Beth could see this would keep Colin nicely out of tinkling range. The garden centre had its own sprinkler system and didn't seem to want any extra help. She led him over and looped his lead across a handy bit of fence.

While she had the assistant's attention, Beth asked lots of questions about what her mother would need to rid herself of the pest Mrs Hills had identified. She was soon armed with all sorts of information and techniques which, together with everything she had already gleaned via her googling, she was pretty sure would mean that Wendy's entire plot would be pristine inside a week. The knotweed would soon be on its way to plant hell.

They then got onto the subject of gardening in general.

Much of it – talk of azaleas and zinnias – was way above Beth's head, though it reminded her of absent friends who'd loved gardening, and made her feel rather melancholy. She shook this off; it just wasn't useful now. She mustn't waste this opportunity to find out more about the Dulwich gardening scene.

With some gentle steering, Beth managed to work things round to the allotments, the Open Garden scheme and all things floral in the area. Luckily, the assistant was chatty and clearly a bit bored. Maybe this wasn't his dream career, or maybe the hours dragged sometimes. He was soon filling Beth in on the arcane rivalries and delicate complications of ministering to highly competitive types armed with trugs and trowels.

'Most of them are fine, yeah?' he said with the teenage upward lilt which usually had Beth gritting her teeth. Now she couldn't get enough of it. 'But there's one or two, yeah? They're seriously out of their trees – trees, ahaha,' he said with a giggle.

Beth managed a smile, hoping he wasn't going to head off-track. 'Anyone in particular you'd say was, erm, worse than the rest?'

The boy fingered his non-existent beard and seemed to be thinking deeply. Beth prayed this wouldn't take too long; she had an unroasted lunch festering in the car, and Wendy was no doubt tapping her foot, waiting for her plants.

'Yeah, I'd say there was one lady, who was, you know, really into it? More so than others, maybe?'

Beth smiled again patiently, thinking it must be exhausting to live in a world where every utterance was a question. As the boy must usually speak to other teenagers, maybe they'd all grown used to never getting a straight answer to anything. 'Do you remember her name, by any chance?'

'I'd probably remember it, if you said it?' he said, shrugging.

Hmm. Beth looked at him for a moment, wondering how on earth that was supposed to help. She couldn't say something she didn't know. Oh well, it had been worth a try.

. . .

At Wendy's house twenty minutes later, Beth disgorged her trove of plants and stood on the doorstep in the expectation of lots of praise.

Wendy took a quick look in each bag as Beth put them in the hall. 'Not many in flower, are there?' she sniffed.

'It's September, Mum. Little is in bloom, I think you'll find.' After her time in the garden centre, she knew this much to be true at any rate. 'How's the Bridge?' she asked, hoping to get onto less contentious ground. Wendy sometimes played with others in between Bridge Club meetings, but now only if she could get someone to pitch in with the bidding.

'Oh, you know, it's fine.' Wendy shrugged. She seemed a little dispirited.

Beth was worried. Maybe her mother wasn't making such a good recovery from her brush with atropine. 'What's up?' she asked.

'Oh, just that *some people* are terribly competitive, you know?'

'Bridge players? No, surely not,' said Beth with heavy irony.

'You can take it too far, Beth,' Wendy said. 'I don't understand people like that. The point is you're supposed to be enjoying the game, not vanquishing all before you.'

Beth's eyes widened. As she knew after their recent stint at Belair House, Wendy could teach Rambo a thing or two about aggression over the green baize.

But Wendy was continuing. 'Trying to win is healthy. But trying to do others down, well, that's just awful, isn't it?'

'Who's doing that?' Beth asked, raising her eyebrows and suddenly feeling a twinge of alarm. 'No one's getting at you, are they?'

Wendy hesitated for a moment. Just then, Beth's phone rang.

She fished it out. 'It's Harry.'

'You'd better get that, dear. And I can't stand on the doorstep all day. I don't want to get a cold, on top of everything else,' Wendy said, shutting the door firmly in Beth's face.

Well, honestly, thought Beth crossly. But she turned back to the call. 'Everything OK?' she said.

'Just wondering if you needed a hand,' said Harry.

Beth felt a surge of affection. It was a kind offer. About an hour and half too late, but it was still enough to perk her up on the way home. She wasn't alone with this dratted lunch tomorrow after all, and that was a good feeling.

TWENTY-TWO

Beth woke up feeling as braced as she possibly could be for a so-called 'relaxed' family lunch. After getting home yesterday with the food, she'd cleaned the house to within an inch of its life, her good work undermined at every step by the combined efforts of Jake, Harry, Colin and Magpie. If she wasn't coming across fresh clumps of cat fluff shed on just-hoovered cushions, she was picking up clots of dried mud from Jake's trainers, or nudging Harry's innumerable paperbacks and newspapers into tidy piles.

In a way, the constant activity kept her occupied and stopped her mulling over why she was dreading the lunch so much. How had it come to the point where she'd be a lot happier having three strangers round than she was dealing with her own brother, mother and, of course, the random girlfriend?

Beth got up and went down to the kitchen, clicking on the kettle and rattling a mug out of the cupboard. She chose a really big one, decorated with a hectic pattern of chickens. Jake had bought it for her for Easter, and the totally unexpected gift never failed to cheer her up. He was a darling, her boy. And surely any gene pool that could produce him couldn't be all bad? Though Beth realised darkly that poor James's side might have been responsible for a lot of Jake's nicer characteristics.

There was nothing wrong with her brother, Josh, there really wasn't. And her mother had a lot of plus points. It was perhaps just that she was so tired, what with Jake trying to find his feet at school, her relationship with Harry up in the air as ever, even Colin – adorable though he was – adding that tiny bit of extra strain. She actually felt close to breaking point, she realised in shock.

And that was without her sense that it was up to her to find out who had killed Alfie Pole and tried to rid the world of Wendy. Because, despite her best efforts to find out where Harry was with the investigation, she was very much afraid that, as usual, he was letting the whole business drop into the massive 'unsolved' folder that seemed to lurk at the centre of the Metropolitan Police like a swirling black hole.

Harry's attitude to Josh was also potentially problematic. So far, they had circled warily around each other like dogs in the park. They'd stopped short of giving each other a thorough sniffing, but only just. Beth knew Josh felt occasional surges of protectiveness towards his little sister. And while she had always been about four times more responsible than him, he was, technically at least, the more grown-up sibling. To some extent, he still seemed to feel he ought to be looking out for her, in lieu of their father. Luckily, this impulse was usually thwarted by the fact he was constantly abroad and had little time to spare from his own concerns.

All this would be complex enough, without the added burden that her mother would be playing the recent poisoning victim like Meryl Streep on steroids to get Josh's full attention. And Josh, Beth was pretty sure, would instinctively disapprove of Jake starting at Wyatt's. What had it ever given him, she could imagine him arguing, except a quiverful of qualifications he didn't use and the bulletproof confidence to sashay through life? Then, like the sprinkles on the top of a cake of trouble, there was the cooking itself. Beth was never at her best in the kitchen, unless it was making tea, she thought, sticking the kettle on again for another cup.

She sighed. While she was at it, she might as well start sorting out the lunch. If she gave herself plenty of prep time, she'd get less stressed and reduce the chances of accidentally giving everyone food poisoning. She turned on the cooker and hefted the chicken out of the fridge. It sat there on the counter, pale, flabby and covered with goosebumps, looking rather like Beth herself on a bad day at the seaside, she thought ruefully.

She sorted out what seemed like a mountain of potatoes, knowing from experience that Jake and Harry between them could put away more than she'd ever thought humanly possible. Wendy, meanwhile, would only pick at a singleton, and would no doubt pass a comment of some sort on the crispiness of Beth's roasting style. Josh would have as many as he could. His girlfriend was an unknown quantity, but based on previous experience, she'd probably exhibit at least one food allergy and might well turn out to be a vegan.

Once the potatoes were done, Beth moved on to carrots, the orange peelings building up around her and dropping all over the floor, reminding her of the flaming acers in Mrs Hills' garden. She mustn't forget to mention the knotweed to Josh. He could at least do something useful while he was in the country.

The time passed pleasantly enough, and Beth was getting into the soothing rhythm of chopping stuff when Magpie peered through the cat flap, checking to see whether Colin was around. Though Beth had caught them having secret love-ins on the sofa when they thought there were no witnesses, in public at least Magpie kept up the pretence that she and the ancient Labrador were mortal enemies. Seeing that the coast was clear, Magpie sidled through the flap, sauntered over to Beth and bit her on her bare ankle.

'Ow! What was that for, Mags? That was just mean!' Beth protested. Magpie looked up at her, green eyes unrepentant, and miaowed loudly. Understanding dawned. 'Oh, your bowl's empty? Sorry, Magpie, I haven't got round to your breakfast yet. I haven't even had mine.'

That cut no ice with the cat, who advanced on Beth again. 'All right, all right, I'm going to feed you,' Beth said, backing away and going into the sitting room where Magpie's stash of priceless cat food lived.

Colin slunk out as Magpie advanced, the two animals exchanging a glance like prison guard and detainee, though Beth wasn't quite sure which was which. She got out the bag with its illustration of a glamorous, fluffy cat who no doubt never bit its owner, rattled the pellets into the cat's bowl and watched as Magpie scarfed them down. She'd certainly been hungry.

Beth more or less forgave her the nip, stroked her for a while as the cat continued to crunch, then wandered back into the kitchen.

Colin was now lying down in the kitchen, looking like a lumpy brown rug. As she passed him, he tried to raise his head but gave up, giving her a strangely remorseful look out of one chocolate brown eye. Beth wondered what that was about, then crossed over to the cooker. The oven was probably hot enough now. It was a little early to put the chicken in, but she could get it ready, rub a bit of paprika on it or something, whatever the posh cooks did these days.

She came to a stop in front of the stove, which was humming away to itself as it heated up. On the hob, where she had left the chicken, there was nothing but an empty space.

The chicken was nowhere to be seen.

TWENTY-THREE

Beth couldn't help thinking that the last-minute table they'd bagged in the Crown and Greyhound pub in Dulwich Village was a bit of a godsend. Technically, she knew she should be furious with Colin. He was outside, his lead tied around a table leg, still looking green after scoffing not only the chicken but also its little polystyrene platter and the clingfilm which covered it, complete with cooking instructions. How a dog, who was ponderous at best, had managed that in the short time she'd been occupied with Magpie in the sitting room, she couldn't imagine. It just showed that, much though she loved the old Labrador, he had much more in common with the playwright Oscar Wilde than she had ever realised before. Both of them could resist anything – except temptation.

Poor Colin was definitely regretting his moment of madness now, having hoicked up a lot of his unexpected windfall in the back garden, along Pickwick Road and even, truly disgustingly, outside the pub. Beth was already dreading what might emerge from the other end, in the hours to come.

But despite it all, she couldn't be too cross with him. The look in his eye was so contrite, so abject, that it would have

taken a harder heart than hers to punish him. His evident
gastric turmoil was payback enough. And nor could Beth escape
the fact she was secretly thrilled. She felt as though she'd been
offered a last-minute reprieve. There had been just about time,
she was now willing to admit, for her to run back to the shop
and get a last-minute alternative to the chicken. But she'd leapt
at Harry's suggestion that they all meet at the pub instead,
thrilled to be let off making a meal over which her mother
would have very much enjoyed judging her, every bit as harshly
as RuPaul contemplating a drag queen in an H&M frock.

Things were even easier because Josh was distracted from
his usual alpha male act with Harry. Instead of the pair clashing
antlers, Josh was completely preoccupied with his new girlfriend, Rose. To Beth's astonishment, for the first time ever he
seemed totally besotted. And the girl seemed quite ordinary,
compared to some of the stunners he'd had fawning over him
before. She was lovely, most definitely, but not a potential
supermodel. She was of average height, normal size, and
wearing a sensible jumper. Best of all, she didn't seem to be
hanging on Josh's every word. Beth really warmed to her. And
Josh immediately agreed to root out Wendy's knotweed,
presumably to impress Rose.

Unfortunately, gazing at Rose, laughing at all her jokes,
holding her hand and making sure she had a drink at all times
did distract Josh a bit from Wendy and her terrific performance
as a frail little old lady. But her mother's sporadic coughs,
sudden claspings of her forehead and occasional complaints (in
a very piercing voice) that she felt a little faint did remind Beth
that she, for one, was still dying to get to the bottom of the
mystery. Her mother might be maddening, but if it was anyone's
job to kill her, it was Beth's.

When they'd all managed to put away very decent helpings
of the Greyhound's respectable take on a roast Sunday lunch –
which Beth was happy to admit was a lot better than anything

she could have served up – she volunteered to go to the bar to get another Coke for Jake. He was dealing with the boredom of so much grown-up chit-chat by playing a game on his uncle's phone.

The place had filled up, and she found herself, as usual, all but invisible behind a crowd of fellow lunchers. Once they were served, she realised she was just a pace behind an elderly lady with a rigid blonde hairdo. It was one of those moments when she knew she'd seen the woman before, yet couldn't for the life of her remember where. So frustrating, thought Beth. Was this what it was going to be like growing old? More and more moments missing? She hoped not.

She racked her brains. The woman was well-turned-out, her shoes were shiny – she could have been the grandmother of anyone in Jake's class. Was that where she knew her from? Beth tried to edge round and glimpse the woman's face, hoping they could solve the mystery together.

Then a stocky man, whom she hadn't noticed as he had been leaning his broad, bullish torso against the counter, turned and spoke a word to the elderly lady. He started waving a twenty-pound note at the busy barman like a picador brandishing a red rag at a bull.

Good God! Beth stepped back in confusion even faster than she had after Magpie's nip that morning. It wasn't just the man's awful manners. He was the last person in Dulwich she wanted to run into.

Beth whipped round immediately, hoping she hadn't been seen. Jake's Coke was just going to have to wait. Sure enough, as she passed a large mirror, she took a quick peek. She'd been right. It was just as she thought. A shiver of horror went right through her.

Sitting back down at the table, Jake's question about the strange non-appearance of his drink was the least of her worries. What on earth was she going to do now?

TWENTY-FOUR

Exactly a day later, Beth was at Wyatt's, still facing the same dilemma. She sat in her office, twirling a pencil, lost in thought. A much-chastened Colin was sitting very quietly in the conference corner. The full ramifications of his short career as a thief were now over, thank goodness, but from the injured look in his eye, Beth knew he'd never quite trust a chicken again. She considered herself lucky that they hadn't had to go to the vet. The old boy had had a very lucky escape – and so, she decided, had she.

Yesterday's lunch had gone much better than she could have predicted, what with Josh being head over heels in love, Harry thus let off the hook, and her mother a little squashed by Josh's inattention, much to Beth's silent amusement. But that sneaked glimpse in the mirror had landed her with a huge decision to make.

Should she say anything? And who on earth to? Harry wouldn't take it seriously, she was sure. With a mammoth effort of will, Beth put the whole issue to the back of her mind. Sometimes things unravelled themselves, she found, if you could distract yourself successfully enough with different issues. Displacement, they called it.

By the time she finished work that day, she'd displaced enough to clear her desk. She'd even got halfway through a plan for her biography of Wyatt, at last. She'd squinted through Jake's homework diary, filched from his bag that morning. He seemed to be getting it done, and everything he'd had back so far, faithfully recorded in the 'marks' section, was in the six or seven out of ten, B+ range where, Beth suspected, he was likely to stay throughout his academic career. Nothing wrong with that, she thought defensively. It was fine.

Beth had even managed to catch up with Katie and have a chat, though the friends seemed a little out of tune with each other. They somehow hadn't got round to the promised discussion of the Billy McKenzie issue. Even walking the dogs together seemed to be out, as Katie had ceded control of Teddy to the dog-walker, but Beth really couldn't blame her for that.

Then Katie had let it slip that there'd been yet another coffee morning that Beth hadn't made the cut for. And she'd sighed very heavily over some Latin prep that, of course, Jake hadn't mentioned. Beth wondered if it was possible that Katie herself was finding the work hard going. Or was she a lot more ambitious over Charlie's marks than Beth? It was mysterious. She certainly seemed to have lost interest entirely in the investigation, though Beth wasn't surprised, given the bullying. And Beth wasn't ready to tell her friend about yesterday's devastating encounter yet.

That fleeting glimpse had filtered into her dreams. With a shiver, she remembered tossing and turning last night, trying to escape nightmares where the same motifs came up, time and time again. The tightly packed balls of yellow petals that she'd seen in Mrs Hills' front garden, blowing across Dulwich Park towards her, mimicking the curiously helmet-like blonde coiffure she'd seen in the pub, which kept popping up everywhere she went. Was the connection really what she thought it was? And how could she ever be sure?

By the time she was packing her handbag and straightening things on her desk, Beth had come to a decision. There was only one way to make absolutely certain that her theory really did hold water. It wasn't going to be easy. But it was necessary.

TWENTY-FIVE

The next day, Beth didn't mind admitting that she was shaking in her pixie boots. The drastic step she was now taking had somehow seemed like the only option when she'd been sitting safely behind her desk at Wyatt's. But now she was here, on the brink of irrevocable action, she wasn't really sure she should – or could – go through with it. And could she really pull it off?

She looked up at the façade of Belair House, smooth and cold and white. This is where it had all started. And where Beth was hoping to bring things to an end.

The house had stood here, impassively beautiful, through over two hundred years of constant change – wars, revolutions, referendums, riots. It had seen worse than the murder of a little old man and a botched attempt on a woman's life. But that didn't mean the events of the past days weren't important. They had been crimes, deadly ones. And Beth was determined that they would be the last to be seen here, for another century at least. She screwed up her courage and went in.

She had the feeling that she'd already glimpsed the truth. Coming here today, she was really just seeking to confirm a gut feeling. And that couldn't be so dangerous, could it?

Dicing with a murderer was never the best idea, though. And this time, it was personal. Beth could almost feel a malign spirit in the air as she grasped the handrail and followed the graceful sweep of the staircase, up, up to the waiting ballroom.

Soon, in a dreamlike state, she found herself taking her seat opposite Wendy again, the now-familiar green baize cloth stretching between them. Behind her, the other five or so tables were spread out for the rest of the Bridge Club. They were gradually filling up. As usual, her position as North meant she was actually in the worst spot for scrutinising the other club members, as she had her back to them. But she'd do the best she could. She listened as people filed in, greeted each other, discussed the weather and took their seats. Could she hear the voice she was dreading, yet eagerly awaiting?

Despite her nerves and her sense that she was on the brink of a discovery, Beth found her mind fleeing to the moment last week, when she'd fanned out her thirteen cards and so many of them had been glorious picture cards. It had been a thrill; she couldn't deny it. Then she'd got so many tricks. She'd loved that.

Could she be a Bridge whiz? She doubted it. But maybe, just maybe, she had a bit of potential. It was ages since she'd taken up anything new and done well at it. She hadn't had time, what with Jake, and poverty, and all the rest of it. And she knew that luck alone was responsible for the amazing fistful of points she'd got last time. But seeing whether she could do as well with another hand... it was tempting, she had to admit.

This time, she was a lot more au fait with some of the peculiar rituals. The bidding, the playing, even Wendy's wincing, all passed off more smoothly. But, sadly, as the games edged by, she found she was making as many mistakes as she had the previous week.

'Don't worry,' said one of their opponents – a nice gentle lady with a golden hairdo, similar to but softer than that which had danced in and out of Beth's subconscious all week. 'I've been playing Bridge for forty years now, and every week I make a different mistake,' she tittered.

Her partner, sitting opposite, seemed to find her comment a little less hilarious, but gamely chimed in. 'Yes, just never play with your husband. All the jokes about people shooting each other after trumping aces are true, you know.'

As a slice of humour, it fell as heavily onto the table as one of Beth's homemade pancakes. Wendy definitely wasn't ready to josh about the lethal aspects of the card game yet and, in her heightened state of nerves, nor was Beth.

Wendy gave the woman a reproachful stare, still very conscious of her special status as a recent invalid, but Beth managed a small polite smile. Then, before the lengthening silence could get too embarrassing, the pair got to their feet, said their goodbyes and moved round to meet their next set of opponents.

They were replaced by the Crofts – the next duo to play against Wendy and Beth, and one of the rare Bridge couples who hadn't apparently yet shot each other (or hid the scars well) over many years of playing together. Both wore zip-up fleeces and cheery smiles, and had the habit of finishing each other's sentences. Beth remembered them from last week's game and had enjoyed their gentle take on Bridge and their indulgence of her newbie mistakes. Mind you, they didn't bear the brunt of them, and in fact benefitted from her erratic bidding and narcoleptic card play.

All of a sudden there was a tinkling from Deidre MacBride's little golden bell, and Beth craned round to see what was going on. The stocky woman was standing in front of the magnificent marble mantelpiece, her salt and pepper hair reflected in the enormous mirror. Her hands were pushed deep into the pockets of her tweedy jacket.

'Thanks for your attention, everybody,' she said in quelling tones. Over in the corner, where there had been a muttered conversation continuing, silence fell reluctantly.

Beth pushed her chair back so that she didn't get a crick in her neck. At this angle, ninety degrees to the rest of the room, she could see everyone for once. Her eyes roved over the tables, smiling as she caught the artist Miriam's eye, nodding to her partner Jules, then suddenly doing a double-take as she spotted the back of one of those smooth, shiny helmets of blonde hair.

Why did this particular iteration of a simple hairstyle – though actually, the spun-sugar creation, whipped up and then nailed down with setting spray, was anything but simple – have this effect on her pulse? It was now racing so hard she could scarcely hear Deirdre MacBride chuntering on about the far-off Bridge Club Christmas buffet lunch and the contribution of £5 expected from each member if they expected to have a spread as lavish as last year.

'Now, as you know, it's also our usual tea break time round about now,' said Deirdre when she'd finished her spiel about the festive shindig. 'But we're running late. So, I suggest that in order to get in our normal number of hands, we have our tea while playing. Who agrees?'

There was a landslide of approval. 'If I could have a few volunteers to bring trays? Some of the more able-bodied?' Deirdre now had to raise her voice again above the din.

Beth thought for a moment, laziness warring with her public-spirited side, then she got to her feet. To her surprise, she'd missed the boat. Several volunteers were already up and on their way out to get the cups. Beth just caught that elusive glint of gold again before Wendy crossly claimed her attention.

'Beth, if you could just concentrate for a second, we might get on a bit better.'

Beth's cheeks were pink as she obediently fished her cards

out of the red container and fanned them out, wishing she could fan her cheeks at the same time. But that would no doubt be frowned upon. She was concentrating so hard on tallying her points that she barely noticed the cup being placed at her elbow, though she muttered an automatic 'Thank you.'

It wasn't until she'd organised the suits and totted up her total – a measly eight points, nothing much she could do with that – that she risked breaking off to take a tiny sip. Ugh! The tea was sweet. She pushed it aside, disappointed. There seemed distressingly few occasions in life when she was presented with a cup of tea out of the blue, so it seemed a terrible waste that it should be undrinkable. But she loathed sugar in tea. Opposite her, Wendy had raised her cup and was also making a face, but as usual for a different reason. Not sweet enough. It was a wonder she had any teeth left, thought Beth. She, too, pushed the cup away. Beth suddenly relaxed. Without quite knowing it, she'd been holding her breath. But why?

Then Mrs Croft to her right picked up Wendy's cup by mistake and took a hearty swig. She saw Beth watching her and misunderstood, smiling at her over the rim. But, as Beth looked on, the woman's mouth suddenly faltered, became strangely rigid and then contorted. She looked confused for a moment, opened her eyes wide and, to Beth's horror, clutched her chest. The cup fell from her hand and bounced once, twice, three times on the table, spilling liquid everywhere, across the green baize, onto the red boards and the bidding boxes, and over the edge of the table to drip steadily onto the parquet.

Her husband stood up, bracing himself too heavily on the flimsy card table, which promptly collapsed under his weight. Cards were suddenly falling everywhere and joining the puddle of tea, and at neighbouring tables, people were standing up and starting to shout.

Beth was to remember the pandemonium for years to come,

and to blame herself for the scenes of chaos. Why hadn't she thought for one second how dangerous it really was to keep on serving refreshments in a group where one person had died from poisoning, and another had been hospitalised? Why had it not occurred to her that desperation might lead to another attempt?

In her ridiculous career as a sleuth, she had sometimes risked her life to resolve a case. This time, unknowingly, she had been responsible for offering up the entire Bridge Club. She'd never forgive herself.

* * *

Beth and Wendy were both toting large bunches of flowers when they met up a few days afterwards. The September wind was biting, and Beth felt it whip right through her black jacket. As usual, Wendy was eyeing Beth's outfit askance.

'Do get that hair out of your eyes, darling. And I'm not sure that colour is very respectful, is it?'

Beth looked down at the offending scarf. It was pale blue – not exactly disco-bright. But maybe it wasn't suitable? She wrinkled her brow. It was true that she was never at her best with the language of clothes.

'That's hardly the most important thing at the moment, is it?' If Wendy got started properly on her daughter's sartorial shortcomings, they could be there for hours. And Beth, for one, had no desire to freeze to death.

'You're right,' said Wendy, and Beth chose sensibly to ignore the unflattering note of surprise in Wendy's voice. 'There are much more important things to think about. This is such a shame.'

'It's really sad,' Beth agreed, glad for once that they were in accord on something.

'A terrible, terrible waste,' Wendy added, shaking her head. 'But she couldn't go on like that. It's a very, very sad loss.'

Wendy stood, looking mournfully down at her tiny black shoes, while Beth tried to look anywhere but at her own bashed-up pixie boots. She certainly didn't want to draw her mother's attention to them. They were in even worse condition than Jake's school shoes, and that was really saying something.

'Well, let's not stand here all day, anyway,' said Wendy, shaking herself a little, and stepping forward. The automatic doors of the hospital opened with a swish and they made their way inside. 'I really don't see why Harry had to be quite so officious. Surely there was no need for an arrest?'

Beth, pretty sure now that Wendy was going to keep up her litany of complaints all the way up to the ward where Mrs Croft was thankfully recovering well from her encounter with atropine, said tersely, 'Mum, I don't think Harry could allow a poisoner to remain on the loose, even if they *were* one of the leading lights of your beloved Bridge Club.'

Wendy tutted, and suddenly Beth felt she'd been pushed too far. 'For God's sake, Mum, you nearly died. Mrs Croft has been really ill, too. How many more people had to be affected before you'd think it was fine to make an arrest?'

'I hear what you're saying, dear. But the Bridge Club is really suffering. First, we lost Alfie, and now all this. People might stop coming, which would just be awful.'

'Oh, for God's sake,' said Beth, but thankfully spared more arguments as they were now approaching Mrs Croft's bedside.

She was sitting up, looking pretty cheery, and playing something that looked suspiciously like Bridge on an iPad. 'My grandson set me up with this and it's making the time fly,' she said with a smile. 'You should give it a try, Wendy.'

As her mother bent her head over the screen and allowed her friend to demonstrate the game, Beth let her thoughts

wander. She could see where Wendy was coming from. It would
be sad for her, and no doubt many of the members, if the Bridge
Club died out. But Beth hoped she'd always keep a demarcation
in her own mind between the convenience of keeping her mother's hobby in play and the incarceration of a murderer.

She also felt a stab of annoyance at her mother's dismissal of
Harry's heroic part in events. Beth herself had been thrilled to
see him so soon after Mrs Croft's collapse, and his actions had
been decisive, effective and extremely efficient. The ballroom
had been surrounded by officers in uniform, the park had been
shut down, the tea things had been sealed into evidence bags
and, most importantly of all, the miscreant had been taken away
in handcuffs. Beth was still in a tiny bit of a swoon at the
thought of it all, which was helping their relationship along
no end.

The fact that, for once, he'd been fairly nearby when her
call came – thanks to her emailed list of suspects – had helped
immeasurably. But still, he'd saved the day, blue-lighting Mrs
Croft to the hospital and overseeing the questioning of all the
players. She did love him when he was striding around sorting
things out.

Wait a minute. Had she used the L-word? Beth's cheeks
grew pinker and pinker, which in itself was ridiculous. No one
else was privy to her train of thought. But had she actually just
made a confession to herself? She'd never thought that anyone
but her late lamented James would be able to tease that word,
that emotion, out of her. It just showed how wrong you could
be. She loved Jake, Magpie and Colin, Katie, her mother, and
Josh too, of course. But that was different.

Beth dragged her mind back to much safer territory –
murder. Her worried frown cleared a little as she mulled over
events at Belair House. But though an arrest had been made
and there was, to Wendy's chagrin, another empty seat at
Bridge, there was a part of Beth that suspected things were not

quite over yet. There were loose ends aplenty, or perhaps, this time around, she should say that there were cards that had yet to be played. She suspected that someone, somewhere in Dulwich, rather thought they held all the trumps. It was still up to Beth to make sure that wasn't so.

TWENTY-SIX

Beth was glad, the next day, to be back in the reassuringly normal, slightly messy surroundings of her beloved archives office. Despite her best efforts, there were always a few straggling play programmes collecting on her desk or in a stack on a shelf, reminding her that even the most OCD people had to keep on top of filing or it would certainly get on top of them. Colin was asleep in the conference corner, lying on the blanket which had won an even larger place in his heart after Janice had sanctified it with her nap. As Beth watched, his back legs quivered as he chased a rabbit over the Rye in his sleep. Not that there were any left on Peckham Rye these days; Beth rather thought they'd all sold their burrows to hipsters for a fortune and retired to Whitstable. And Beth hadn't been anywhere near the Rye for ages. She shuddered at the thought.

She didn't know whether it was because she was watching him but, all of a sudden, Colin shot to his feet. He didn't even take forever about it, as he usually did; bracing arthritic limbs and shaking the stiffness out of his tail. No. This time, he was lying prone one minute, then upright the next. Even more astonishingly still, he was growling deep in his doggy throat.

The hackles on the back of Beth's neck rose in unison with the dog's – she'd never heard him make this noise before, and it was utterly terrifying. A kind, sweet creature like Colin might well drown you in slobber, yes, but he wouldn't ever dream of harming anyone, so this was completely extraordinary. He was glaring fixedly at the entrance to the office. Then he barked sharply, once, twice, and moved from paw to paw, like Roger Federer about to return a demon serve.

Beth just about had time to push herself back from her desk and scrabble to her own feet, when the door was bashed in. The crash was huge in the still, calm office, as the thick fire door whacked into the wall and chunks of plaster fell to the floor. But for once Beth wasn't worrying about the mess. Her eyes were riveted on the panting, red-faced man who now dominated the doorway, cutting off her only exit route, his meaty hands clasping the frame and his horrible mouth wide in triumph.

It was Tom Seasons, the bursar of Wyatt's. So much for his sabbatical. He seemed to be back with a vengeance, like the villain that refused to die in some superhero movie. Beth had rather hoped he might have left for good, moved to another school, left the area even. But quite clearly, that had been wishful thinking. He must have been hanging around, biding his time. Dulwich was a very small place, as she'd always known. And now her office too was shrinking by the second, as the man, six-feet-something of steaming anger, advanced towards her. She backed away but came up against the edge of her chair and sat down involuntarily, in an undignified heap. Great. Now she was even shorter, compared to this beefy giant bearing down on her. Where was Harry when she really needed him?

Just then, a familiar head popped round the door. Thank the Lord, it was Janice. Beth took a deep breath – the first she was conscious of drawing since Seasons had darkened her doorway.

'Janice!' she piped, her voice so much higher than normal that it was like the squeak of a strangled bat. Colin in the corner suspended his growling for a moment to wince.

On the one hand, Beth was so pleased to see the school secretary that she felt like dancing a little jig. On the other, she was now terrified that Seasons would attack Janice too. She immediately started fumbling for her phone, which was on the desk. Seasons' eyes tracked her movement, and for a horrible second she thought he was going to wrench it right out of her hand.

But she needn't have panicked. Janice's appearance, and even Beth's own movement, seemed to have woken Seasons out of his rage-filled trance. He marched into the room and steadied himself on the chair in front of Beth's desk, and immediately he was just a rather tired, rather heavy, very red-faced middle-aged man, not the rampaging hulk who'd just confronted her. Even Colin started to relax, the growl fading away, and he slowly lay down again, although with one suspicious brown eye fixed on the big man as if to warn him not to make any false moves.

'Come in, Janice, please. And Tom, erm, what's all this about?' asked Beth, relieved that her voice now seemed to have sunk several octaves to its normal pitch.

Seasons, though, seemed to be having trouble getting out any words at all. His face was still the colour of a traffic light stuck on stop, while sweat patches were gathering under the arms of his shirt with all the ominous darkness of storm clouds.

Beth knew she was being a little disingenuous. She had a fair idea why Seasons was here. And if she was completely honest, she'd been expecting something from him. But she'd hoped it would be a tersely worded email, not the man himself, apparently dangerously close to having a stroke right in front of her in her office.

'Sit down, Tom. Let me get you some water,' she said, getting up and edging towards her conference corner. There were rather dusty glasses and one of Wyatt's branded bottles of mineral water on the table. They'd been waiting patiently there for Beth to organise her first proper meeting. Today, it looked as though their moment had finally come.

'No!' said Seasons suddenly, stopping Beth in her tracks.

Both she and Janice looked at the man expectantly, but his head had flopped down. He braced his hands on the back of the chair, seeming to struggle with himself, working out what to say. At least, Beth hoped it was that and not some sort of cardiac incident still brewing. Colin stirred warily over on his blanket, though he thumped his tail when he caught Janice's eye. She smiled at him reassuringly and he put his head on his paws again.

'This is all very well, Tom, and it's, um, good to see you after all this time, but I do actually have some things to be getting—'

'Beth. Please,' said Tom.

Her bursting into speech seemed to have been the cue he was waiting for. Typical, thought Beth. He'd always been one of those men who loved the sound of his own voice and could never resist interrupting a woman. Well, she didn't work for him any more. Janice was her line manager, and to all intents and purposes he was supposed to be on sabbatical. She could speak if she wanted to, in her own office.

'I'm sorry, Tom, but I'm pushed for time,' she said more forcefully. 'I'm not sure what this is about, but unless you'd like to talk right now, I'll have to ask you to make an appointment and, erm, come back another time.' Beth's wide-open, slightly terrified eyes met Janice's, and the other woman nodded her encouragement. This gave Beth the strength to carry on. 'So, Tom? What's it to be?'

At that, the man sat down heavily opposite Beth. He dropped his hefty forearms onto the wooden surface of her desk and then steepled his fingers under his chin. He eyed Beth. The hectic flush was still spread across his jowls, but he was now just this side of tomato. Nevertheless, Beth shrank away. Janice moving further into the room and taking the seat next to Seasons helped a lot. Over in the corner, Colin stirred, raised an ear, then seemed to slip back into standby mode which, to the uninitiated, looked exactly like a nap.

Beth didn't want to keep repeating herself, but she'd had enough of this. She cleared her throat, ready for another attempt to get Seasons to explain himself or leave. Again, he seemed to sense that she was going to speak and dived in to forestall her.

'I've been wondering about all this for months, Beth. Well, years now. Since you first started at Wyatt's, in fact. Because that's what it's all about, isn't it, Beth *Haldane*?' he said, dripping venom as he lingered on her surname. 'It's all about your father, isn't it?'

TWENTY-SEVEN

There was silence in the office. Not the comfortable sort of pause you get between old colleagues; not even the little thinking space you might expect when someone's asked a rather challenging question. This was the sort of humming, highly charged silence that fell when a diver was about to jump off a high board, or a jury was waiting to deliver its verdict.

Of all the questions Beth had been expecting from Seasons, it had certainly not been this. She looked at him, her jaw slack. Meanwhile, Janice was staring over at her, eyebrows sky-high in enquiry. Beth turned her gaze slightly so she didn't have to catch her friend's eye. Janice hadn't actually spoken, but Beth could almost see her words hanging in the air. '*What on earth is he on about?*'

Now it was Beth's turn to pause. And even to sweat. She sat there, in her swivel chair, her mind whirling with possibilities, with things she could say, with explanations. None of them was easy. None of them seemed to cover the magnitude of what had been going on. Her own armpits began to prickle, and she could feel her face growing hot.

Seasons, now returned to his normal shade of underdone-pork, was clearly rejoicing that the pressure was off him. 'Not such fun when it's you in the hot seat, is it, Beth? Cat got your tongue? Or, should I say, moth-eaten dog?'

That was enough. It was all very well Seasons attacking her. To an extent, after what he'd been through, she could understand it. But having a go at Colin was beneath contempt. Beth burst into speech at last.

'Look, I can see how you might take all this personally...'

'*All this*? What do you mean by that?' Instantly, the man was jumping down her throat, demanding clarification. He wasn't going to make this easy.

Beth squirmed in her seat. 'Well, there's been a lot going on in Dulwich. And you've often been at the centre of it... probably through no fault of your own,' she tacked on hastily. Seasons harrumphed and seemed to be about to say something else. Beth continued quickly.

'Look, I know your wife, well, ex-wife, was involved with the first case I had to investigate, right here at Wyatt's. And things that I brought up then might well have, er, caused you pain. But it's not fair to say that was my fault. I didn't encourage your wife to, um, do whatever she did...' Beth stumbled on, only for Seasons to interject again.

'No one's saying you did. And I'm not concerned with that matter—'

Beth had no compunction about interrupting the man. He'd asked for answers. Now he could jolly well listen to them. 'Then your girlfriend, later on. When there was that, ahem, issue I looked into in Herne Hill. Well, that was all very unfortunate, wasn't it? But again, not my fault,' said Beth as forcefully as she could, shaking her ponytail for emphasis. 'And then, a few days ago...'

Now they were really coming to it, Beth decided. She wasn't sure whether to continue, as the tell-tale red tide was sweeping up Seasons' face again. His blood pressure must be

going through the roof, and this was after his scarlet-faced erup-
tion into her room in the first place. If he wasn't on medication
already, he certainly should be.

Beth wriggled again, but it was impossible to get comfortable in her chair under such an angry gaze. Even Janice, her
stalwart friend, was looking decidedly askance, as though she
knew there was a secret at the heart of all this that Beth
wasn't getting to. Beth decided there was nothing for it but to
go on.

'Your mother. Look, I'm sorry she turned out to be the
poisoner. But the evidence was insurmountable. She tried to kill
my mother twice, she tried to poison me. And she did kill off my
mother's poor old Bridge partner, Alfie Pole.'

This wasn't news, to Janice or to Seasons. The handcuffs
had been slapped on in public, and Mrs Hadley, with her
blonde helmet of hair, had been led off to the Camberwell
police station by Harry in full view of the entire Bridge Club.
Presumably, Seasons had since visited her in custody, arranged
lawyers, all that stuff.

Beth leant forward and tried to look as sympathetic as she
could. After all, the man didn't choose his mother. It wasn't his
fault she was a homicidal maniac. But Beth did think Seasons'
judgement on marriage partners and girlfriends was seriously
flawed.

'I'm sorry you seem to have been involved, however tangentially, in so many of the mysteries I've got roped into. But the
fact that people around you seem to have a distinct propensity
to kill is just not my fault. Is it?'

Beth looked from Janice to Seasons and back again, hoping
for understanding, for support, for clemency. From Janice, she
got confused sympathy. The woman looked as though she was
blundering through foggy woods, trying to find her way, and
having only limited success. She'd pricked up her ears at the
mention of Seasons' mother. Although the arrest itself was

common currency in Dulwich, no one knew the full inside story of the Bridge poisonings yet.

Beth took a steadying breath and addressed Janice directly. 'As you know, Tom's mum, Rosemarie Hadley, was behind it all. She masterminded the poisoning. Harry is still trying to work out exactly why. I won't go into everything because it's a live investigation, but it's clear that she had some strange grudge against, well, against my mother.'

Seasons, as before, looked ready to burst a corpuscle or two. But, looking her right in the eye, he took his two meaty paws and slapped them together in a slow handclap, the sound reverberating around the room like gunshots.

'Oh, very good, Beth. Very smart. But then you Haldanes always are, aren't you? Distraction. Such a clever technique. But let's come back to the central issue. Not my mother, as you well know. No, all along, it's been something quite different behind all this, hasn't it? I'll say it again. *Your father.*'

Janice turned her head to look at Beth again, and shrugged her shoulders. What on earth was all this about? It was clear she didn't have the first clue.

Beth, sitting in her beloved swivel chair, wished for a mad moment that she could simply corkscrew round and round, faster and faster, until she took off and flew out of here, across the immaculate Wyatt's lawn, down Calton Avenue, up the high street and back to the blessed safety of Pickwick Road. She wanted to shut herself in her tiny house and never come out again. But there was a problem – how would she get Colin back? He was too enormous and much too badly coordinated to get onto the chair with her. She couldn't leave him, could she? It was tempting but, as she looked over at his unsuspecting chocolatey head, she knew the answer was no.

She was going to have to tough it out. Explain everything. People always said it felt better to get stuff off your chest. Beth didn't believe it for one second, but it looked as though she was about to find out if it was true.

She cleared her throat. And then shrugged her own shoulders. 'All right, then. Yes, it's true. My mother has always said that there was a reason why my dad died so young. And that reason was – your father.'

Opposite her, Janice took a sharp breath in, but Beth continued, fixing Seasons with an angry glare. 'Your father, Geoff Seasons, was my dad's boss at the accountancy firm. Dad was just a middle manager, really. He wasn't a high flyer. He was a nice, kind man, who always did his best. But that wasn't good enough for your bully of a father, was it? He always had it in for mine. Made him work late. Criticised his figures. Undermined his confidence. Made him feel a failure. And then, when Geoff himself made a catastrophic mistake, who did he blame it on? Dad. He harried him, night and day, until my dad died of a heart attack. When I was only eleven. If you think I'm going to forget about that, if you think I'll ever stop thinking about my father and how he suffered, and how *you* and your family deprived me of so much, then you're wrong.'

'So you admit it?' said Seasons, a perverse delight spreading across his pudgy face. 'This has all been about revenge. All the accusations, all the scandals you've dragged my name into, all the charges made—'

'No! No. Not at all!' Beth sat up straight in her chair, and shouted Seasons down. 'Not a bit of it! Your family is guilty as charged. Your wife, your girlfriend, your mother, the whole lot of them. There's no doubt in my mind about that. And more to the point, there's no doubt in the Crown Prosecution Service's mind. This has not been a vendetta. Not a bit of it. Though it might suit you to think it was,' she said, exhausted now, and suddenly afraid to catch Janice's eye.

What on earth would her friend think of her now? There was so much she'd never told her. She hadn't concealed it, exactly. It had just never come up. Maybe she should have said, when she'd first met Seasons at her job interview so long ago... but back then, she'd never expected to get the position. She'd been astonished when she was told she'd beaten off hot competition from a stream of better-qualified candidates.

She thought quickly, and finally decided to put a long-held suspicion into words. She'd never have a better opportunity than this. And she didn't have much left to lose. 'I think you recognised my name when you interviewed me. But I didn't know you. My mother never really said who *Geoff* was. As far as I was concerned, he was just Dad's nasty, mean boss. I didn't know his surname. But you! You've got ten years on me, at least. I bet you knew everything about my dad, and the part your own father played in disgracing him. There aren't many Haldanes in Dulwich. Did you choose me for the job on purpose?'

It was Seasons' turn to look uncomfortable now. Janice, meanwhile, switched her gaze to him and gawped as though she'd never met him before.

'You certainly weren't the best candidate,' sneered Seasons. 'God, you were a shambles. Tongue-tied, incoherent, badly dressed... it brought back all the times when my father had to haul yours over the carpet for his latest shoddy bit of work. I admit, it amused me to think I could have you here, where I could keep an eye on you. But there was something else—' He stopped short, seeming almost embarrassed.

'What? What was it? Surely you're not going to stop there, after all the awful things you've said?'

Seasons looked up and caught Beth's eye. 'I suppose the truth is, I felt sorry for you. Your dad might have been a bit ineffectual, but his death was a shock, I admit. I don't think my father had been expecting him to just peg out like that. I know he felt... responsible. I suppose when you walked into my office that day, well, I saw a way to make amends. It was clear that you weren't doing brilliantly financially. I thought you could cope with being the number two in a department as obscure as the archives office. Little did I know what was going to happen to your boss. And, at the time, no one had a clue you'd stumble on that discovery about Wyatt's involvement in slavery, and make the archives a much bigger deal than they'd ever been before. No, back then, it seemed like there wasn't too much danger of you messing up. But I've been paid back handsomely for my philanthropy,' he said bitterly.

Beth didn't know what to say. On the one hand, it explained her lingering sense of surprise that she'd ever landed such a great job in the first place. But it was hard to believe it had been thanks to Seasons' benevolence. There had been other people involved in the choice, and some of them – including the head-master, who was no fool – must have given her the post on her merits. She had to cling to that thought. Being beholden to this horrible man would be too much.

'I can see it might look like I've, somehow, had it in for you. But I can assure you that has never been the case,' Beth faltered. 'There's history between us, that's a fact. But you can't deny that your family has been involved, up to the hilt, in all these cases that have come my way. That's not my fault. And it's nothing to do with what happened in the past.'

'You keep telling yourself that,' said Seasons with a curl of his lip. 'I know you're just seeking revenge. Your father was a weak man, and you're a coward. Why don't you just come out and say that you've got it in for me and my family?'

'But I haven't,' Beth said simply, her palms upwards. 'It isn't true. The stuff with our fathers is just coincidence. I must admit, it looks odd when you dredge it all up into the light of day, but I haven't thought about it for years. Whereas the stuff involving your family members is actually happening now – your mother, for instance. Why don't you just admit that she, and the rest of them, are all guilty of what they've been accused of?'

There was another weighty pause. Then Seasons spoke again, more quietly this time.

'Maybe they were forced into it. By circumstances. By this place.'

'What, by Dulwich itself?' said Beth sarcastically.

'Why not?'

A heavy silence fell. Beth now tried to catch Janice's eye, she wanted to gauge how all this was going down, but her friend seemed to be looking very busily at her shoes. Finally, Seasons sighed, then spoke again. His voice was so quiet this time that it took Beth a while to decipher what he'd said.

'*It's time I got out.*'

TWENTY-EIGHT

'But I can't believe it was that evil Seasons' *mother*! And that it was all just spite. Poor Alfie, murdered just to get at Wendy. It's crackers,' said Katie, her eyes wide. For once, she hadn't even complained about coming to Aurora's for coffee after dropping off the boys. 'I've been itching to know what went on. But every rumour I've heard has been madder than the next.'

'Well, this time the explanation really is pretty cuckoo. But I suppose the main thing is that it's been a *whydunit*, not a whodunit this time. If I'd just been more on the case, I could have realised much sooner that it must have been Mrs Hadley – Seasons' mother. Although my mother was sure she'd seen someone at the time Alfie was drinking the poisoned tea, she thought it was one of the other women who have the same helmet hairdo. They all look the same from the back. And then Harry caught her red-handed on her third attempt.'

'But is what they're saying true?'

Beth stirred her coffee. 'What are they saying?' she asked quietly.

Katie didn't speak for a moment. She looked around the empty café, the low energy lightbulb and subdued autumnal sun outside doing their best to illuminate her soft blonde hair. Beth hoped fervently she'd never take to hairspray in years to come.

'Well – that you brought it all on yourself. I'm sorry, Beth,' she added quickly, before her friend could break in. 'But that's the story. You had a grudge against Seasons, so you got his wife, girlfriend and mother into trouble. Because he was mean to your dad?'

Beth sighed. 'Wow. Look, I know you're not a gossip. But can you do your best to counteract that? I truly didn't connect Seasons' father with my dad. *He* was the one who chose to employ *me*. And then, let's just say, he's not a great judge of character.'

'Apart from hiring you. And there wasn't much he could do about his mother, I suppose.'

'No. She must have had to listen to him ranting about me so much that it drove her literally crazy. I didn't realise she'd married again after his father died. If I'd heard that name, Seasons, from the start, I might have got on to things a lot sooner. Then Mum, and Mrs Croft, wouldn't have had to suffer. And poor old Alfie wouldn't have died. Of course, all the stuff about the allotments, the Open Garden events, and even about Alfie's daughter Venetia, turned out to be completely irrelevant in the end.'

'How did Seasons' mother get her hands on the poison?'

'Atropine? Believe it or not, it's in prescription eyedrops, used to treat inflammation. I should have realised. She has those great big bulging eyes.'

'You can't be expected to see everything, Beth. You're not a doctor. And you were on your own in this. I promised I'd help but, well, in the end, I just felt I had to put Charlie first. If I'd known that woman would try and kill Wendy, and you, and your whole Bridge table...' Katie looked as close to murderous as

Beth had ever seen her, and she found it rather comforting. 'What will happen to her now?' Katie asked.

'Psychiatric reports. Honestly, she's as mad as a box of badgers. I thought her son was bad enough – he always seemed one shout away from an aneurism – but she's gone up, up and away since it all happened. She won't go to a normal prison.'

'Still, you must feel a lot safer with them out of Dulwich.'

'Absolutely!' smiled Beth. 'I'm not sure where Seasons will go. But it can't be far enough for me. Now. How's the Billy situation?'

Katie sighed. 'I've decided on a charm offensive. We're going to ask him over, as often as Charlie will let me, and I'm going to monitor everything and come down on him like a ton of bricks if he puts a toe out of line.'

'Do you think that will work?' Beth put her head on one side. She was sceptical – and also worried that Jake would get left out. What with this, and all the coffee mornings Beth wasn't being asked to, not to mention the rumours now swirling about her, she was beginning to feel as though the Haldanes might be on the back foot in Dulwich, despite the removal of the evil Seasons clan.

'I've got to give it a try. But I'll be with you all the way on your next case,' Katie said with a smile.

Beth drank up the dregs of her horrible coffee and gave an answering grin. 'Don't hold your breath. What else could possibly happen around here?'

* * *

Back home in Pickwick Road that evening, with the comfort of four familiar walls around her, Beth was feeling happier than she had for a long time. So what if there was a bit of talk? Such things were five-minute wonders in SE21. She'd be knocked off the gossip agenda as soon as Belinda got a new handbag.

In the meantime, Wyatt's had a new, benign atmosphere she was revelling in. It was a blessed relief that Seasons would never corner her again, and doubly so that her boy could now wander the school without falling under the moody, malevolent scrutiny of a man who wished her family ill.

And another enormous plus – everyone now turned a blind eye to Colin's presence about the school. After Beth had managed to catch up with Janice and make a clean breast of everything, she knew that her friend was still on her side, still her protector, and still one of the ageing Labrador's biggest fans. The old boy was now fast becoming a bit of a school mascot. True, the payback for Janice's forbearance might be Beth coming good on her rash promise to babysit young Elizabeth, but Beth was braced for that. More or less.

Lazily swirling her hand in the post-supper washing-up water and taking out a tea-stained mug, Beth held it up to the light for a second and then scrubbed it out thoroughly. Had Seasons, or his family, been the worm in the bud all the time, as far as Dulwich was concerned? And had she herself unknow-ingly been pursuing some sort of feud against her father's perse-cutor? She'd much rather believe that Seasons and his family had brought it all upon themselves. But maybe there was some-thing about Dulwich which drove people to extremes. Not her, obviously, she thought, polishing the mug until it shone.

Beth did a final sweep of the sitting room for cups and plates, finding a couple of strays. Hands full, she passed Jake's horribly scuffed school shoes in the hall and nudged them into a neater alignment using her foot. Back in the kitchen, she slid the last of the dishes into the water. Harry and Jake had just played their last PS4 game before bedtime, and she heard Harry thud-ding down the stairs after shooing the boy off to sleep.

The whole house shook as usual. The heavy footsteps continued down the hall, stopping at the threshold of the kitchen. Magpie hurtled out of her cat flap like a scud missile.

Harry hesitated in the doorway, looming uncertainly. Beth looked at him in surprise, her favourite tea towel decorated with the flora and fauna of Dulwich Park in her hand. He wasn't usually a ditherer.

'I've been thinking. Maybe we should move in together. Get a bigger place.'

Beth, amazed, knew her eyes must be as big as the saucers she'd just been rinsing. It was quite an offer. Her heart leapt. Harry, so big, so tall, so wonderful in his gorgeously huggable Aran jumper, had bashful uncertainty writ large all over him for the first time in living memory.

'But we couldn't possibly afford it. You know what houses go for round here,' she said. Even as she spoke the sensible words, a wide and bewitching smile spread across her face, turning her, at a stroke, from doughty Shetland pony to the most enchanting little unicorn.

Harry strode over to the sink with a single pace, bent low and took her into his arms. 'We could, if we moved out of Dulwich. It's not the only place in the world, you know,' he whispered into her ear.

Shocked, Beth looked up into blue, blue eyes. The teacup she'd been drying so carefully slipped from her fingers and smashed into a million pieces on the floor.

A LETTER FROM ALICE

Thank you so much for choosing to read my book. I love writing about Beth Haldane and I hope you've enjoyed finding out what she got up to this time. If you'd like to know what happens to Beth next, please sign up at the email link below. Your email address will never be shared and you can unsubscribe at any time.

www.bookouture.com/alice-castle

If you enjoyed the story, I would be very grateful if you could write a review. I'd love to hear what you think. I always read reviews and I take careful account of what people say. My aim is always to make the books a better read! Leaving a review also helps new readers to discover my books for the first time. I'm also on Twitter, Facebook and Goodreads, often sharing pictures of cats that look like Magpie. Do get in touch if that's your sort of thing. Thanks so much again, and I really hope to see you soon for Beth's next adventure. Happy reading!

Alice Castle

Alicecastleauthor.com

Printed in Great Britain
by Amazon

16118758R00144